BLOOD COUNTRY

BLOOD COUNTRY

Ivan Ruff

Walker and Company
New York

Published in the United States of America in 1989
by Walker Publishing Company, Inc.

Published simultaneously in Canada by Thomas Allen & Son
Canada, Limited, Markham, Ontario.

Library of Congress Cataloging-in-Publication Data

Ruff, Ivan.
Blood country / Ivan Ruff.
p.   cm.
ISBN 0-8027-1066-2
PR6068.U45B5   1989
813′.54—dc19   88-26694
CIP

Printed in the United States of America

10 9 8 7 6 5 4 3 2 1

To Jenny

Chapter One

Fatigue now, more than hunger, more even than despair and fear, a dead weariness, had started to bring on hallucinations, and he knew he would have to give up soon.

A leaden coastal mist had shut down the daylight, and as the night thickened around him he knew that he could stretch his sleeping-bag out in a ditch anywhere here and grab the few hours' sleep that he needed to save him. But the compulsion to keep on the move drove him forward.

If he came to a road he got off it again immediately, pushing on blindly across open country. In places the land was rocky, and the thin soles of the second-hand shoes he wore gave little protection against the jagged flints. Elsewhere he found himself forced to wrench his legs through hollows of swampy mud, refusing to retrace a single yard, using his night-adjusted vision and his feel for the terrain to guide him back on to solid ground.

And always beyond the last ridge, the sea hung out there like a black hole at the far end of the night, inexorably sucking everything towards it. The persistent cool wind declared the sea's nearness, and the night was restless with the suppressed roar of a distant swell. A harsh, even monstrous presence, but in all this landscape it was the friendliest thing he knew.

As if to offset the total blackness around him, small savage eruptions of flame burst repeatedly on to his fading, sleep-starved consciousness. Petrol bombs on the streets of Belfast,

1

the shattering glass and the sudden lascivious lick of fire at your body, the yelling chaos of people high on terror, the twitching dread of what might come at you next from those stinking, shuttered buildings – his mind lacked the energy now to fight these images off. Worse, he also saw, as achingly as a mirage ahead of him, the yachts in a Mediterranean port, sunlight rippling on their canvas from a flawless blue sky, the relaxed easy bounce of perfectly brown topless girls, and everywhere the effortless raunch of money that flowed like sex, with nobody caring where it came from or where it went.

He was painfully thirsty, and the pictures that overprinted his mental screen seemed to get to his clogged, sticky throat more than any other part of his body. But he left the water ration in his bag untouched. He had known this phase would come, and he knew how to handle it.

The cloud cover was starting to drift and break up, and a fitful moonlight washed around the sky. It was not much help for seeing, because it deepened the shadows and made contrasts which were deceptive. It also made him more visible. Moonlight he could do without.

More disturbing, he had hit a path, a firm track in a place where there seemed no reason for a path to be. Maybe it was some old footway kept open by weekend ramblers, nothing more sinister than that. He stayed with it for a while. The sea was closer now, still beyond the last ridge of the coast, but the lazy crash of each wave was distinct, as was the rattling tremor of the gravel beach the tide came in on.

Some distance from the path, in what seemed to be an uncultivated field, he made out the whitish stone of a ruined farm outbuilding. For a moment he stopped to check things through – himself, his reasons for being there, the security of the place for a few hours' sleep, the potential for escape if he should need it.

None of it felt good, but he knew this night would throw up nothing better. The derelict byre was further than it looked, across a broken pasture choked by dry ranks of thistle and entanglements of briar. The crudely cut stones from the ruin

2

were scattered over a larger radius than the usual slow decay of such buildings would account for, but by now he was only thinking of sleep. Against a half-collapsed wall, the damp cob crumbling from between the fractured layers of stone, he unfolded his lightweight bag and got as comfortable as he could on the remains of a flagstone floor. The place stank like a foxes' latrine, but suddenly it was a good place to be. He took five mouthfuls of water from his flask, no more, then replaced it.

He used his rucksack as a pillow, and before his mind blanked out he allowed himself one brief smile. He had earned it.

Daylight woke him, still early. It had not rained, and there was even a trace of sun in the sky somewhere. He flexed the ache out of his body in a minute, and got ready to go. He could eat on the way. His rations were down to chocolate bars and water, and they required no mealtime formalities.

As he picked his way back across the tangled meadow he noticed some fifty yards off and oblique to his own direction a trail of small wooden posts, knee-high, diagonally striped with black and yellow. There was a signpost too, although from where he stood he could only see its back.

Taking great care, he made for the nearest point in the line of posts, then followed them until he reached the gravel path again. As he went by he glanced at the face of the sign, but he had already inferred its message. In white letters on red it proclaimed, THERE ARE BOMBS AND UNEXPLODED SHELLS HERE. THEY CAN KILL YOU. KEEP OUT. He tossed a screwed up chocolate-bar wrapper at the sign and went on.

He knew where he was now. Christ, of all the places to have landed. Under cover of night he must have strayed inside the boundary without realising it, and just kept going. Too bloody right – no wonder there were so few roads, no traffic, no lights anywhere. But now it was daylight the whole place could be crawling with military within minutes. They wouldn't know who he was, just somebody who shouldn't be

3

there. He wouldn't want to test their mood if they saw him.

He had never been as far along the coast as this, although he had heard of the place. But how in Christ's name did you get out of a territory which had been sealed off by the Army decades ago, its population evicted and its buildings left to ruin, a whole ghost area?

The cliffs had to be the answer, so he headed for the grey-green ridge the other side of which he could hear, smell, feel the sea. On his right he left behind the village which was the centre of this desolate valley. It gave him the creeps, and he hardly glanced at the rows of cottages with their windows and timbers stove in, the overgrown village street chevroned with the tyre-marks of military vehicles, the deathly silence. This was how the world would be after the bomb. You could almost feel it had already happened.

As if even now some pitiful mutant might crawl from the rubble and cry to him for help, he got away fast, all the time scanning the heights that enveloped the valley for signs of movement, always aware that somewhere up there field glasses or a rifle might already be trained on him. On the cliffs he would get out of this death-trap, out of the biggest ghost-town in Britain. And then he would be on his home run.

The area called Macemoor covered thousands of acres of unreclaimed, unreclaimable land, the tail-end of a once vast moor broken up by marsh, by scrubby coppice, by the minor flows of larger rivers that meandered further inland. There were single houses rather than villages here, and the nearest real town was thirty miles away. The only definition Macemoor had was its border with the sea, and here the land was more imposing, graced on all the maps with evocative names. 'But places here,' Martin Ritchie had written, 'are called generically – people talk about the Rock, the Inlet, the Bank, the Moor, and since it's obvious what's being referred to, proper names would be redundant, a concession to outsiders . . .'

Those letters, Laura Sondergard remembered. As she

looked at the cliffs, and at the sea blue and calm beyond the pale grey cliffs, she had the idea of taking out the letters and reading them in sequence here, as a symbolic gesture. The moment passed, and she left them packed with the other stuff in the boot of the car. But when she asked herself how the hell this situation had come about, it was the letters that gave the answer.

She had left her London flat unsold, and that was symbolic too. Today was the final stage in joining Martin at Macemoor, but she had let the Clapham flat to a friend, left her furniture there, not sold up or made a complete break. Perhaps later. But as of today her home was here. She had come a day early, unknown to Martin, and that was something else again.

At forty, somehow, one explained less. She still felt good about being forty, and it was the right time for Martin to have re-entered her life. Fifteen years, a marriage and divorce, a successful career as an illustrator, now working freelance and getting good commissions, many relationships, but mainly the monumental slab of that fifteen years, should have made seeing Martin again impossible. But it was the easiest, sweetest thing that had ever happened to her.

First the letters, then they had met, then the weekends together and the increasingly difficult goodbyes. Then a time when they both cried and Laura said, 'I've got to live with you.'

Martin had become embarrassed – it was a bleak place, his cottage was modest, he had been on his own for three widowed years now and had lost the ability to accept things from other people. Especially he could not accept the gift of her life. It provoked instant fear in him, and beneath the fear, guilt.

Laura reassured him. 'I can work from here. I love the place. I've got enough track record and contacts, I can get all the work I want. I need to change my life. I'd like to change it with you.' Staccato, impassioned, her style. And here she was, a self-possessed woman who at forty still liked herself but had a recurrent impulse to try and out-think experience.

Hence the arrival a day early.

Laura wanted to drive around this area and absorb some of its elusive, brooding character without the imprint of Martin's constant direction. It was his world, she had never known anyone who went so perfectly with a particular landscape, a man who had created his own world and was living out an awkward, original integrity which not many people attained. Maybe he was too real, and she needed to acquaint herself privately with some corners of what, after all, was *his* landscape.

She pushed back the shoulder-length blonde hair which the sea wind blew across her face. She had learnt, on many Martin-led treks along these cliffs, to dress for the terrain and the weather, but today she was wearing a skirt, light shoes, normal town clothes, as a way of reminding herself that her identity was something she wanted to extend, not abandon. There would be plenty of time for jeans and woolly hats.

As Laura watched, squadrons of guillemots launched themselves from the cliff-face and tumbled seawards just for the fun of it. The ubiquitous herring-gulls drifted by on thermals, screaming into the wind. An occasional black-back planed above it all. On a small crescent of lonely beach, a long way below, Laura caught sight of someone, a slight figure with a rucksack, apparently exploring the rocks. He was too far down for her to discern any features. She thought no more of it and turned to the path that led back to her car.

Later the same day, driving back from Faulston where he had recorded his weekly nature programme for the local radio station, Martin Ritchie took a couple of hours out on the cliffs. He had spent most of the day at the cottage, alternately working on a children's ecological encyclopaedia and setting up the room which was to be Laura's. This he had emptied over the months, decorated, fixed shelving in, and equipped, as a surprise welcome present, with an artist's desk with wide drawers for storing her work. It was ready, she would arrive the next day, and he needed some air. He had become very tense.

6

He went to a spot on the cliffs where, almost a year earlier, he had passed an interminable day trying to nerve himself to phone Laura. Driven by a strange obsession, he had traced an embarrassed course through a chain of old acquaintances till he found her new name and current address, and in diffident, uncertain terms, had written to her. After the exchange of a few tentative letters, a day came when his guts clenched and his concentration lost its grip, and he could not rest until he heard her voice again.

That first conversation had been stiff, full of wary silences, the over-anxious chat of people who could no longer visualise each other. But there was no going back. For Martin the sound of Laura's voice was like a blood transfusion, wiping out the years. And since then, for him this part of the coast would never again be free, as long as he lived at Macemoor, of the association with that first telephone call. And he was here for life.

He was tracking a peregrine falcon. They were so rare that he almost certainly knew which nest it had come from. He watched as it stooped for the kill, falling with bunched wings through a vertiginous diagonal to smash a rock dove's spine. One of this year's young, still brown rather than grey, it was already murdering like an old hand. Martin watched it zoom away to some private feeding ledge out on the limestone hump of Saltmayne, and then his eyes moved reflectively to the sea's crawling surface two hundred feet below. He took a deep breath and settled down on the short spiky grass. His hands were trembling slightly, and he watched the occasional whitecap lifting out on the water and told himself it was getting cold, but he knew that was not why his hands were shaking.

About to put his glasses away, Martin noticed a submarine heading out for the open sea. In spite of a desire to ignore the humped sinister black shape, he swung the glasses up again. It was one of the nukes, 'a big steel cigar loaded with the four horsemen of the Apocalypse', as John Vayro always called them. Even as Martin watched, the submarine glissaded below sea in a long slow-motion knife-thrust, leaving only a momentary wake behind it. They always went like that as they slipped away from the Inlet, under sealed orders which gave a destination known only to their commander. Martin contrasted the submarine's stealthy passage unfavourably with the peregrine's dizzy public slaughtering, then zipped up his anorak and stumped slowly back down the cliff path.

The cottage was a rambling brick building, decrepit when Martin moved there three years ago. Once the timbers were repaired and the roof renewed, he had worked his way through it room by room, using such skills as he had and learning more as he went. It was neither attractive nor ugly, an unpretentious and comfortable place with a central front door and large sash windows. Outside the wall of the garden, which Martin had let run wild, there was a small patch of hard-standing for vehicles, and from here a dirt track led out into the moorland.

One of the feral cats that haunted the cottage sat watching from a sill as Martin approached, then crept away into the dead scrub at the end of the garden. It was about to rain. Martin put the kettle on and went into the annexe which he had had built on to the cottage as a study.

This room seemed to have no character in common with the rest of the house. Apart from the word-processor in the corner, everything was of wood – the shiny floorboards, the simple furniture, and the walls that were lined with racks of folding cases within which Martin filed his collection of the insect life of Macemoor. In the few gaps where the wall itself showed through there were framed prints from early nineteenth-century natural history works, and a photograph of Laura. The study had the quiet and the eerie sense of unrevealed treasure of a pharaonic tomb. Half a lifetime of research and observation was now condensed into the computer file in the corner, but Martin still missed the company of his battered notebooks, which he had been unable to throw out and had almost shamefully boxed up and hidden away.

He made some tea and typed that day's details on to a disk. It was ironic that so much technology stood at the service of wildflower spread-patterns and insect frequencies, and might even help these natural phenomena outrun the agencies of their destruction. It was raining now. He took out the disk and switched off the screen. In the lamplight from behind the machine he reread some of Laura's letters. It was a pity that, living together, they would no longer write to each other. Or perhaps they still would. He liked the idea and lingered over it. He wondered why even now he could hardly recapture what those letters had meant to him at the time.

I can't believe you're really alive – that sounds ridiculous, as if I had thought you were dead, which God knows I hadn't – I had thought about you, often, but in a kind of limbo, as someone I would never see again, and could never see again – and now here you are, and I feel, I don't know, glad and (silly word) impressed . . .

He heard a car engine, distant, but for the moment went on reading.

You gather from my change of name that I was married to a Swede. Since you found out where I was, you may have turned up other details, so I don't know how much to tell you. Briefly, I had two miscarriages, and we drifted into a declining relationship, and in the end Andy left. I guess one of us had to. Neither of us wanted to keep in touch, and it's been maybe two years since I wondered what happened to him. Why is it so easy to tell you all this?

Drizzle misted the headlamps as Laura bumped up the unmade track to the cottage. Martin was already outside when she stopped.

'I couldn't wait,' she said, but he was already laughing and as excited as a boy.

He grabbed a bag and ushered her in out of the rain. Inside they began caressing each other with an urgency that took no

9

account of the fact that now, now at last, Laura was here for good.

It had begun with a dream. Some friends had invited Martin over – an awkward, interesting man, on his own a lot since his wife had died three years before – and there was someone they wanted him to meet. Later he described the dream to Laura.

I dreamed it was you I was going to meet the next day. I walked into their house and my friends said, this is Laura, and the person who stood up was you. They, of course, had no idea that we had known each other fifteen years ago.

Anyway, when I woke up, there was a half-conscious interval in which I believed that this meeting had actually happened, and I experienced a happiness that was quite strange to me, a lightening of burdens and a warmth all around, so potent that it took a whole day to force myself to accept that this encounter had not taken place in reality. For some days after this, I slipped deeper into a mixture of depression and anxiety which I thought time and my normal routine would clear away. But in fact it tightened its grip on me and began to poison my life. And that originated my determination to find you again . . .

By the time Martin wrote this, Laura was already a real person once more, a name in the phone book, handwriting on an envelope, a signature, the word *love* over her name.

In the lamplight of his workroom, shrouded by miles of silence outside, Martin had considered what Laura would find if she saw him again.

His cheeks had become sunken, and the flesh had settled somewhere down the jaw. The lines in his skin were no longer finely etched, but had become features in themselves, and a slight puffiness was emerging below his eyes. But the eyes themselves were still clear, and the one gap in his teeth was not visible except when he laughed. He practised in front of a mirror the extent to which he would have to laugh for that

10

space in his upper maxilla to show. The gesture strained his face and made him realise how little he was in the habit of laughing like that any more.

Another time, he wrote:

How did we let each other go, fifteen years back? I don't know. But since then I doubt that a month has gone by without me thinking about you, and a number of times I've wanted to write without finding the words or the occasion. I thought the idea of tracking you down would pass, but it became an obsession. Until I knew where you were, how you were, my life couldn't go on . . .

They met, finally, where they had met for their first day together, by the tube station at Marble Arch. Re-enacting the *then* seemed to make the *now* easier.

On his way there, Martin moved through the London crowds and noise without confidence. He no longer had that excited sense, from other times in his life, of the city whirling in orbit around him, but felt that it washed him along blindly like a scrap of the omnipresent litter. Worse, he felt a deep and nagging lack of glamour in himself. Laura was now a career woman whose mail came from an address near Clapham Common, and he felt an absence of things to impress her with. He was forty-seven, still fit, but forty-seven none the less, and his nonchalance had gone. He had bought a new pair of jeans, and wore them with an indescribable jacket and a mixture of garments of random style, anything to avoid the impression that he had tarted up for this reunion. At the same time he was afraid that he would make Laura look too dressy and unable to have lunch anywhere with this middle-aged hick who had come up to town for the day looking fresh from the cattle-market. Attempts to judge the image he had achieved irritated him, and he tried, and totally failed, to dismiss the whole bloody thing.

At Marble Arch he was early, nervous in advance at the possibility that he might not recognise Laura any more, that

11

she would pass through his line of vision without breaking it. A moment of comic nightmare hovered over the swarming, tourist-dominated junction, in which they would both circle desperately around, unable to make positive identifications of each other. He kept looking across to the Park Lane subway, because the first time they had met there he had watched her descend below ground and approach him from that direction. The ability of life to repeat itself seemed the only security he had.

When she was a minute late Martin faced the prospect that she might have decided to abort the meeting – OK, he would give it five minutes, then go. He would get back to his proper life. They could gloss it over from a distance, or just forget it. He would give it five minutes, that was all a serious man with serious work to do should spare.

'Hello, Martin.'

She had come from behind him. Martin turned. As he looked at her his face was instantly alive and vulnerable, also anxious, also happy. All the emotions they had hoarded for this meeting ran together in one powerful current. Without banalities, without a word, they opened their arms to each other in an embrace of transcendent warmth. They kissed almost-formal cheek-kisses suitable for the street, but still soft and accepting, and stared at each other in wonder as at people given up for lost and incredibly saved. In the end they needed words to break the spell.

'You look terrific.'

'You look young.'

They laughed. Impassioned tears pricked at the back of Laura's eyes. Martin looked down at this fair-haired woman, her face thin and becoming lined now, but still lit up by that same mixture of delicacy and sensuality, and he knew that this was the great love of his life. To love and be loved by this woman would fulfil him more than anything else ever could.

Their kisses now let in a complex flood of desire. Eventually, somehow, they walked away from the crowds, along side-streets where they didn't have to care where they were

12

going. Her left breast nestled against his right ribcage, with a familiar physical ease that no time could ever change.

On her first visit to Macemoor it was the kitchen that impressed Laura most. It was a lived-in, pine-panelled room, no showpiece, but clearly the domain of someone who knew how to cook and enjoyed it. The string of garlic bulbs, the dried herbs from the garden, the jams and chutney made by himself, the good utensils all decently marked by use, revealed a Martin Laura had not encountered in the fast-moving months when their earlier lives had briefly come together. Whereas that Martin had shrugged off cookery as a trifling business hardly justified by the ten minutes it took to consume the average plate of food, he now had a freezer and a food processor, he made his own dough, slapping it around with a skilled exuberance, and put meals together like someone in the daily habit of feeding guests with pleasure and skill.

Laura wondered at it, both in the sense of marvelling and needing to question. The kitchen prompted her first mention of Martin's dead wife.

'Did Eleanor teach you to cook?'

Martin paused from chopping some vegetables. He insisted on doing the entire meal himself, dominating the range like a proud Frenchman. He gave an amicable shrug. It had struck Laura once or twice before, how in middle age there was something Gallic about him, alternately serious and droll, letting his body speak a lot.

'I taught myself,' he said. 'Slowly, painfully – maybe in response to living with Eleanor.'

'Not wanting to be dependent?'

'Yes. Also, she was a good cook, and I don't like watching someone do a thing so well when I can't do it at all.'

'If you don't want to talk about her,' Laura said, 'it's all right.'

Martin poured them both some wine, and sat down beside her to drink it.

'I don't need to talk about Eleanor,' he said. 'It wasn't perfect, but we were reasonably happy together. There's no hidden tragedy waiting to come out.' He smiled and touched her wrist. 'Maybe it's because we never lived together here.'

'I didn't realise,' Laura said.

'I moved here after she died. We lived thirty miles along the coast from here. I'd always had an eye on this place, and it was cheap, needed working on, and I suppose it's been my companion for three years as well as my shelter. This is the place I never want to leave.'

'Never's a long time,' Laura said.

Martin's eyes were dark and intense, and his face glowed from the half-concealed kitchen light. 'There's no such thing as time here,' he said.

Later, they dozed and woke, and slept again, and forgot about time and place, luxuriating in the salt-marsh, moist-flour sexual warmth of the bedclothes. Suddenly there was no need to hurry. Ever again.

Chapter Two

On the twenty-storey office block in south London even the name – Concordia House – appeared only once, chiselled into a concrete plaque beside the main door, which was itself at the side of the building. From the busy traffic route over which the block towered, the main visual effect was of a grim hinterland of corrugated-iron sheeting which shut off the functional site from the acreage of housing redevelopment behind. The corrugated iron screened off the car park which lay open to view through the ferroconcrete stilts that supported Concordia House's smaller four-storey brother at the other end of the site. The smaller and larger buildings were joined by a three-storey bridge. In what passed for a forecourt, a small patch of earth crowded by concrete, two plane trees shrugged off their dead leaves.

Concordia House lacked any designation, genuine or phoney, of the business conducted there. It towered above its immediate district, unapproached by any similar block that might have threatened its privacy. From a distance it was twenty floors of grey concrete fascia divided by what appeared to be strips of opaque yellow glass. The window glass was in fact plain, and the effect of yellowing was caused by net curtains stretched across every pane. The twenty layers of discoloured net curtains through which only fluorescent striplights dimly penetrated, together with the architectural mediocrity of the building, gave the Intelligence headquarters a peculiarly British aura of unassertive respectability.

Wearing the dark suit and white raincoat which he always adopted for visits here, Harry Teal left the smaller of the two buildings by the concealed doorway in the dark covered area, and walked away, a bulky undistinguished man with reddish skin and a face almost expressionless except for a suggestion of anger somewhere, an anger constantly searching for a target. Solitary but anonymous, he soon blended into the concrete and tarmac of the city street.

A country job, they said. Why had they given him an assignment in the country? The *bloody* country, he thought, and before he could boil himself up any higher on this subject he noticed an estate agent's, crossed the road, and went in.

A smiling receptionist greeted him. Unbothered by manners, yielding to some deep internal pressure, Teal said, 'I want to sell a house.'

He insisted that they came to look at it the same day, since he would be out of town for a while. They could have the keys and take care of the sale. The sooner the better. His was the only name on the deeds. It would not be complicated.

Teal felt cleaner for this, and as he walked up towards Waterloo he considered again whether this country job had anything to do with his wife leaving him. By the time he got back out to Malden he was convinced of it.

The semi-detached house, stolidly prosperous in the 1930s, was cramped and pretentious now, with its small leaded windows (front only) and its token Tudoresque gable, its dingy pebbledash, the frosted front door with the panel of stained glass. Teal went in. The normal smell of the house, old cooking mostly, mingled with the chemical base of the new stair-carpet. Then the familiar objects, all in place. It was very much a house where things had places. The letter in Maureen's writing was still propped up on the phone shelf.

I can't stand it any longer. It's no good trying to talk to you. I'm going up the wall, and you don't care. Every time you

16

come home you check that I've done everything, you make me account for every minute of my time. You're not interested in anything I'm thinking, so long as it isn't subversive. I feel a cow doing it like this, but to your face you'd only argue and put me in the wrong, which is what you do all the time. Don't try to find me. There is someone else. You wouldn't understand.

Teal stared at the letter for a very long time, still looking for a weak spot. Maureen was not good with words, and things committed to paper always made Teal edgy. The word 'subversive' was underlined three times. 'There is someone else' – put in for effect, probably. Maureen with a bit on the side, an improbable idea. But it was two months now, and although he had not heard from her since the night he had come home and discovered the letter, he had felt compelled to notify Administration.

Changes of personal circumstances had to be notified. Divorce, even separation, would mean a revetting. 'There is someone else' – Maureen's new man would have to be traced and put through the machinery. 'Estranged wife consorts with known communist sympathiser/trade union activist/peace movement subversive' – they could bury your career under epitaphs like that, and unknown to Teal the rottenness could seep from his file to every aspect of his life. Life and file were anagrams of each other, and somehow it was not accidental. They would never tell him, but he would be moved delicately into a siding, the passing years would be a desert of failure, and he would degenerate into one of those helpless figures crippled by a hint of scandal in their past, pitied and avoided.

For the country job they had provided him with a Browning automatic, a clip of thirteen rounds, and a semi-retired member of the firm who happened to be living out that way. And, Teal had no doubt, an opportunity to fight off the compromise of his own personal security clearance caused by the departure of his stupid bitch of a wife. That was the way he was going to take it.

*

17

On the same day that Laura came to live at Macemoor, Harry Teal checked into the Roebuck Hotel in the small town of Barnbrook. He was registered under the name of Greenwood. He required no time to settle in. Although his stay had no limit written into it, he had no wish to feel at home here. The sooner he was back in London the better. Half an hour after his arrival Pilkington would be here. They would eat dinner together, then go for a drive, and while he waited, Teal drank a vodka, plain, unchilled, tasteless, the way he liked it.

Pilkington, a little rubicund man, nervy, with an over-friendly manner, resembling a rustic estate agent, was punctual. They ate at the Roebuck, with no interest in the food except to finish it. They avoided names. Afterwards, as Pilkington drove them both out of Barnbrook, he said, 'Of course, very exciting for me, this. Officially retired and all that – glad the old firm thought my local knowledge might be useful.'

'They said you were still true-blue,' Teal said.

'Absolutely,' Pilkington said, with a middle-aged giggle. 'Couldn't be truer or bluer.'

Teal had the absent-mindedness of someone whose ulcer is troubling him. In fact what bothered him was having to work with a part-timer who was technically his superior officer. And, which was worse, who knew his way around here. At the first sign of incompetence, Teal would dump him.

'I'll brief you then,' Teal said.

Pilkington asked, 'Shall I stop?'

'No, keep driving.'

A minute elapsed as Teal ordered his thoughts. Pilkington flicked the car lights on and kept the speed down.

'There was a body,' Teal began. 'We don't know whether chummy found the body or did it himself. Anyway, apart from the poor fit, forensic established that the clothes were a switch. And on the clothes we found evidence that linked their original owner to a very important man whose disappearance we were just getting worried about. The police did well for us on this one, because we soon tied the owner of the clothes to a railway station, and –'

'How was that?' Pilkington interrupted.

'Just let me brief you, OK? I'll cover the points.'

Pilkington beamed sideways. 'Of course. Sorry.'

'He was leaving a trail. That's obvious. He had a long discussion at the ticket office, so the clerk remembered him and the ticket he bought. They identified the train, and from there they found one witness our friend had a conversation with, after which he disappeared. We know he went all the way because the witness saw him leave the train at the end. Even spoke to him. But nobody else even remembered the guy. Probably spent most of the journey in the toilet. But we know he came out here. Then vanished. Dead trail. No more police for the moment, unless we ask for them. Just you and me. And this.'

Pilkington took the Browning, two pounds plus of hand-tailored steel, and massaged it in his podgy fingers. The automatic was instantly familiar, comfortable.

He smiled slightly and asked, 'Do we know why we're hunting him?'

'No,' Teal said. 'But the people who give me orders want him so bad it's making their teeth ache. Any other questions?'

'No,' Pilkington said. 'It sounds like a super game.'

Night was falling over the countryside. Teal felt his own teeth starting to throb.

At the end of Laura's first day at Macemoor, when the sky was flushed with early evening sunlight, they went out and walked along the cliffs, too elated to eat, too alive to sit still.

They came to a place where the cliffs buckled away in a frozen agony of contorted igneous strata down to a micro-scopically distant shingle beach. A solitary, stocky figure in swimming trunks was wading from the sea, pumping his thighs against the tide. As Laura noticed him he also looked up and waved. Martin waved back and said, 'That's John Vayro. He goes in the water every day, sometimes more than once a day, right through the year.'

The swimmer was already towelled down and briskly

getting dressed. As they walked on he came up the cliff by an oblique hidden path, heading towards them.

Martin explained, 'John's a retired civil servant. He used to work at the Underwater Weapons Establishment on the Rock.' He pointed to the great limestone hump of Saltmayne across the bay, purple in the evening light. 'Now he lives alone along the coast here. I sometimes cook him dinner. He seems a perfectly contented man, so he's not terribly interesting, but he's friendly –'

'Contented people aren't interesting?' Laura asked, feline. The humorous fire rose and died again in her eyes.

Martin smiled. 'Perhaps only to themselves.'

He kissed her mouth. They were hardly able to stop kissing as Vayro approached, a short strongly built man with an open gaze, round red patches on his cheeks, and frizzy steel-wire hair haloing a shiny forehead.

His voice was surprisingly high-pitched. 'Mr Ritchie!' he called. 'And what's this, no field glasses I see, senility setting in no doubt. And a handsome woman on your arm. This is not the dedicated man of science I used to know.'

Martin greeted Vayro with an affectionate grin and introduced the two strangers.

'Welcome to this place, my dear,' Vayro said. 'I hope you love it as much as I do, and as this man does.'

'I've fallen for it already,' Laura said. She felt his candid blue eyes searching her out.

Martin asked, 'How was the sea, John?'

'The sea is life,' Vayro said. He looked at Laura and repeated, 'Life. Always the same and always different. I embrace it and test myself against it every day, and on the last day of my life I shall set out into that water down there, swim as far as I'm able, then let the sea take me. Who could ask for more? I'm sorry, my dear,' he added, making a small concession to Laura's polite smile, 'but you didn't come to this part of the world for small talk, did you?'

His manner was so open that Laura relaxed and laughed. Martin asked if Vayro fancied a drink, but he was already walking away, cocking an eye at a bank of indigo cloud rising above the downland.

'Thanks, no. Another time. Enjoy yourselves. Rain in half an hour,' he called. He waved and disappeared along a clifftop track.

'Strange man,' Laura said.

'Total sanity can be very disconcerting,' Martin said. 'But he does know about weather. Let's go home.'

Home. The offshore wind razored the clifftops and made conversation hard. Only when they came back in sight of the cottage Martin said, 'I loved Eleanor, but I never stopped loving you.'

Laura looked up at his battered, wind-reddened face, and a wave of affection and sensuality went through her. She could have lain down in the coarse heather and opened her body to him then and there. She hugged him and said, 'I'm so happy.'

Martin had rearranged the shelves to make room for Laura's books, and the new grouping drew her attention to things she had not come across before. The change had forced Martin to rationalise the publications with his own name on, mostly monographs or contributions to various naturalist or scientific journals, together with several books ranging from special-ised to popular works from which he made most of his meagre living. Laura took out a copy of the regional magazine devoted to the reactor at Caunder, which in the cover headline was referred to as 'our nuclear neighbour'. She browsed what Martin had written about the wildlife to be found inside the thousand-acre power-station site.

As she was reading, Martin came in from a bath, naked, and sat down on his towel in front of the fire. He reached a chunk of pine on to the grate. His chest and belly wrinkled laterally as he leaned forward. He would never be fat, but in middle age his chest was assuming a comfortable barrel shape, which with the domed forehead left by his receding hair seemed to characterise the man he had always been destined to become.

21

Laura looked at him, and he threw his hands across his naked front in mock timidity.

'At fifty,' he said, 'you have the body you deserve. Only three more years.'

'Wrong,' Laura said. 'At fifty, you have the body *I* deserve.'

In a moment of despondent candour, Martin said, 'Look, if ever you find me boring, sod off back to London. Like a good girl. For both our sakes.'

'I couldn't find you boring,' Laura said.

'You haven't been here long.'

'Long enough.'

'It's a long time since I had to care what anybody thought of me,' Martin said. 'And now I care a whole lot what one person thinks of me. I'm afraid I may start behaving strangely.'

'You're an eminent man,' Laura said. 'So if you're going to act strangely, at least be eminently strange.'

'What gave you that idea?' Martin asked.

She indicated the shelf of publications which carried his name.

'Oh, that. A record of observations. I was a dedicated train-spotter as a boy, when they had real trains, and I graduated from there. I just like writing things down in notebooks.'

Laura rolled forward from her chair to kneel beside him and kiss the generous flesh of his body, his round lugubrious headmaster's face, his large but fine-fingered hands.

'How do you feel about this?' she asked, indicating the magazine with the 'nuclear neighbour' headline.

She was hoping he would express indignation at such a blatant public relations exercise – various well-meaning people being used to proclaim the plant's contribution to the local economy, its peerless safety record, its social life, its environmental 'cleanness', and, in Martin's case, the plant and animal life that thrived unthreatened within its five-mile perimeter fence.

'Well,' he said, 'it's a popular magazine. My article was a general interest piece. I do surveys at the plant from time to time.'

Laura's face was blank, and he read it correctly.

'What's bothering you?'

'It's just a big PR job, can't you see that? Your cosy neighbourhood nuclear plant, the gentle giant – can't you see what that kind of stuff is doing?'

'Oh, I know,' Martin said.

He looked at her in a way that said, I've been through all this a hundred times, and I'm not going to argue with you.

'Listen,' he went on, 'thirty years ago they began using pesticides. Over that time the poisons have got stronger, but there's a growing number of insect species now which are resistant to them. Life fights back. And now a lot of farmers are returning to organic methods, not for idealistic motives, but because the chemicals are self-defeating.'

'Life fights back,' Laura mocked. 'Great if you're dead.'

Martin remained genial and said, 'We'll go over to Caunder, and I'll show you the reactor. It stands in a big expanse of heathland, just off the coast, totally swallowed up. You don't even notice it. And in a few decades they'll concrete it over – look, two hundred years ago they were mining everything around here, coal, tin, chalk, ball-clay, anything they could scrape out of the ground – all gone now, back to grass. And one day the Caunder reactor will vanish and return to waste –'

'Sure,' Laura said, 'nuclear waste.'

'You'll see,' Martin said.

All gone back to grass. After the initial infatuation Laura went out for some days with map, binoculars and sketchbook and drove around on her own, and slowly and remorselessly the country started to eat away at her.

Country, my country, *the* country – the word, like the landscape itself, became more elusive as you tried to close in on it. Having grown up in towns Laura searched unsuccessfully for the definition always possessed by the dullest streets. *Country* was space and light, land as the silent, invisible repository of thousands of years of human and non-human life, the earth as a geological accident which yet, changing more slowly than those who passed over it, embodied the inevitability of a stable environment. And then it was a machine for rearing and killing, and the tracts of land on to which Laura was projecting spirit and mystery were also, as she knew, the empires of agribusiness, every acre a costed item on some distant balance sheet.

Yet it would always be there. Martin was right, the country had its own stubborn identity, irreducible and challenging. He had found comfort in it. She was beginning to learn.

That hill, for instance. A rounded hill on which an outcrop of chalk lightened the soil, suggesting the shine on a bald head. She drew it, and felt lucky at the moment of perception that had caused her to stop the car. How many other people, she wondered, over centuries had looked at that hill in that way? She opened the map, hoping the place would not be called Bald Man Hill or something trite like that. She was relieved that the spot was unmarked.

But mentally it was going to be a long haul. Streets were easy, they handed you a package, every one different but limited by their design, whatever jumble of structures people had lined them with. For the artist a street was easy. Whereas the country was fluid. You could bathe, swim – drown? – in it, but getting it on paper was different.

She was glad of the house she saw in the distance, glimpsed through a declivity in the hillside, far off and bravely golden in the sunlight, a lonely monument to style in the middle of nowhere. Laura instinctively liked something about the people who had put, or kept, it there. On the map it said simply, Scardale.

Great cauliflowers of cloud, Martin scribbled in his notebook. He could use the phrase in an article or a radio talk. The micro-recorder sat snugly in one of the many pockets of his

lightweight all-weather coat, but for these small impression-
istic touches he always found that longhand was necessary to
conserve the mental warmth of the idea. His own voice on
tape still made him uneasy.

After a bite of lunch he would record some thoughts on the
dead she-otter he had found that morning, killed while
crossing a road. He had carried the body, strangely unbloody,
the neck broken, and put it in the back of the Land-Rover. He
planned to set it down behind the cottage and record the
process of decomposition. The discovery had saddened him,
and as he ate his sandwiches he let memories of forty years
ago well up in him, recalling an otter family playing among
the exposed roots of an overgrown river bank, in the dusk of
his boyhood. For some people childhood was summer days,
for Martin it was twilights, the kingdom of bats and owls, the
rare treat of a nightjar or the otter family. He would turn it
into words when the thoughts had washed through him. And
much as he mourned the dead otter, he knew that it signified
others in the area. He would do a little detective work on
where the animal had been heading –

'Martin!'

A deep, assured voice, a voice out of the hills and the wind.
Martin looked round and scrambled to his feet as a large man
in sheepskin jacket, denims and leather boots laced up the
shin came down the flinty path towards him.

'Hello, Godfrey.'

They shook hands. Martin made no attempt to compete
with the bigger man's grip.

Godfrey Knapp's strong ivory-like teeth grinned through a
well-tended growth of facial hair.

'Saw you from way back there, Martin. Knew it had to be
you. I've been in the States for three months, and my first
outing when I get back I find you here. Then I know the place
has been guarded while I was away. Good feeling.'

'I'm always around,' Martin said. Usually the dominator
himself, with Knapp Martin always felt restored to a boyish
diffidence which was only partly accounted for by the dozen
years' gap between them.

25

Knapp took out an antique silver hip flask and proffered it. To be companionable Martin took a drink. Without wiping the rim Knapp then raised it to his own mouth.

'This place –' he said, with a gesture.

Far off, the sea, the promontory of Saltmayne only a gentle shadow on the water. Between, miles of rough countryside, barren and repellent except to those who had learned to love it.

'Are you doing anything this afternoon?' Martin said. But already his eyes narrowed at the sky. Knapp's head also turned upwards as Martin muttered, 'Buzzard.'

They watched the raptor's silhouette spiral against the clouds, and Knapp intoned, 'Forgive me that I have not eagle's wings.'

Before Martin could respond to the sudden intrusion of poetry, Knapp added, 'This afternoon – afraid not. On my way back to the car. Have to address the fat burghers of Barnbrook tonight on the subject of preserving this beautiful region. The unique contribution they can make with their cheque books and so on. But I'll see you at Scardale, Martin. Soon. Be in touch.'

And he was gone, with a wave, soon disappearing into a combe further down the hillside.

Martin sat down again, behind the rock which he used as a windbreak. So Godfrey Knapp was around again. It was a strange relationship the two men had, never really at ease with each other, both in their way loners, almost mystically attached to this landscape, and Knapp in his way as conversant with natural history as he seemed to be with so many other things. Yet their congeniality never became friendship, but was always overcast by a wariness that Martin could not explain.

He was not sorry about this. Knapp was too many people in one, and his directness of approach, his apparent intimacy, hid more than it revealed. Knapp knew too many people, perhaps that was it, from the Lord Lieutenant of the county to the barmaids of the pubs on Barnbrook's market square. He knew everybody, used everybody, was often happy to be used by them in return, but made sure that nobody ever came out ahead of him.

Then there were many things Martin did not know or wish to know about Knapp – where his money came from, what he did in his frequent absences from Scardale, where he derived his influence from. Martin was suspicious of him, and he felt that Knapp chose it to be like that. Yet on practical issues the man was invaluable, a wire-puller, a fixer. You could trust him with anything except yourself.

But behind all his *bonhomie* Martin sensed a loneliness, a disappointment with life, that shaded into contempt. Yet who else would shout poetry at a wheeling buzzard? Martin smiled and shook his head. Knapp was one of life's one-off people, and in the end they were the people you had to depend on.

Pausing for another pull at his flask, once he was down the slope and out of sight, Godfrey Knapp let his eyes rest on the landscape around him. But his mind was turned inwards.

It was two years since he had last heard from them. And now they were calling again, that plummy ageless voice at the other end, always glad to hear from him 'if there was anything'. There never was, these days.

So why had they resumed contact?

Chapter Three

'We'll walk the new boots in at Ashcot,' Martin said. 'It's a good place for new boots.'

'What's Ashcot?'

'It's a very special place. Any day you don't feel like working, we'll try out the Rover's new guts as well.'

The Rover was an ex-Army Land-Rover which Martin serviced himself, sometimes aided by a mechanic he knew whose passion in life was moths. They met rarely, contacted mainly by phone, trading expertise on Lepidoptera and auto parts. This sort of place, Laura had noticed, was full of odd relationships like that.

The Land-Rover, its khaki blotched with blue where the rust bubbles had been sanded off and retouched, rolled easily through the country on a day when vast blocks of cumulus hurtled dizzyingly across an open sky. The road seemed to lead nowhere, but that was another thing you got used to around here.

'Martin, stop!'

Martin smiled and drove on. Laura said, 'Did you see that sign?'

'Yes.'

'It said the road was closed.' She spoke the words with some disbelief. 'By the Army.'

'Bugger the Army,' Martin said. 'I don't like armies. Do you?'

28

A smile played around his lips as he rocked the Land-Rover to a stop where the narrow road was now very firmly gated off by an iron five-bar with a large well-painted sign, black on white, declaring that there was no admission except on Army business.

Laura gave Martin a quizzical look. Before she could voice what she felt, he climbed down from the jeep. She decided not to protest, studying the road ahead. But the narrow tarmac strip disappeared into a cluster of interlocking downs, beyond which the sea made a glittering slate roof across the entire horizon.

A field telephone, a primitive box on a wooden stump, stood sheltered by a small clump of bushes. Martin jangled his key ring, then looked up at the sound of an oncoming vehicle. A new and shiny Army jeep rounded the hill and stopped abruptly at the gate, the engine purring as it idled. From the cab a trim-moustached sergeant, black beret glued to his head, looked down.

'Morning, Mr Ritchie.'

Laura tried not to gape as Martin answered, 'Morning, sar'nt. Can we go through?'

'You've got about three hours before they start doing it for real.'

'OK, we'll be gone by then.'

The sergeant unlocked the gate, reversed on to grass while Martin drove inside the prohibited area, and as Laura caught his eyes, gave her an informal but respectful salute.

She frowned and said quietly, 'Martin, what am I getting into?'

Martin grinned. 'What do you mean?'

'I feel like visiting royalty. What the hell is this?'

'Darling, you're the queen of a strange country. Just wait a minute.'

Laura remembered a piece Martin had written – 'Ashcot, the Flowers of Unpoisoned Ground'. She had looked no further into it. But Ashcot now unfolded the first of its haunting, obscene secrets to her eyes.

It lay in a valley, which they approached from above, so it was easy to see the random layout of a small village of grey houses scattered among trees along a secluded coomb. The buildings were without roofs, the windows gaped black and empty, and in some cases the façades were crumbled away, exposing what had once been bedrooms. Most stood open to the sky, but on some houses pathetic remains of rafters still supported clutches of dislodged tiles. Some houses had been blasted open, and in the ruin of their humble interiors sprouted banks of rosebay and greedy red-green saplings.

Silent, Martin and Laura drove along what had been the main village street, little more than a lane, on part of which the tarmac was suspiciously fresh. The dead houses stared mutely, like fragments of broken bone sticking out of the earth.

'My God,' Laura said. 'What happened?'

'The Army took it over for a test range in the war.' He made the ghost of a shrug. 'They never handed it back.'

'You mean people lived here?'

'It's a long story.'

Laura said, 'I get the feeling that around here everything's just one long story.'

A short way through the village Martin pulled the Land-Rover on to a green that was three-quarters closed off with wooden bollards. It bore signs of regular use as a vehicle park.

'Under here,' he said, 'the people of Ashcot buried their dead after the Black Death.'

'Martin, you sure know how to create a mood.'

Martin smiled. 'It's quite a place, isn't it?'

Laura, frowning, said, 'It lacks innocence.'

Martin looked into her eyes and said nothing.

They walked along the devastated, silent village street. On some cottages the doors and windows were planked over with boards that were now themselves rotting away, while above them the skeletal buildings had been caved in and left to die of their wounds.

'How did they do all this?' Laura asked.

30

'Tank shells,' Martin said. 'Hand-grenades, mortars – they use the place for battle practice.'

'And the people who lived here?'

'They moved them out and rehoused them in '43. They've never been allowed back.'

Laura followed Martin on a footpath out of the village. The path was wired off, and signs in white on red warned of unexploded bombs and shells in the adjacent fields.

'I noticed you got in without any trouble,' Laura said.

Martin grimaced, apologetic yet self-satisfied. The scene at the roadblock had gratified him, Laura had observed.

'It's a –'

'Don't tell me,' she said. 'A long story.'

'No, it's simple for once. For years people campaigned against the Army's occupation of this valley, so in the end they gave limited access – some weekends, holidays. But even before that they came to the interesting conclusion, not unassisted by me, that their seizure of this land had protected it from forty years of intensive farming, erosion, chemical debasement. It's a genuine wilderness. I've written about it a lot – that's how the Army know me. I've become a sort of resident naturalist here. Over a hundred plant species grow in the fields you're looking at now.'

Martin waved with a sort of paternal pride, and reeled off some names, whether uncommon or everyday Laura had no idea, but the names had magic in them. Carline thistle, restharrow, yellow archangel, chervil, monkey orchid, agrimony, fritillary, pasque-flower – he spoke them with the reflective emotion of someone naming their children. And with the flower names the spectre of an old, dead England passed before Laura's eyes, a fleeting vision that however did nothing to soften the loneliness of the gutted houses below them.

'So everybody likes the Army because of their conservation work,' Laura said. 'I think I understand now.'

'They're not the world's tidiest people,' Martin said, pointing across the valley, 'but they're not as bad as they're painted.'

31

The place he had indicated, revealed above a distant wooded stream as they climbed a steep rocky way up the scarp, was an overgrown field in whose deep rank grass the rusting hulls of tanks lay littered about, some overturned, some with turret and gun twisted and accusing, others burnt out and rounded, humping shyly out of the long meadow-grass, their function smashed into extinction, gradually fading back into nature.

'Gunnery practice,' Martin said.

Laura didn't reply. As they went higher to turn along the ridge which had been their skyline for an interminable time, the view unfolded and the isolation of this remote village struck her with great force, its frozen-in-time pathos, its monument-like spirit. She thought of Samuel Palmer's *Valley of Vision*. But you would need a strong stomach to draw or paint these exploded stumps of houses, aching as they did with the depopulation on which all those other things depended.

They clasped hands to complete the last steep stretch, and to celebrate what they found up there. What breath the sea-powered wind left them was snatched by the landscape that rippled away all around them. The coastline, bay after bay of buckled rock-strata, gave on to a greenish-blue sea that washed in a white foam on to crescents of pebbled beaches. A buzzard drifted by, on a level with their eyes, playing with the air, making the sea its wallpaper. And Ashcot itself was suddenly a long way back, shielded from the sea by patchy areas of woodland, and now looked small, dreamlike, an apparition of a medieval hamlet which time, disease, poverty had gradually wasted. Yet along the valley, more visible now, were more derelict buildings, farmhouses that had been substantial once, fishermen's cottages or boathouses hard against the sea's breakers, all of them gutted or crumbled to the foundations.

Although the wind chilled her lips, and its force obliged them to shout, Laura said, 'I once went to Dachau – on holiday in Germany – you know, the concentration camp. It was my husband's idea. I got the same feeling – I'm not saying this is the same thing as Dachau, but – you just don't know what to say in the end –'

Enigmatically, leaving Laura to think about it, which she did for a long time after, Martin shouted into the wind, 'People die, but places go on living.'

The Roebuck Hotel in Barnbrook had been named that way, according to a plaque in its modernised foyer, since 1678. The plaque was Victorian tile, incongruous in the aseptic new surroundings, but Harry Teal appreciated the detail. He took his environment at face value, and he liked a place that made these little attempts to impress. Likewise in his room he found a *Pilgrim's Progress*, bound in red leather and copperplated on the flyleaf, 'Valentine Elwes, HMS *Vortigern*, October 1918'. Teal liked the resonance of the date and the trusting way in which the book reposed in this homely but comfortable hotel room. He made an attempt to read it, but failed, so just admired it as a piece of superior furnishing, part of that indefinable classy feel which some of these country places possessed. All the same he hoped not to be there too much longer. Although he was not eager to return to his wifeless house, he wanted this job to be quick and recorded as a success on his file. As the days had gone by, this mission had become identified with his rehabilitation.

He checked his room key in at the desk, and the girl said, 'Thank you, Mr Greenwood.' Wearing his discreet check suit and highly polished veldschoen, Teal left the hotel. He switched himself mentally into the character mode that said, 'Man of invisible means – some years spent abroad – enjoying mature affair with British countryside – maybe writing a book or studying some area of natural history – not a back-packing coast-walker, but the kind of man you come across in many wild locations, gazing silently, part of the stillness, impossible to place and yet perfectly at home –'

It was an easy image to assume. Teal sniffed cynically and revved his Volvo. The Volvo, like the roll of flab around his middle and his incipient double chin, went with check suits and thinning, tousled hair, a package that could go anywhere and not arouse suspicion. Priceless, and Teal ought to know. Not arousing suspicion was his trade, his art. His love.

The limestone hump of Saltmayne, known locally as the Rock, had an area of five square miles, but when approached along the clifftop road that led to the causeway it looked small and self-effacing, tapering down into the grey sea-water like a dead whale about to be sucked under. But from the causeway itself, at sea-level, the Rock suddenly reared up, raising near-vertical walls of jagged almost grassless limestone, all shades of blue and grey from white through indigo, a petrified tidal wave.

In its time Saltmayne had been everything. For several thousand years it had been a human settlement, and was one still, although except for lobsters for the luxury market the fishing had died out, and the work had gone elsewhere, across to the mainland. Still Saltmayne lived on like an ageing but indomitable body, gradually dying in some parts but fighting back in others. It had been a fortress, a prison, a quarry, a naval base, a site for secret weapons research, and it remained all of these things, although over the years the emphasis varied. The one thing it had never become was a tourist attraction, even when parts of the mainland began to summon wilderness-lovers. Something about Saltmayne repelled even the mainlanders – there was not a single tree on the so-called island, the people who lived there were dour and elusive, for centuries it got its living from plundering ship-wrecks, and the atmosphere of the place still brooded with the spirit of convict labour-gangs and bloated bodies washed up on the rocky foreshores.

Yet the zigzag road from the causeway up on to the heights of Saltmayne was one of the great sights of Europe. Probably only the lack of sunshine had stopped it being covered with casinos. That was fine by Harry Teal. He preferred the sun to be an aeroplane trip away, so he could leave it when he got bored with it. Overcast skies spelt better security.

On top of the Rock the main church stood out prominently above the fields of tough grass and quarry waste. It was a plain building of square-cut ashlar and clear Venetian windows, constructed by inmates of the Victorian gaol system who quarried, cut and dragged the blocks to their place of consecration. Teal parked the Volvo and stepped through the dry grass of the burial ground. It was his first visit, and would be his last, but at least what he had come for was easy to find.

The wreath drew his attention, fading and ragged now, a unique spot of colour in the muted surroundings. Against a headstone which, for all the date being 1891, was still clean and unweathered, the circle of flowers carried the message 'From The Boys'. The legend on the stone commemorated Michael O'Connor Maguire, and all around lay the graves of other members of the Fenian Brotherhood, incarcerated here for life by Victorian England, malnourished and worked to anonymous deaths, until the IRA had recently made the spot a place of pilgrimage and gained a brief moment for it on the national TV news.

Ironic, Teal thought. Hardly a week goes by without some centenary being forced on the public, but the one nobody heard about was the Special Branch's big birthday in 1983, having been founded a hundred years earlier to crack down on the Irish malcontents who lay at his feet now. Ironic that only the IRA had garlanded their end of the occasion, and sickening too, because what self-respecting country would leave its finest servants uncommemorated? A dark anger began to rise in him as he stared at the modest gravestones.

Teal started, aware of another person in the churchyard, a well-dressed woman with straight blonde hair, her face pinched by the unremitting onshore winds that raked the heights of Saltmayne. She looked too smart for a local, and anyway these graves were old and showed no sign of being visited. So her presence was suspect. Teal decided to move on. He raised his eyes momentarily to the woman as he passed, but said nothing, and went by. Her car was parked in the road, a powder-blue Dyane with a CND sticker in the rear window. He memorised the number plate.

From the top of Saltmayne, the sheep-cropped ridge behind the prison, Teal stared out at the indented coastline. A man of limited imagination and a tendency to take things personally, he ground his teeth as he thought of chummy out there somewhere, defying them to come and get him. Well, he couldn't eat defiance. They'd soon put him away.

The thin man with the rucksack Laura had glimpsed from the cliffs on that first day remembered the caves from an exercise with the marines years ago. There was no beach at this point, and no access from the land side except for natural breaks in the rock which offered hand- and footholds only to experienced climbers whose nerves were indifferent to the wind-clawed drop, a hundred feet to the jagged sea-lapped boulders below. You could either do it or you couldn't. As it happened he could.

The caves were little more than eroded fissures in the rock, and as soon as he made it there a heavy depression overcame him, stronger even than the need for endless sleep which his mind and body had begun to plead for. He kicked his way out of this downward spiral by repeatedly telling himself why he was there, how long for, and what options he still had open.

He would live on tinned food and bottled water. He had enough for two days. Before that was up he had to find a source of replacement. That would be the first test.

The neolithic hill-fort of Lendra was curiously small in the distance as the Land-Rover skirted the uplands whose top the ancient earthwork crowned. Laura kept seeing what Martin meant about things being swallowed up here, devoured by space, by contours, by sky and sea. The oilfield was a prime case – Britain's largest onshore reserves, the storage drums screened by trees, the hardtop sites carefully constructed in unvisited glades, the pipelines buried or under sea.

The oil had been another masterpiece of public relations, and she was aware of Martin's role in the exercise. The oil company had funded studies of its – so far – minimal impact on the environment, and they undertook no new work without consulting local naturalists. Martin himself still earned occasional consultancy fees from them.

As they drove he asked, 'You don't feel you've wasted your time, coming here?' It was a perpetual anxiety with him, now the honeymoon was passing.

Laura said, 'No, the images are fantastic. Some days I can't unload my head of all the impressions I've taken. I realise how stale I'd got.'

'Good,' Martin said.

'So you can stop apologising. I love it here. I love you too.'

'I'll stop apologising.'

'And as for the nuclear power, and the submarines, and the oilfield, and the Army – Martin, there's more fucking PR out here than in the West End.'

With a wry smile Martin said, 'You're right, of course.'

They left the car and walked some way on the cliffs.

'Look.'

Laura pointed to the figure and handed Martin the binoculars.

'It's Vayro. What's he doing down there?'

In a cove where the rocks merged with a strip of pale sand, John Vayro was walking about, fully dressed, not purpose-fully like a man going somewhere or hunting for something, but in an aimless distracted way, retreading the small beach with shambling steps that lacked his usual energy.

Laura said, 'Should we go and see?'

Evening was approaching, but there was still an hour or two of usable daylight. Martin said, 'Yes, let's go.'

They followed the winding track down. The sea came barking in, its noise beating off the concave cliffs. The tideline was marked by a dark rim along the sand, minute globules of tar which washed up casually every day, sorted into an orderly layer by the tide. Until they came close Vayro did not notice them.

Martin forced his voice above the sea-roar and called to

Vayro, who turned briefly but kept his eyes fixed on the sea as if he did not dare look away.

'You all right, John?'

Vayro stumbled away, over to a chain of rocks, disregarding the slippery layers of brown seaweed which showed how far they lay below water at full tide, and leaned carefully against them. His square, alert face looked grey. His distress was evident, and Martin went close and put a hand on his shoulder. He urged questions on him. Vayro's answers were reluctant, and the wind scattered them.

'Terrible weakness – feel fine one minute, then can't move – nearly drowned the other day – out in the water, couldn't swim any more – had to float back, nearly hit the rocks – nearly didn't make it –'

'You shouldn't be here,' Martin said.

'I had to. You know how it is.'

'Come back with us,' Laura said. 'Have some dinner and stay over.'

Vayro gave a tight-lipped smile and shook his head. Martin and Laura concealed their helplessness by staring out at the sea. His stocky figure was like a symbol of resilience as the anorak hood flapped behind his wiry grey hair and the wind glanced off his weatherbeaten face. But suddenly his control gave way, and the tears rolled down his leathery cheeks.

'Oh Christ,' he said, the inflexion of his voice conveying apology. 'I feel so weak.'

They took one arm each and led him back along the shore. Vayro was docile and grateful, as if a great tension had been lifted from him. It was starting to rain. He let them lead him slowly back up the cliff, as helpless and trusting as a child. They left him at the hospital in Barnbrook. There was no question of taking him home, although he protested. It transpired that he had already been having blood tests. The hospital kept him, they said, for overnight observation.

For a while Vayro was mentally on top of what was happening to him. The word 'leukaemia' was not mentioned, although

38

the doctors had told him, and since he had designated Martin as the person closest to him, they had told Martin too. But for the two men it was something to be kept out of sight.

For a short time he still looked curable. The muscular body was not shrunken, and apart from skin pallor and a blankness in the eyes, he remained the same man he had been.

'I still intend to die in the ocean,' he said. 'If these bastards can't do anything for me, I want you to get me down there.'

Martin said, 'We'll plan a break-out.'

'I mean it,' Vayro said.

They both knew he was too weak to cross the room, but he meant it.

Vayro was in a room by himself, in protective isolation from routine infections. They saw and heard of no other visitors, and wondered at the strange solitude in which he must have spent his life. For a few days Laura had a cold and was not allowed to see him. On one visit during this time Vayro roused himself, his mind unusually active.

'Could you get that document from the table?'

There was only one. Martin reached for it.

'It's a will, all witnessed and everything. You're the sole beneficiary. All I have is my house, a few quid in the bank. It all goes to you.'

Martin had begun protesting.

Vayro went on, 'If you don't need it, I know you'll use the money for something good. Now that's done I'm glad.' He sank back into the pillow, eyes closed.

Martin bit back on his emotion and pressed Vayro's hand. The older man eventually blinked his eyes open and in a near-whisper continued, 'Once I'm dead, not before, go to the house and take care of everything. Go alone. Try to understand.'

Martin wondered at the last imperative, but said, 'You can trust me.'

At the end of the day the thin dark young man from the cliffs travelled the several miles of coastal paths to the small but

39

sprawling township which lay at the back of the naval base. He had been here himself during his days as one of Her Majesty's defenders of the realm, and he knew the kind of place it was, poor housing littered across the hillsides that rose away from the Inlet, a large number of scabby drinking-holes, chip shops and pinball arcades for the drunken sailors with money in their pockets and nowhere to go. A piss-awful climate too, no decent women, fights with the sub boys stir-crazy from a month underwater. A hell of a hole.

But he would be less conspicuous there than in the pretty villages and genteel towns inland. All he needed was a supermarket where he could load up with tinned meat and other wrapped, preserved food that required no cooking, some carry-packs of spring water, and away again.

He had cleaned himself up as best he could, and the growth on his face almost felt like a proper beard now. But he still looked dirty, dishevelled, and was starting to smell bad. He needed all his water for drinking, so washing and shaving had to go. From a comfort point of view, he was indifferent. He just didn't want the attention that scruffiness and body odour were likely to attract.

Still, he could get enough for a week. The streets, those bloody, faceless streets of so many British towns, were already glooming over as he found the right sort of shop for what he wanted. He was not in there three minutes, but several people looked, and the checkout woman maybe remarked the crispness of the note he handed over, and how it contrasted with the rest of him. He was prepared for all that.

Worst case – she would pick up a phone and call the police, who would recognise the description. Then what? A man-hunt? By the county constabulary? In the gathering dark-ness? With no idea what direction he would be taking? And for what crime? Being shabby in charge of a ten-pound note? Was that a crime these days? Probably.

But assume all of that, and take action accordingly. He was away from the place in minutes, blending with the dark. Tonight he would sleep rough. He needed daylight to negotiate the caves. He had found a small copse and secreted his sleeping-bag there under the fallen leaves. That would see him through another night.

But eventually he would let himself be seen by somebody. Deliberately, carefully. That was the whole object. Otherwise he would never know if his plan had worked.

The chemotherapy took effect, swift and disastrous, and the approach of death now assumed a surreal ugliness. Vayro's face became inflamed and swollen, and his hair, the bristling grey hair that had always seemed an emblem of his strength, fell out in the course of a day. Martin and Laura went at their regular times, but now the occasions when they found him sedated were a relief.

Martin told Laura about the will, but kept quiet about Vayro's strictures on going to the house. For many years Vayro had worked at the Underwater Weapons Research Establishment on Saltmayne, and the prohibition must be connected with that fact. Vayro was hardly a spy, and he had retired from the Establishment several years ago, and yet he asked for understanding of what Martin would find at the house. Understanding of what?

The fear that somebody else might discover it first, perhaps even while Vayro was alive, finally drove Martin to go there. It was bad faith, but the old man was clearly dying now, and Martin wanted to know all there was to know about his old friend before he saw him out of this world. He had a house-key on the ring he had taken when they reclaimed Vayro's car from the clifftop.

Only after he returned from the small, tidy house did he tell Laura about the episode.

'It wasn't secret documents. The place was full of homosexual pin-up magazines. He must have been keeping quiet about that for years. For a lifetime.'

'Why should he?'

'This isn't London. Besides, the Weapons Establishment is a very tight-security place. If he'd been active, even suspected, they'd have got rid of him, and on his papers it would just say "security risk". You can see the problem.'

'I can see a wasted life,' Laura said. 'Can't you?'

Martin answered, 'That's a judgment I can't make.'

After an hour on the same tract of heathland, Martin made his third sighting of the kite in a week. This time Laura was with him. They followed the bird, watching as it vanished and reappeared.

'I have this certainty,' Martin said, 'that it's the same one I saw in the spring. I thought it was a vagrant from Wales, but maybe they're checking out a new breeding-ground. In medieval London kites used to scavenge the streets, the original shite-hawks. Now they're about as common as eagles.'

The kite soared away, wings and forked tail languidly extended on the air-current, and withdrew to another, more distant landscape.

'You think they'll be back next spring?' Laura asked.

'Could be. I sort of hope not.'

'Why?'

'Their eggs are worth a lot of money. Every birdwatcher within a hundred miles would be here. Continuous guard would have to be mounted on the nest. The kites would raise their young in conditions of greater security than the submarine base over there. Ironic, isn't it?'

Their attention was caught by a figure walking towards them on the same stone-littered track across the heath. It was strange how the kite could disappear so easily in a pale wilderness of sky, yet a solitary human advancing through acres of varied countryside could stand out like a tower.

He was a plumpish man in a check suit, swinging a straight ashplant and looking directly at them as the space between narrowed – no eyes fixed to the ground, no furtive glances then looking away.

He did not speak, and for some reason Martin, usually affable, said nothing. Laura knew she had seen him before,

42

but it was some minutes before she remembered the grave-yard on Saltmayne. After he had passed, Laura's eyes asked, *who?* Martin's shrug said, I've never seen him before. After some distance he added, 'I don't know who he is, but he doesn't live here.'

Here meant a whole region. She asked, 'How do you know?'

'You can always tell.'

Beside the mellowing greens and browns of a woodland autumn the red flag looked smart, jaunty, flickering a little in the breeze, a huge rectangular poppy. Further along the road, against a hillside of corn-stubble, another red flag, this time a fluent patch of blood in the sky, snapped dramatically at miles of rolling country.

'I can never get used to them,' Laura said. 'I always think the revolution has broken out.'

The flags marked the outer reaches of the gunnery no-go area, and were accompanied by the omnipresent smaller signs warning trespassers of unexploded shells that might lie in the undergrowth. But most of the shells were fired out over the sea. Every view, every line of thought, led to the sea, to Vayro, as unremittingly as the road they were on led to Barnbrook, to the hospital, the isolation room in which he lay dying.

This particular day he woke for their visit. A perky but barely rational light danced in his eyes. At times he seemed to know them, at others he was fixed on some vision in his own mind.

'It was the sea in the end,' he said. His voice was feeble. They strained to hear.

Martin repeated, 'The sea?'

'The sea killed me.'

A terrible croaking laugh rattled in his throat. Martin's intestines constricted. He knew what Vayro was getting at. All along he had hoped to avoid it. But he refused to cheat the dying man with silence.

'How's that, John?'

'The Caunder outflow.'

'Caunder?'

'The waste they pump into the sea. The water's radioactive. Don't you believe that?'

'It's very low level, John.'

'It's killed me. Every day, swimming in radioactive water. Look at me now. This is how I've got to die.'

Vayro did not speak again. They waited till he dozed off, then Martin kissed his blotchy, bald head, and Laura pressed his hand, and they crept away from the sickroom. They felt a shame stronger even than sorrow.

When they called the next day, Vayro was dead.

The body had already been removed from the room. Technically they could ask to see what remained of the old swimmer, but they let it go. They had known it all along, somehow, but had driven over there rather than receive the news starkly across the phone. Going there was a dumb, hopeless way of saying a final goodbye. As they drove home again in grim silence the red flags gashed the air against a backdrop of slate-purple storm-clouds.

Chapter Four

In her workroom Laura re-created the familiar space of her
London studio, except that now instead of cramped and
overgrown gardens her window gave out on to miles of
moorland above which, on days when either sunshine or
storm-clouds clarified the light, the sea appeared to sleep.
Martin had insisted that she have a phone extension in the
room. Totally unnecessary, Laura said, and yet once it was
installed she felt better having it there, and she realised that
he had spotted something which she herself had not admitted,
the need not to feel cut off. She knew he was afraid of the pull
of London, and moments came when she also feared it.

The mail brought constant recall of what she had left.
People invited her back to stay, wanted to meet Martin, were
having parties, even hinted at coming down to see her. This
forced Laura to consider exactly what transition she had
made. It was not just a physical move, a break out of London
all the better to enjoy it when she moved back again. It was a
change of life, but as yet she could not even explain to herself
what shape it would finally assume.

Certainly, the place offered her images which London
could never provide, and many of them were still working
their way through her consciousness weeks after she first
encountered them. She had one book commission at the
moment, a children's book for which she had a known and
perfected style. The project was fun, but she needed to work

on another side, exploring these new images. Lately she had been preoccupied with the sight of a lone figure walking towards her across the open moor.

From regular sly checks on her drawing-board Martin knew what impressions she was taking. Laura asked him for critical advice. He had no artistic skill beyond a gift for accurate biological draughtsmanship, and this made him a useful commentator.

'Why do you keep redrawing the same picture?' he asked. 'The one with the figure in the distance.'

'The thing you can't convey in the picture,' Laura said, 'is that the man is moving through a landscape which is still. In reality, you see the figure moving towards you, maybe two miles away, but it gets bigger only very slowly – yet you *know* it's moving, and the figure dominates the landscape. The problem is to convey that in the drawing without destroying the perspective.'

'I was in Finland once,' Martin said, 'actually Lapland, on a survey, and I was crossing a long stretch of tundra with a Finnish ecologist. Places like that make Macemoor seem like Hyde Park. Anyway, we saw someone approaching us. You couldn't tell how far away he was, but it took forty minutes for us to reach each other. It was a lonely place, and I felt very intimidated by this character. But when we came up, he didn't even make eye contact. He just stared ahead, continued his even-paced walking, and passed us. My Finnish friend had done the same to him. When I looked surprised, he said, "If he wanted company, he wouldn't be here." Apparently it was normal behaviour, people showing respect for their chosen isolation. It altered the way I saw my own life.'

Laura hesitated before changing the subject. 'I thought I'd go to London next week.'

Martin said, 'Good.'

'You don't mind?'

'Of course not. It's time you went.'

'I'll have to stay over.'

'Good idea. I'll go out with Batman while you're away.'

'Batman?'

'His name's Arnold Moloney. He studies bats all around here. Everybody calls him Batman.' Martin paused. 'I miss you already.'

'Me too,' Laura said.

Before the leaving day came, Laura found herself once again walking towards a lone figure in the middle distance. This time it was on the coast, where she had spent an hour drawing the folds of some interesting limestone anticlines. Crossing the down with the sea behind her, to where she had left her car, Laura again saw a solitary man coming towards her from half a kilometre away. She slowed down and watched him carefully, trying to work out the dynamics of the figure's blending with scenery which, as it came closer, it dominated.

Even at that range, she knew it was not the man she and Martin had seen on the day John Vayro died. That stranger had been fleshy, assertive, arrogant, all plain from the way he walked. The person she now saw coming towards her recalled the stranger Martin had described trudging across the tundra of Lapland. Maybe that, or something self-effacing in his walk, made her fix her eyes on the ground as she came within twenty yards of the man. She flashed only one glance at him before firmly averting her eyes.

Whoever he was, he did not belong there. Although you met a great diversity of people in these remote areas, there were certain identifying features common to them all – items of clothing, a style of walking, even the way they looked or didn't look around them. The man Laura passed was dressed wrong. The only detail she registered was his thin-soled town shoes, but nothing else about him was right either. His demeanour was furtive, he had his hands in his pockets and his shoulders hunched, and he was underdressed for the winds that always blew over the coastal downland.

She sensed that he did not want to be looked at or spoken to, and although she had relaxed a little since leaving London, the possibility of rape or assault when alone in an isolated place like this suddenly came back as potently as on a deserted city street at night. After passing the stranger she walked faster and for a while was tense at the thought that he had followed her. But when she looked round he had gone.

She mentioned the meeting to Martin. He thought it was probably somebody from the housing estates around the submarine base along the coast. They were a small, inbred population, a passive workforce captive to the Royal Navy, and sometimes a few of them got drunk for the weekend and drifted off their normal trackways. Usually no problem.

The solicitors had written. Since John Vayro had planned his own tough-minded marine suicide, he had left no alternative funeral instructions. Laura and Martin organised a non-religious burial, with the coffin simply delivered to the municipal cemetery at Barnbrook, where they watched as it was lowered into the ground, on a day when the sea drove in an iron, unremitting rain over the land. They said their goodbyes without pity but with a lingering guilt at the way he had died, then walked back through the dripping pines to the road.

After that, the will was faultless, and Martin was officially informed that Vayro's house would be transferred to his ownership. While Laura was away he drove the five miles to the house to check it for an idea he had been formulating.

Embarrassment at benefiting from a friend's death had provoked him to think of converting the place to a field centre, and the potential of that kept catching light in his mind. The lonely dwelling, its back against a small copse of holm oak and stunted conifers leading to an acre of marsh colonised by bogbean and sundew, was perfect for a weather-shelter, a meeting place, an observation post, and most importantly a record station, where every local sighting could be logged for all other visiting naturalists to follow up. It was an exciting picture, and Martin also had a vision of a carved stone lintel over the plain front door commemorating Vayro and his gift. The old swimmer would have been well pleased.

48

From an upstairs room in the house Martin was sweeping the country with his telescope, playing with designs of enlarging windows and converting the inside of the roof to a watching post. In the distance, perhaps a mile away, he saw someone walking, a youngish man he did not recognise, who after a minute's observation, brought back Laura's description of the man she had seen two days earlier.

Across that moorland space no detail was clear except an impression of thinness, of a slight dark man in a suit, ambling along at a pace that declared aimlessness. But out here nobody could be aimless, any more than a rare bird of passage could be 'lost'. A need to find out who the man was, and a wish to find out how far he could cover the moor without himself being spotted, prompted Martin to sling his field glasses and leave the house, pulling on his anorak as he went.

He knew every swell of the ground, and as he strode along the flinty tracks he was simultaneously assessing the likely position of the stranger and his own possible visibility as a rise in the land rolled him into prominence again. Much of this he could neutralise by angling his walk towards patches of scrawny thicket or outcrops of rock. The price of his own concealment was to lose sight of the stranger for a while, but he travelled fast and banked on the inhospitable country not to swallow his quarry up too readily.

The clouds parted and let through a quick flash of sunlight as Martin climbed a rise from which he could see the area he had been surveying from Vayro's house. The stranger had gone. Refusing to believe he had lost him, Martin walked on. The sea opened up in the distance, and the land swept away to meet it.

He uncased his field glasses and had just hooked the strap round his neck when he became aware of movement behind him. As he turned he saw the stranger heading away from him. So he had misjudged something as he crossed the moor. That, or the stranger had altered his direction. Martin went after him, his boots quiet on the wiry turf. The stranger showed no awareness of being followed. Martin waited till he was parallel before speaking.

'Afternoon,' he said, slowing his pace.

'Hello,' the stranger answered, not curt, but not inviting conversation. He started as he spoke, but somehow Martin was not convinced by the expression of surprise.

'You staying round here?'

A pause, then, 'Yes.'

'Some very good walking routes.'

This was so irrelevant as to sound like sarcasm. Martin frowned uncomfortably.

The stranger was wearing a discreetly patterned lounge suit which did not belong in the country or, Martin guessed from its size, to him. His shirt was open-necked and not too clean, his shoes cheap and about to give way. The wind untidied everybody's hair out here, but below the straight dark hair the stranger's face was taut and pale and carried a growth of at least three days' ugly black stubble. The mouth was wide, an expressive mouth somehow devoid of expression, and the eyes were long and narrow, shrewd lidless eyes which only permitted a one-way view.

To the comment about walking he said, 'Yes.'

Martin was pretending to match his pace to the stranger's, but it was awkward.

'Where are you headed?'

'I'm just walking around.'

'It's a nice place.'

'Yes, nice.'

The stranger's accent was classless, in other words the speech of a man who was used to dealing with his betters but without servility.

'Can I give you any directions?'

'No, I'll be all right, thanks.'

'Good luck, then.'

'Cheers,' the stranger said. He seemed fit, for all his out of place clothes, and was soon some distance away.

Martin had stopped there because it was a spot with a wide view of the land around, and he wanted to train his glasses on the stranger for a while. He wondered about the man. He was obviously sleeping in the open, his clothes had the crumpled look of being slept in, the rest of him looked worn and hungry. Yet his speech was controlled and gave no clue as to why he was wandering around here like this.

When he finally disappeared from Martin's range of vision, it was in the direction of the cliffs, suddenly and even efficiently. Martin again had an impulse to follow, but killed it. The man didn't seem to want help, so what was the point?

Laura had been back a few hours. In the kitchen she was listening to the local radio station, although on the Faul peninsula even local radio seemed to deal with a remote outside world. She called, 'Martin, Martin!'

'What?'

'Come and listen to this.'

Martin clattered downstairs and was in time for the last half of the news item.

'. . . from the mental hospital at Faulston. He is in his early thirties, with dark hair and a pale complexion. His manner may be charming, but this can be deceptive, and if he feels threatened he could become dangerous. Members of the public who suspect that they have seen this man are advised to alert the police as soon as possible . . .'

'The man I saw,' Laura said.

Martin said, 'I saw him too.'

'You didn't tell me.'

'Do you remember what we've been doing since you got back?'

Laura laughed. 'OK.'

'I met him yesterday, tried to speak to him, but he didn't want to talk. It had to be the same man you saw.'

Laura gestured at the radio. 'Him?'

'Must be.'

'What do we do? Tell the police?'

Martin grimaced unfavourably. 'A manhunt all over Macemoor? I'm not crazy about it. Let's see if we can find him again tomorrow.'

'Then what?'

Martin thought a moment, disregarding her question.

'You know,' he said, 'I had this uncanny feeling that he was living there. Not just dossing in the fields, but actually – living there.'

They took the two points where they had met the stranger, mediated the distance between, and drove there. On the way Laura said, 'Of course, he could be someone else.'

'Who for instance?'

'I don't know – a criminal, a spy –'

'Then why don't they say so?'

'Making him a lunatic might encourage people to look out for him.'

Martin laughed. 'I can't think of anything less likely to catch this guy. The point is, what are we going to do if we see him? I've no experience with madmen, criminals or spies.'

'Offer him food. He must be starving out there.'

'Why should we get involved at all?'

The question hung coldly in the air. The Dyane churned up a long gradient. Laura looked sideways.

'I know why you're involved,' she said.

'Go on then. Why?'

'Because someone you don't know has invaded your territory, and you want to get rid of him.'

After a pause Martin nodded and said, 'You're right.'

They walked little-used tracks over the coastal hinterland for an hour, then Martin spotted someone. As they got closer it was clearly the man they were looking for. He saw them coming, but made no attempt to change his direction or to get out of sight.

'What do we do?' Laura asked. 'What do we say?'

Martin kept his eyes on the approaching figure. 'I don't know.'

As soon as they were near enough, Martin tried to catch his eye, but the stranger held his head furtively down and was going to shuffle past them.

52

In a hearty extrovert voice Martin called, 'Hello!'

He had tried to sound unthreatening. The stranger looked baffled but returned the hello. They drew level.

'We met the other day.'

The stranger's shambling pace slackened, and he peered at Martin from under lowered brows.

'You remember?'

Slowly the stranger said, 'Yes.'

'My friend and I' – Martin indicated Laura – 'were just going to have lunch.' He cocked his head at the nylon bag he carried on his back. 'We wondered if you'd like to have some with us.'

The stranger was silent.

'Just a picnic,' Laura said. She opened the bag and took out a pork pie, spreading back the greaseproof paper to reveal the golden crust. It was a good move. The stranger said, 'Thank you.' They laid out a groundsheet and sat down to eat. This was the part they had not rehearsed. After a few common-place remarks about the beauty of the scenery, Martin said, 'It's quite a skill, living in the open.'

The stranger looked from one to the other of them, fleetingly and with a nervous control that allowed him to meet their eyes briefly without giving anything away. He ate slowly, thoughtfully, not ravenously like a starving man, but with the controlled appetite of someone used to rations. Eventually he answered, 'I don't know.'

'I'm Martin, this is Laura.'

The stranger's white face creased in a minimal social gesture and a brief nod at both of them. Martin asked if he had a name, as gently as he could, but it still sounded intimidating.

Laura gave him a look of warning. The stranger ignored the question, became impenetrable behind a veil of self-absorption, as if at that moment he found himself alone with the cliffs and the sea, everything else a delusion. He even stopped eating. Laura offered him a drink from a flask of coffee and said, 'You don't have to talk if you don't want to.'

A minute's silence. Then Martin said, 'If you're in any trouble, we'd like to help.'

Again the words hung stillborn for a moment, then the wind shredded them. What could have been spray but was in fact a light, prickly rain, began to blow in off the sea.

'What do you do when it rains?' Martin asked. 'You shelter? There are some good caves near here.'

He winced as he said it. Showing off his mastery of the area, he had told the stranger that no hiding place was safe. Bugger, he thought, and hoped the words had made no impact.

Laura suggested, 'Shall we go and sit in the car?'

'It isn't a trap,' Martin said, again perhaps too quickly. 'You're quite free to come and go.'

But of course they would say that, wouldn't they? The rain was more intense and stinging now. They gathered the things back into the rucksack and zipped their jackets. The synthetic material of the stranger's suit was already darkening as the rain soaked in.

'You can't stay out here,' Laura said. 'Come back with us.'

He looked at them through narrow eyes, suspicious and knowing, then shook his head.

'Please,' Laura said.

'No.' His voice was pleasant, detached, but final.

Through the sheet of mist and rain which had blotted out sea and sky and reduced them to three blurred figures in a tiny storm-centre, Martin shouted, 'You'll die out here.'

'I'm all right,' the stranger said. It was the first personal remark he had made.

'Listen,' Martin told him, 'we'll be here, same place, same time tomorrow.' He looked at his watch for effect. 'One o'clock. We'll be alone.'

There was nothing more to say. The stranger watched them in silence. Even before they hurried away, he seemed to be fading into the grey sheet of rain.

'He might be the man they're looking for,' Martin said, 'but he's no more insane than you are.'

'Schizophrenic?' Laura asked. 'They said he could be dangerous.'

'Maybe.'

The wipers pushed the rain off the windscreen long enough to give a glimpse of the poor visibility outside. They drove across country towards a pub Martin knew, where the fire was open and the food good. The weather had made the pork pie inadequate.

'Are you going to tell – *them*?'

'No, I said we'd be alone.'

'You don't think today was a bit pointless?'

'Well, I learnt one thing.'

'What?'

'He might be an escaped madman, but he knows how to live wild.'

'How do you tell?'

'He didn't care about getting wet.'

'So?'

'You and I were diving into our waterproofs. And we're only a short drive away from a fire and a change of clothes. Our friend the nutter, who appears to be living like an animal, seemed in no hurry to get out of the rain.'

'I don't follow you.'

'He must have some way of getting dry. That means a fire, shelter, where he wouldn't be too easily detected. One of the caves, I'd guess.'

'Wouldn't people notice the smoke?'

'You've never seen the caves. They're only accessible from the sea for a short time each day, between tides. Even then, you'd need to be bloody good with a boat. From the land, only for very good climbers. If he had a fire down there, the smoke would just get chewed up by the sea. The breakers come in like fury all along there. The more interesting question is how the hell he gets down there.'

'So how do you see tomorrow?' Laura asked.

'I don't know. We may have scared him off. If he's not there tomorrow I suppose we have to report it.'

55

'And if he is there?'

'That's an even bigger problem.'

They arrived in pouring rain at the remote pub which Martin used as a canteen when he was working in that direction. The barman knew him and made friendly chat, but Martin didn't introduce Laura, and she sensed that he was still shy about her. They drank quietly in a corner, content to be together and warm.

A bluff man in his fifties, who might have been an agricultural rep or a forestry manager, came in, beating the rain from his clothes.

While waiting for his beer and pie he said, 'See the enemy are in here today, Frank.'

He spoke ostensibly to the barman, but in fact to the occupants of the bar. The barman smiled noncommittally as at a joke which he couldn't grasp. But in the customer's face there was something outraged and provocative.

'The enemy,' he repeated, this time looking round.

Laura looked at Martin, who shrugged.

'Who's he?' she asked.

Martin shook his head, uncertain.

The barman asked, 'You all right, Charlie?'

The bar was hushed. A clock chimed a tinny half-hour.

'I'm bloody all right,' Charlie exclaimed. 'I just wonder what that kind of people are doing round here.'

He drained half his pint pot. In his world you didn't normally have to say a lot by way of explanation. Then he pointed an angry finger.

'Out there, in that bloody car park. A motor with one of them bloody CND badge things in the window.'

'Don't let it worry you, Charlie,' the barman said.

Martin's eyes flashed at Laura. Then he got up and walked across to the bar. With a long stare at Charlie he said, 'Maybe you'd better tell me your objection.'

Charlie was a pompous, dignified, decent man who would never give ground. He demanded, 'That your car?'

'It's my car,' Laura said, getting up. Her crisp, received-

56

pronunciation voice struck an uncommon, wrong note in the room. The hostility was instant.

'She with you?' Charlie said to Martin, who was also getting angry now and answered, 'No, I'm with her.'

For a moment Laura had an urge to laugh at these two big men and their poor apology for a John Wayne act. But it was too painful, too heavy.

'Look,' she said, 'it's my car, I put the sticker in it. What's bothering you?'

'Are you against nuclear power?'

'Why?' Laura said. She could see Charlie's self-respect about to depend on his ability to slap this posh bitch down.

Charlie looked round, aware of support in the rest of the bar.

'A lot of people around here make their living from nuclear power. You'd best be careful what you go round shouting from your car window, little lady.'

Laura grinned derisively. Martin said, 'It's none of your business.' His voice growled, but she could feel the uneasiness in him. He was a much *nicer* person than her, she kept noticing.

Uninhibited, she said, 'Are you really telling me I can't have a sticker in my window? Are you the local secret police or something?'

'Listen,' Charlie said, 'a lot of folk around here work in nuclear power, or for the Army, and they do well out of it, and they don't like smart-arse townies like you coming out here making them feel like criminals. If you want to make friends around here, you'd best get rid of that badge.'

'Or what? Somebody's going to bomb the car?'

Charlie looked at Martin, silently appealing to him to squash the little woman or drag her away for her own good. Martin tried to look aloof and amused, but awkwardness betrayed itself in strained facial muscles and arms folded too tight.

'It's a sensitive issue, Mr Ritchie,' the barman, who was also the landlord, said apologetically.

So in this pub, Laura observed, Martin was *Mr Ritchie*, addressed in respectful tones as an arbiter.

'Do you want me to take the sticker out?' she asked him.

'Of course I don't,' Martin said. 'Not only that, I don't like being labelled somebody's enemy. Especially by a loud-mouthed piss-artist.'

They got their coats and left. Running through the rain Laura shouted, 'Thanks.'

Scrambling for the car, Martin shouted back, 'My privilege.'

'Martin, they've found him.'

'I'm listening.'

They stood frozen while the radio news gave details of when and where the escaper from the Faulston mental hospital had been retaken. It seemed that after a week of hiding he had all but given himself up. The radio's urgent rattle hurried on to the next item. Laura switched it off.

'I don't know why, but I feel sad.'

'Would it cheer you up,' Martin said, 'to know that they haven't caught him?'

'What do you mean?'

'They may have caught *a* nutter, but they haven't caught *our* nutter.'

'How do you know?'

'The place they mentioned is thirty miles from where we were yesterday. And the storm lasted all night. It's not the same man.'

'So he's not an escaped lunatic.'

'Maybe there's another one.'

'An Army deserter?'

'Perhaps we'll never find out.'

'I really wonder who he is, you know.'

Martin frowned. 'We have a visitor.'

'What?'

'And beneath that enticing robe you're not wearing a thing.'

58

'Martin, what are you talking about?'

'Listen.'

Laura listened, shrugged, pulled the robe a little tighter across her chest.

Martin said, 'When you've lived here longer you'll find you can pick up sound over a greater distance. If you can hear a car from this house, it's coming this way. Out here there's nowhere else to go.'

Laura went to change. From the bedroom she called down, 'What are we going to do? About him?'

'We still have to go there. Or we could just forget it.'

'I think you should go alone.'

The oncoming car was very audible.

'Maybe we're about to learn something. Why me alone?'

'The two of us seemed to put him off. I felt he might open up more to you.'

From Laura's workroom Martin stole a look outside.

'It's Godfrey.'

'Who's Godfrey?'

'Godfrey Knapp. You remember, the master of Scardale. He must have come to bellow at you.'

'Did you know he was coming?'

'No, people don't make appointments out here. They drive fifty miles, then say, I was just passing –'

Laura straightened her hair and still looked sceptical. A magisterial triple knock shook the front door.

Chapter Five

Life had prepared Godfrey Knapp for an old age of loud
check suits and yellow waistcoats, and he defied this by
wearing, at least when in the country, corduroy jeans, denim
shirts, sheepskin jackets. He had a round, bearded, Edward
VII face, and a booming voice which made his slightest word
reverberate off the nearest plane surface. This power of
vocally outgunning anybody else had long since persuaded
him of the superior value of whatever he said.

An aura of cigar smoke hung around him, but he knew
Martin Ritchie's habits and had jettisoned the panatella in a
ragged bank by the garden wall. Cigars were vegetable
matter, he was as good an ecologist as the next man, it would
rot down, what the hell.

'My dear Martin!'

'Hello, Godfrey.'

'I heard you're married.'

His eyes had a shrewd, even malicious twinkle, that said:
you thought you could keep a secret from me.

'Well, not exactly – as good as –'

'I wished to bring my congratulations and welcome the lady
to this ravishing place.'

Laura hovered in the background, fighting embarrassment,
trying to maintain her anxious smile. Martin brought the
visitor in and made the introductions.

Godfrey Knapp had one of those macho handshakes which

Laura always refused to acknowledge, offering her hand with minimal pressure as an instrument of touch only. Knapp was not her kind of person, she knew it in the instinctive way that no amount of further acquaintance could ever change.

But she also knew instantly that, physically at least, she was very much his kind of person, and she felt that he now knew everything about her that he was interested to know.

'A drink, Godfrey?'

'A Scotch, Martin.'

Laura was staggered. Martin hardly ever drank, he certainly never drank before the evening, and here he was at 10 a.m. sharing whisky with someone whose name he had hardly ever mentioned. If she had poured herself a drink at ten in the morning it would have been an issue between them, yet he was about to relax with this booming, bearded oaf with his open-necked denim shirt revealing a fine gold chain resting on an upward-thrusting mat of grey chest-hair.

She declined a drink for herself and sat down with a forced smile to make conversation. After a few exploratory pleasantries Knapp said, 'You heard about the runaway madman, I suppose. They picked him up last night. When I told Harold, he said "Will that be one guest less for dinner, sir?" Bloody funny, eh?'

His laughter was loud and torrential, impossible to do more than smile along with politely.

'We just heard,' Martin said.

'On my land, as a matter of fact. One of my tenants had a break-in, some food stolen. Poor devil.'

It was not clear who he was referring to. The phrase 'my land' had been used with the casualness of habit, but Laura felt it was directed at her.

'Godfrey has an estate,' Martin explained.

'Inherited mostly, I admit apologetically. I make up for that by doing what I can to maintain it well, leave something more than a few thousand acres of garbage after I'm gone. I watch my farmers very closely. Don't want people naming a dust-bowl after me.'

61

'Godfrey has done terrific work with the oil companies,' Martin said. 'This place would look like Texas now if it wasn't for him.'

'I have contacts in the *City*,' Knapp said directly to Laura, whispering the last word to lend it a wicked emphasis. He was being pompously ironic and enjoying it.

His eye kept glancing obliquely at her, momentarily tracing the shape of her body beneath the shape of her clothes. Laura could summarise this kind of man instantly, the sixty-year-old whose virility had one more campaign left in it, and a catalogue of still-unrealised fantasies stewing around and demanding tribute. Her life had been littered with them. In London men coming on to her had always been a fact of life, and she had rebuffed it, played with it, reciprocated it, as her feelings took her. It had never felt disturbing in the way these sidelong glances from Godfrey Knapp disturbed her.

When he left he shook her hand again, this time gentler and more lingering. He contrived to be looking at Martin while absent-mindedly brushing her palm, and Laura found it amusing.

'You must come to dinner and have a look round Scardale. I'll check my engagement book and phone you back.'

Laura said it would be lovely. She and Martin watched the dark blue Jaguar glide down the unmade road and out of view.

'How did you ever meet him?' she asked.

'You can't avoid him if you live round here,' Martin said. 'He's the school bully.'

'I seem to have missed him so far,' Laura said. But she remembered her distant glimpse of Scardale, its classical warmth in the autumn sunshine.

'I feel those days may be over,' Martin said. His voice gave nothing away.

Martin went to the rendezvous with the stranger unaccompanied. Disbelieving that the man they had met was a mental case, he now tried to formulate a new explanation for him. A deserter, Laura had suggested, but the last place on earth a deserter would come was here. Half the region was controlled by the Ministry of Defence, in its various guises. No, whatever he had left behind him, it was not the Army.

An eccentric of some kind, maybe, on the run from the law, although which law was not so easy to guess at. But the cities, distant and festering, which Martin was puritanically inclined to see as kingdoms of anarchy and corruption, offered more protection than the spaces out here. More generally, Martin was less happy about their involvement with the stranger now. Assuming him to be a mental patient, they had been out to help him, doing their duty as citizens and so on. An element of sympathy lay behind it all. None of that figured now.

It made more sense to forget him, turn the Land-Rover round and get back to something more important. But a streak of resentment had started to permeate Martin's feelings about this thin, cool vagrant. Laura was right, he wanted to clear the place of an intruder.

He remembered when an Alsatian had gone wild and was leaving the savaged corpses of sheep across the hillsides. The animal had been hunted down and shot. Martin had seen its body thrown over the nearest cliff, and recalled the cheer which went up at that moment. Ugly – but so was the ripped, bare flesh of the dead ewes and their lambs on the spring slopes. There was ugly and ugly.

Once he remembered the mad Alsatian and the anguish it had created along that stretch of coast, he understood his present feelings better.

The place they had appointed was the reverse slope of the down that fronted the sea. Martin walked a hollow that was not quite a valley, sheep pasture mostly, coarse grass chequered with dark islands of gorse. The paths criss-crossed away from the dried-out bed of an ancient stream, and Martin headed for the exact point where they had left the stranger in yesterday's storm.

A curlew rose from the scrub and flapped away into a sky of

scudding cloud. The doleful two-note cry chilled Martin's blood, as it had whenever he heard it since he was a boy of thirteen, on holiday in the Lake District. He was lying in bed with a smuggled bottle of beer, puzzled and frustrated at having forgotten to bring an opener, when a curlew flew over the house. Its call made him shiver with emotion. From that moment, 'nature' ceased to be a hobby and became the country of his blood. Ever since then hearing a curlew returned him to that moment when the secret of his life had been made plain to him.

He kept his eyes sharp for the stranger, but there was no sign of him. Perhaps he had taken the hint, realised that people were getting uncomfortably close, and moved on. A good result, Martin thought. Get the bastard out. Strange, but since the escaped lunatic idea had gone dead, charity seemed to have died with it.

Then he was there. He had suddenly appeared, in such a way that Martin knew he had been watching him for some time. He came into view deliberately, he was the one in control. And Martin recognised another source of dislike of this man, the way he was far more on top of things than his pathetic, down-at-heel image suggested. Ignoring this for the moment, Martin lifted his hand in a brusque greeting. The stranger dropped from sight, waiting for Martin in a spot where the path dipped behind a small rise in the ground.

He looked the same, the facial stubble a little heavier, the incongruous lounge suit that much more crumpled and dirty, but otherwise wiry and alert. He stank of wood smoke.

'You survived last night, then?'

The stranger found it less remarkable. 'Sure.'

'Must have been quite a storm here.'

'Very bad.'

'I've got some food, if you want to eat.'

'OK.'

Martin put down a groundsheet and held out a plastic box. He saw the reluctant, almost puzzled look at the moss-like flan-fillings inside. 'Spinach,' he said, and added, 'with eggs.

64

Sesame seeds. I made them.'

The stranger took a slice and bit carefully into it, then started to eat eagerly.

'Were you planning to stay out here long?'

The stranger shrugged.

'You'll never survive the winter. It gets very tough along this coast.' Martin watched the younger man's face. 'Do you have a home to go to?'

A shake of the head. Martin insisted, 'You must come from somewhere.'

The stranger's self-possession began to get maddening. A prickle of bourgeois indignation went through Martin: he's happy to eat my food, he can bloody well answer my questions.

'You know what will happen if you stay here much longer? People will see you, somebody will tell the police, and they'll come looking for you.'

'Is that what you're going to do?' The question was passive, even gentle.

'No. But somebody will.'

'Is it a crime, living here?'

'They'll find a way of making it a crime.'

'Why are you telling me this?'

'I'd like to help you in some way. But first I need to know who you are. Why you're here.'

There was a long wait. The stranger tugged up a few pieces of dry grass.

'I don't know.'

Martin allowed a similar pause. 'What exactly don't you know?'

'I don't know who I am.'

'You mean you just found yourself living out here, with no identification, no memory?'

'That's all I can say.'

Martin looked at the stranger again. His first impulse was to suspect. But why? Amnesia was a fact, people did go missing, separated from their previous lives by the blank aftermath of trauma. Why should he be lying, when all that was at stake was this animalistic survival in the rocky wastes of a hostile coastline? His pinched face, his abject clothes, the filthy smell that came off him, were genuine. It was no affectation. And amnesia would explain his uncanny calm, his strange lack of discomfort or regret.

'You must try to do something about it,' Martin said.

The stranger said, 'I thought if I stayed here a while something might come back to me.'

'Have you thought about the police?'

He showed no alarm, simply saying, 'What can they do?'

'They have lists of missing persons. They might be able to match you up and get you back into your life.'

'I don't trust the police.'

'Why not?'

'Do you?'

'Where else can you turn?'

'I'm all right like this. Why are you so interested?'

His eyes started to check all the visible distance around where they were sitting.

Martin protested, 'It's all right, I didn't bring anyone with me. You're in no danger.' He paused. 'Laura and I would like to help you.'

'How?'

It was a good question. Fortunately this conversation marked by silences gave Martin time to think about what he meant. He felt bad about his suspicion of the stranger, his impulses to reject him. If it were a sick animal – once he had nursed a rat with a broken leg, looking after it tenderly for weeks, slimy tail, yellow teeth, fleas, the lot. And even when he released it, healed, the rat bared its teeth in rage at him before slithering away. He would do it all over again. Yet a damaged fellow-human . . .

'We could put you up for a few days. Nothing special, but you could eat properly, we'd get you some clothes, maybe you'd begin to remember something.'

'Why should I trust you?'

'Why do you have to trust me? I'm trying to help you. I don't want anything from you.'

The stranger's face looked wolfish, unconvinced. Martin was always irritated by any suggestion that he was trying to sell anybody anything. If he doesn't accept, he thought, I'll go to the police.

'What does your wife think?'

'She isn't my wife – but yes, she agrees.'

This was not true, they had not discussed the stranger moving in, even for a night or two. But Martin was already rehearsing the conversation with Laura, and planning what things they would have to move to release the spare divan.

The stranger said, 'If you don't change your mind, and you come back here when it's getting dark, and I'm still here, then I'll come with you. If I'm not here, forget that you ever saw me.'

'If you don't want him here, that's it. I won't go back.'

'I'm quite happy,' Laura said.

She sensed that now, when it became a practical issue, Martin was keener to help the stranger than she was. But it was also like a test of her adaptability.

'A couple of days.'

'You don't think he's clinically ill?'

'He may be.'

'What if we can't get rid of him?'

Martin said, 'I think the problem will be keeping him here. He's like a wild animal, and I've no wish to tame him. We'll clean him up, make him fit for the real world, and that's it, he's on his way.'

'Wait till he sees your tent. He'll probably just steal it and go back to the cliffs.'

'I mentioned the police in passing. He didn't like it.'

'You think he's a criminal?'

'No. Because this is the one place you'd never come to hide. He can't be running from anything, because this is one place you're sure to be seen.'

The stranger was waiting in the dusk, an odd urban-looking figure, a shabby city-street loser transposed to an area of 'outstanding natural beauty', an actor who had wandered on to the wrong film set.

'Do you have anything to bring?' Martin asked.

The stranger shook his head. Martin led him to the empty Land-Rover.

'We've got to call you something. Do you have a name that you can remember?'

'The name Ray keeps coming into my head.'

'First name or last name? Sorry, stupid question.'

'I don't know, anyway.'

'Can we call you Ray?'

'Yes, it's OK.'

They drove off, out across the darkening expanse of Macemoor. Martin navigated its unlit, unmarked roads without even thinking. He felt confident, suddenly in control of something that had been agitating him. When the startled eyes of a roe deer shone back at him from his headlights, he instantly slowed the jeep to a crawl until the deer calmly stepped back into the darkness. The speed of his reflexes at moments like that was always an index of his general state of being.

They fed Ray, and by prior agreement asked no questions and made no conversation outside immediate domestic matters. He spent a long time in the bathroom, obviously with the windows open, because there was no trace of condensation when he finished. Everything was perfectly clean, and apart from a wet towel he left no mark of his presence there. Martin lent him some roughly fitting clothes until the next day, and his old things were bagged up for burning. Then he asked to sleep.

'Thank you for looking after me like this.'

'We'll see you for breakfast,' Martin said. They wished him goodnight.

Downstairs, they were careful not to talk about Ray, not

even to mention him. The cottage walls were thick, but in this place, Martin claimed, with experience you could hear the gnats mating.

The trip to Barnbrook to buy clothes was difficult, like taking an overgrown teenage son to be kitted out for the new school term. Ray seemed to realise this, and efficiently chose some neutral, unfussy gear that suited the country. They trailed around the shops with him because of the amnesia, and he made no protest, blankly ignoring the assistant's strange looks as Martin hastily signed a cheque.

The change in Ray's appearance was dramatic. The washed hair and clean-shaven face made him more human, and the new clothes allowed through a certain physical authority which the ludicrous ill-fitting suit had concealed. Having eaten and slept well, he looked sharp, still lean but in a rippling fit way that heightened the vacancy of his mental condition. His face, with its freshly revealed clean lines, spoke of a greater intelligence than his long trance-like silences and his halting answers suggested.

He spent a lot of time alone, immobile and reflective in an armchair, seeming not to need stimulants, exercise or diversion. He had noticed the telescope and asked if he could use it. He liked to sit up in Martin's workroom, staring out at the moorland. They had agreed that for this one day they would let Ray relax and recover some human dignity, before broaching the subject of his next move.

They had plans for the next day which would mean leaving the house, and that would now mean leaving Ray alone there. The weather forecast was good, and they fought off an uptight inclination to scrap the programme out of a reluctance to take this risk. They told him if the phone rang to let it go unanswered, but otherwise they wanted it to be clear they trusted him. It felt right and seemed the least they could do.

The rock of Saltmayne was like the petrified hand of a drowned giant, tapering down to one long bony finger sunk in a year-round ferment of cold and treacherous water. From closer, the smoothness of this tip broke up into a promontory of jagged stone, cuboid boulders that had been tilted crazily against each other for millennia, jarring planes of kelp-greasy rock which the sea swallowed and regurgitated twice daily. Yet this sombre world's end was a staging-post for millions of migrant birds on their way north to breed, or now in autumnal passage bound for the warmth of an exotic winter.

Martin came here every year, usually for a succession of days, staying all hours of light. The phenomenon never failed to stir him, this delicate and touching, yet primevally powerful earth-movement of wave after wave of small birds heading out into nothing, many of them to die the death John Vayro had wanted, unseen in the dark sea-wastes, many others to make landfall on the Mediterranean and feel the warmth of Africa coming to meet them.

Laura kept out of the serious birdwatching. She could identify the main species now, and liked the visual effect of the flocks of migrants, but she avoided the fine distinctions, the need to verify whether a small bird was a moustached or only a sedge warbler before it became one of a thousand silhouettes again.

One moment stood out from all the others. Martin began shaking as he tracked a medium-sized, fork-tailed bird, down from a telegraph pole and across an open field. Laura followed as he scrambled towards it, crawling behind a dry-stone wall for a better view. The light was behind them and gave a perfect sighting. His breath tight, Martin passed Laura the glasses and showed her where to look.

The bird Laura saw could have been anything. For a moment she thought she had the wrong one. It was brownish, she would have called it a thrush or something.

'What is it?' she whispered.

'A pratincole.' Martin's voice was hushed, almost solemn.

Laura said, 'A prat what?'

'Pratincole,' he muttered. 'Pratum, meadow, incola,

70

inhabitant – inhabitant of the meadow, a graceful accompanist of the Roman Empire.'

'Right,' Laura said, hardly daring to smile.

In the air it was less ordinary, with arched wings and a deep fork in the tail, a sharp silhouette as it flew towards the horizon. Wheeling the glasses after the bird, Martin became aware that another birdwatcher had spotted it from the other side of the field.

'Pratincole! Pratincole!' he shouted.

'Yes!' Martin yelled back. 'Yes!'

Martin waved his arms and fists in the air, and the other birder did a kind of jubilant dance. A rare vagrant, instantly corroborated, a day made unforgettable. Martin's eyes shone with tears and his face coloured with feeling.

'As ornithologists,' Laura said, 'you lot make great football hooligans.'

They walked back down to Saltmayne Point, and Martin tried to explain what a catch this kind of sighting had been. After a while they were approached by another birdwatcher, a small rotund man, bespectacled, in a battered fisherman's hat. He asked for any news, and was impressed by the report of the pratincole. Martin indicated where he might still get a view of the bird. A day like this was full of these casual encounters, exchanges of observations. Eventually Martin said, 'I haven't seen you here before.'

'No, no, I'm on holiday. I came specially for the migrants. That and a small piece of family business.'

Nobody took up his cue, so he went on. 'I have a brother who seems to have disappeared. We suspect he may be in these parts. He could be suffering from loss of memory. We've been trying to trace him.'

From behind rimless lenses his eyes glanced softly from Martin to Laura and back again.

'You wouldn't have heard anything? I know it's a small world out here.'

Martin shook his head, perhaps a little too definitely. 'What does he look like?'

71

'About thirty, thin, very dark. We're completely unlike, him and me. I think you'd know if you came across him. He's probably very disturbed.'

'We haven't met anybody like that,' Martin said. He looked at Laura, whose face was wary. He only met her eye for a moment.

'Well, if you do, the local police are in touch with me. We'd like to find him. He needs help.'

'We'll keep our eyes open,' Martin said.

'Thank you. Brave little creatures, aren't they?' he said, as another flock of martins launched themselves into the un-favourable wind. 'Well, goodbye,' he called. 'I'll keep an eye open for the pratincole.' He headed up the path that led along the western edge of Saltmayne, past the tall electrified fence and the squat 1950s council-style building of the Underwater Weapons Establishment, mundane and anonymous on the Rock's higher reaches.

When he was well out of earshot, Laura asked, 'Why didn't you tell him?'

'I don't know. Instinct.'

'You didn't believe him?'

'I'm not sure why, but no, I didn't.'

'He's a genuine birdwatcher?'

'Oh yes, he went to great lengths to let us know that.'

'Why should he be lying?'

'But why us?' Martin said.

'He's probably been going round the island all day saying the same thing to people. Look, why don't we just ask –?'

Martin shook his head. 'I think we should speak to our friend Ray first.'

'The news might scare him off.'

Martin looked almost satisfied. 'That's up to him.'

The birdwatcher returned to the secluded village where he was renting a room, bed and breakfast, for a short orni-thological holiday. The landlady discreetly tended her rhubarb patch while he made use of the phone, putting

72

through a call to the Roebuck Hotel in Barnbrook.

He asked for a Mr Greenwood. The muted, uncommunicative 'Hello' of Harry Teal finally answered.

'Hello, this is Pilkington. I've spotted him.'

'You're sure?'

'Certain.'

'Good,' Teal said. 'Tell me about it.'

Chapter Six

Scardale in autumn, Godfrey Knapp thought, and let his eyes dwell on the pastures rolling down to the lake and the wooded hills beyond, a whole thought in itself, needing no dressing, a complete paragraph.

I love it, yet hate it, it breaks my heart every time – *'qui me ronge, o la vie et la mort de mon coeur'*. Christ, what reflex in me quotes Baudelaire, against my will, against my better judgment, another stinking aborted foetus from my past. To have picked up so much knowledge, so effortlessly that I didn't value it at the time and feel disturbed by it now, like the memory of laughing teenage girls shagged on the edge of poppy-littered fields and discarded with the condoms that divided us – how they haunt me now, at the end of a life which has brought me everything except one thing – certainty of who I am, what man I want others to see in me.

Sixty approaches. Forty was wonderful, and even at fifty I was full of running. Why does the start of my seventh decade depress me like this? Got to shake it off. There's no way out but down, the gravitational pull to that hole in the ground. Got to shake it off.

Where's that bloody journalist got to? And why can't I stop thinking about that woman I met at Ritchie's place – Laura, can't remember her second name, but something touched me that I haven't felt in years, an appetite whose resolution is not just to *fuck*, but a kind of hunger and thirst for peace of the spirit. Why did she awake all that? How bloody inconvenient, for a start.

And where's this sodding journalist got to? I know her type from the phone call, thinks we're a load of provincial drongos whose tongues loll out at a visit from a metropolitan media princess. It was certainly a very sweet call she made, but did she realise that the people who put her on to me had also tipped me off about her? Still, village idiot she wants, village idiot she'll get. I just hope she checked her knicker elastic today – ah! –

Godfrey Knapp truncated his reverie and turned at a sound of activity in the hall behind him, although he knew already what it was. Harold, the old closet queen he employed as a factotum, was carrying two suitcases out to the BMW, followed by Dorothy Knapp, a woman who still wore fur round her shoulders and a neat feathered hat from below which she looked at the world with imperious, blameless eyes that loved nothing except good breeding points in dogs and horses.

Godfrey detested her heavy, expensive clothes, unchanged by fashion or season, her wide tubular ankles and the thick tan nylon that encased them, the embalmer's fluid she called scent, the dry powder that coated her marshmallow skin. Yet he coughed on his cigar as she arrived on the terrace, and shifted his position uneasily. She still had this power to unnerve him. They had not shared a bedroom, a bed, a sexual experience, for twenty-two years. It was exactly Dorothy's sexlessness that made her so formidable.

'I shall be away for three days,' she told him, although he already knew.

'I'll be away when you get back. A week or so,' Godfrey answered.

'My regards to Dr and Mrs Bonney,' Dorothy said.

Godfrey took the necessary two steps forward and kissed her cheek. It was a strange, sad ritual, and he resented it every time he did it, but never to the point of not doing it.

No further words were required. The BMW, expertly

handled, slid over the gravel and along the shrub-lined road to disappear into the estate. Harold went back into the house, and a melancholy spaniel that had been hanging around Knapp's feet seemed to find the change of company agreeable, and followed him in.

The kisses were a pain in the arse, you didn't need lips like rose-petals to feel how meaningless they were. Yet every goodbye, every hello, and when they were under the same roof, every bedtime, was sanctified with that momentary flesh-creeping contact. Dorothy seemed to expect it, he had never asked her why. With the pragmatism of a lifelong connoisseur of female flesh, Godfrey just knew it was easier to do it.

Maybe it represented a tribute to the large sums of money that had flowed together when they married, or perhaps a sporting gesture in the face of marital defeat – no hard-on feelings, and all that. For Godfrey divorce had never been a practicable option – Dorothy had cash, and a lot of pull, and for reasons of respectability and security, the security of Scardale for a start, he had managed his life better by staying with her.

For her part Dorothy did not object to the hundreds of women he had laid since their last night together, when in addition to refusing his bizarre requests, she announced that from then on she would be refusing the normal ones too. After that the subject seemed banished from her consciousness. For some years Godfrey felt like a gawky adolescent with permanent uncontrollable erections, and loathed her accordingly. Widely travelled, for many years he had collected women like whisky miniatures, with the ambition of screwing every nationality in the world, but this wearied in the end, ethnically if not physically. He knew that there would always be some obscure racial sub-group beyond his geographical, financial or libidinous range. The only constant in his life remained the Dorothy kisses, which had become like the last seals on an Egyptian tomb, something he kept up in case their absence brought the whole structure of his life crashing down.

The tragedy of growing old was that inside you remained young. Everybody knew this. Even some old wheezer in his club, last time he was in town, had said it to him, drooling over his port with a weak smile. How could something so banal be so painful?

And that woman he had met at Ritchie's kept returning to his mind, like one of those people you think you have met somewhere before. He hadn't met her, of course, but she seemed to point a direction which somehow his life had never taken, towards a region of gentleness and complexity, of dark rich colours and subtle arousals. He had spent his life trapped inside this imposing physical frame, this voice that could flatten people against walls, and it had served him well. But again, he was the victim of it. This was not the man he wished to be for the last phase of his life. He wanted to admit a feminine side to his nature, to lie in a twilit room with an intelligent woman who would dominate him, to feel silk against his skin, to wear French underwear and be the passive, explored partner, awaking to the teasing touch of a masterful, deliciously horny woman.

He lit another cigar and blew the smoke away on the wind. Certain encounters with Dorothy always started him off like this. Bloody woman. Not at Scardale, of course. The one place his fantasies must never come to life was here.

Ah, that bloody journalist person was on her way at last, unless he was mistaken. He checked his watch. She wasn't late at all. It was just his own impatience.

From a mile off, and without knowing anything about architecture, Sarah Keeling could see that Scardale was the sort of run-in-the-family place that conferred on the owner the sort of wealth of background that mere money could never buy. She had primed herself with all the stories: how the Knapps had held on to it by judicious marriages, how the roof only stayed on because the death-watch beetles were all holding hands. The occupants of such houses were either shrivelled genteel ancients mouldering away in dusty rooms,

77

or larger than life figures born several centuries too late, plotting Elizabethan fantasies of theme parks and hamburger concessions. If this was Godfrey Knapp waiting for her at the top of those steps, he certainly wasn't the first type.

Sarah Keeling wore large round glasses, her make-up was precise, her dark hair was highlighted and cut to the minute, and she hadn't modified her London style one bit for this rustic assignment. People always knew when you were posing, and anyway the glamour bit pleased some people and got them to open up.

A very loud voice from that barrel chest greeted her. 'My dear Miss Keeling.'

Or did he say 'Ms'? The jeans and cowboy boots, the aggressively jutting cigar, the gold chain and hairy face, weren't the normal run. She made a mental note: ageing hippy.

'Mr Knapp.' He didn't order her to call him Godfrey. That was a relief. 'I was told you're the man to see.'

'That depends what you want.'

'That depends what you're prepared to tell me.'

Knapp guffawed in exaggerated appreciation of her repartee. He suggested a drive round the estate before they went into the house. The Jaguar had streaks of mud along the sides, splashes received at high speed, and he hadn't bothered to have it cleaned off for the press. That was style.

'Remind me,' Knapp said. 'The name of your series.'

'*Living With the Nukes*.' Sarah grimaced. 'It wasn't my title.'

'The nukes! I know more about newts than nukes. Conservation's my thing now. Didn't they tell you that, these informants who told you I was the man to see?'

'Yes, but I also understand that there's a local organisation which in the event of a nuclear alert –'

'All of these things are set up by government, surely?'

'Well, not entirely.'

'But yes, they are. All clearly laid down, from region to sub-region to local level –'

78

'Oh look,' Sarah said, 'I know all about borough treasurers and planning officers who have their secret directives to lock themselves in a basement and control the country while the rest of us are dying of radiation sickness. That's just a joke, isn't it?'

'Depends what you make of it. I hear the Swiss, for example, are very good at these things.'

'What I'm trying to get at,' Sarah said, fiddling with the passenger-side air-vent to try and escape the cigar smoke, 'is the point where the civilian population becomes involved – not civil servants who'd snuff it without their luncheon vouchers, but the real power and talent in the community. I don't believe that if a nuclear alert goes off, or whatever nuclear alerts do, someone like you is going to sit on his backside waiting for a local government officer to tell him where to go for his food stamps.'

'Well, Miss Keeling,' Knapp said, 'you're quite a guy.'

'We're both very busy. I thought I'd come to the point.'

'What, then, do you see me doing in the kind of event you describe?'

'I see you having your own organisation, maybe with some government input discreetly filtered through – I see it being arranged informally, recruitment based on local knowledge and confidentiality, a hand-picked team working in secrecy. You would have your own shelter on an estate like this. I don't see you waiting on the government, somehow.'

'A charming but nebulous idea,' Knapp boomed genially. 'But I really can't see it working.'

Sara asked, 'You know nothing of such organisations?'

'I dare say I've heard every rumour you have, and a few more besides, some of them bloody silly.'

'You don't have a bunker on your estate, then?'

'Did someone tell you I have?'

'As a matter of fact, yes.'

'I'm afraid they were speculating. You know, all this stuff about nuclear alerts has been overdone, in my opinion. As for me, I've had a long and active life, so what should I care? *Après moi l'Apocalypse.*'

79

Sarah persisted, 'But it isn't about war, is it? There are a lot of things short of total destruction. People are preparing for them, and our futures are going to be determined by those preparations.'

Knapp drove with one hand on the wheel. The other rested on his passenger-side knee, towards Sarah's right thigh.

'You know more than I do about this, frankly,' he said. 'All right, so there's a nuclear alert. First somebody checks that it isn't a kamikaze pigeon obliterating itself on the tracking dish. Then what?'

'Round up all the dissidents, maybe?'

'Whoever they are. And from what information source?'

'Come on, everybody knows who they are.'

'To do what with the dissidents?'

Sarah suggested innocently, 'Shoot them?'

Knapp roared with laughter. 'Miss Keeling, you're dangerous but exciting company. Come back to the house and I'll get us both a drink.'

Ray opened the door of the cottage as the Dyane stopped on the patch of hard-standing outside the garden.

'I saw you from upstairs.'

They went in. For a moment it was as if they were guests, Ray welcoming them for a visit.

'You've been cleaning,' Martin said. It sounded like an accusation, and he added, 'Well done,' more heartily. But for some reason he could never find the right register or tone with this peculiar young man.

Not that the place had been filthy, but it rarely had the dustless shine they saw before them now. Ray said, 'I wanted to do something for you. You've been very good to me. I hope you don't mind, but I also cooked you a meal.'

He looked from one to the other, unsure whose culinary approval to seek.

'It's in the oven. I'll turn it up now. It'll be half an hour.'

The kitchen was also immaculate, the table laid, a warm smell of cooking meat. Martin and Laura went to have a bath,

80

astonished, amused, enjoying the experience.

'I raided your freezer,' Ray explained as he was serving the food. 'You're sure you don't mind?'

They both concurred that it was absolutely lovely. Martin told Ray about the pratincole. He took a polite but remote interest. They ate for a while. He had used some frozen kidney, green pepper, modest ingredients. It was the work of someone who knew how to cook, who could make a basic meal from anything. The brown rice was slightly puddingy, but seemed just right like that. They ate with pleasure, but there was a layer of unease below the surface.

As if to test this out, Ray said, 'So you had a good expedition?'

Martin said, 'Yes, interesting.' He stared at his plate. He had lived alone too long to be adept at pretending with other eyes on him.

'How are you – generally?' he asked. He barked the question, in a way that Laura had noticed he always did when he was agitated.

'I feel good. You've helped me a lot.'

'Has anything – come back?'

Ray looked furtive and said, 'No.'

A silence intervened. Being a couple weakened the joint approach Martin and Laura had worked out as they travelled back. Neither knew who should say what, and by avoiding facial communication across the table they had lost touch with each other's feelings.

'I thought I'd go tomorrow,' Ray said.

Martin asked, 'Do you know where?'

Ray shook his head. 'Maybe it'll come to me at the station – is there a station near here?'

'It's Barnbrook. I'll take you there. The line only goes one way.'

'That narrows it down, then.'

'Do you remember having any family?' Laura asked.

Ray didn't remember.

Laura exchanged glances with Martin. 'Do you have a

81

brother?' she asked. 'A small man with glasses? Rimless glasses,' she added, in case the detail assisted recall.

'I don't remember anybody like that.'

'Listen, it may be a coincidence,' Martin said, 'but we met somebody today who was looking for – he said – his brother, who he thought had disappeared around this area and might be suffering from loss of memory.'

Ray's reaction to this news was less apprehensive than they had expected. His question was almost disingenuously dumb.

'You think it could be me?'

'We didn't tell him about you. He told us to contact the police if we heard anything.'

Ray asked, 'Why didn't you tell him?'

'I'm not sure.'

'Perhaps I should meet him.'

'Surely if he was anything to do with you, you'd remember,' Laura said.

'I suppose I should,' Ray said. 'But I don't.'

'He's a birdwatcher,' Martin said. 'No?'

'Means nothing.'

'Shall we bring you two together?'

To their surprise Ray said, 'It might be a good idea. Can we fix it up in the morning?'

After that the meal wound down agreeably. Martin and Laura insisted on clearing up. Ray excused himself and turned in.

The next morning he was gone. He had vanished silently, leaving no trace of his existence there. He had left his bedroom door open, a last polite touch to let them know immediately that he had gone, not to cheat them with a closed door and a forced entry.

'I'm Sarah Keeling. We talked on the phone.'

'Come in,' Laura said.

The introductions made and the social drinks proffered, Sarah launched into her usual patter.

'It's called *Living with the Nukes* – that's a bit trivialising, and not my title – we've taken an area where you have a large nuclear presence – the reactor at Caunder, the submarines, and we want to look into how people see these things – the dangers, the benefits, the moral questions.'

'I haven't been here long,' Laura said. 'You'd better ask Martin about all that.'

Martin sat very still in his armchair, nursing a diminutive sherry. The dark stillness of his eyes and his physical calm were like a deliberate counterweight to Sarah Keeling's over-fluent chat and slightly manic style. It looked ominous.

'You moved here recently?' Sarah asked. 'That's interesting. Where from?'

'London.'

'Which part?'

Laura gave her Clapham address, and Sarah's eyes widened a little in familiar recognition.

'When you came here – did you think much about living side by side with nuclear power and Polaris submarines?'

'I never gave it a thought.'

'Right.' Sarah turned to Martin. 'You're a naturalist. How does a naturalist feel about nuclear pollution?'

Martin's stillness now had about it the tautness of a spring wound as tight as it would go. A look which Laura had learned to know, a sort of iron concentration, sharpened his features.

'I'm not sure what to answer,' he said, 'because I'm not sure what you understand about these subjects. There's hardly any point in me saying nuclear pollution is bad. You didn't come here for that, surely.'

'I'm interested in people,' Sarah said. She had a pen and notebook at the ready, which usually gave her an advantage, but here she felt weakened by them.

'Well, speaking as a person,' Martin said, 'I feel that nature – life, if you like – is a dynamic process. What's the worst you can imagine? Nuclear war, followed by nuclear winter, annihilation of the world as we know it? But eventually life would re-emerge. Not necessarily human life, of course. But

83

then why are we so hung up on human life? Man's domination of the planet doesn't have to last for ever.'

Sarah quickly made a few notes and said, 'So you're a nature mystic.'

'There's a point where science is far more mystical than any religion ever was.'

'Does that mean you don't care what happens to people?'

'That,' Martin said, 'is a ridiculous question.'

He could already see it in some colour magazine: 'Nature-lover Says Anything that Destroys People is Good'. He hated the glibness of people like Sarah Keeling, their rapacious search for the out-of-context quote, the leading questions, their crude way of turning everything into a headline.

'How do you feel about the high incidence of leukaemia around here?' Sarah asked.

She had a thin, elegantly made-up face, nice hair, good clothes, an attractive front. Martin felt shabby and vulnerable in comparison. She was hitting him harder shots all the time. Why did her faultless manners convey such ruthlessness? She was seeking to trap him. He had practically dared her to do it.

He said, 'You have figures?'

Sarah's hand twitched for her notebook. She had figures all right.

'For the whole country,' she said. 'And this area has an abnormally high leukaemia rate – I'm sure you have the picture as well as I do.'

'A matter of interpretation,' Martin said gruffly, ashamed at taking refuge in such a feeble defence.

'You think it's a false correlation, leukaemia and nuclear reactors?'

'A correlation doesn't prove anything.'

Images of John Vayro, raw and swollen from chemotherapy, of the outflow pipe from Caunder into the sea, troubled Martin. They were not thoughts he wanted to share, but he resented them being stirred up by this smart, impersonal yuppie. Perhaps she sensed it, but he knew she would ask her next question.

84

'Do you know anyone who has died of leukaemia?'

'Yes.'

The vulture, he thought, the bloody vulture. His anger, hurt, voiceless anger at the questions was now clear. The interview had nowhere left to go.

Sarah said, 'Can I ask one last thing? How easy would it be for people in this kind of area to oppose nuclear power? I suppose what I mean is, you find that most opponents of the world of nukes don't live anywhere near it. The closer you get to those areas, the more passive people become, the more willing to believe all the propaganda. It's a weird trend.' She smiled briefly. 'I'm sorry, that isn't a question that can be answered –'

Sarah stood up. She had ended the performance smoothly, at least by her own criteria. Nobody had egg or blood on their face.

'Thanks for your time.'

Martin got up but said nothing. Laura grimly ushered the journalist to the door, and the two women parted, with the required minimum of courtesy, no more.

In the summer they had lain here, in a stretch of the dunes where people rarely came, naked on a sun-facing side of a dip in the rolling sand. In the acres of duneland around them each rise was crowned with marram grass that susurrated in the incessant breeze. Martin had noticed the resemblance between a marram-crested dune and the female pubic mound. The memory always came back when they returned there, of a relaxed, sensual and apparently endless summer.

Now the clouds were sheets of ponderous grey, and the wind was harsher, stiffer, as it howled off the sea. The marram was dry, creaking as the wind raked through it.

They had come here to walk off their confusion after Sarah Keeling's visit. Laura tried to stand back from the issue. Martin had got worked up so far that he had to wind himself down again. Attempts to talk him through it would fail, she had been through that before. And she felt a secret sympathy with Sarah Keeling and the dexterity with which she had exposed this thin spot in his enamel. But Martin was burning from it, and she felt for him too. Walking the dunes was the easiest way out.

A flush of what she took for suppressed rage reddened his face, accentuated by an unnatural pallor around the mouth and eyes. When they halted for a rest in the lee side of a dune, Laura saw a film of fine sweat-beads glistening on his cheeks and upper lip. He huddled inside his jacket, and his eyes looked faraway. She put an arm round him. 'Are you all right?'

He nodded at the distant shadowy bulk of Saltmayne across the water, greying into the horizon.

'They ringed eleven storm petrels there last week.' His voice was faint and unconvincing.

'Martin –'

She could feel him shivering. 'Help me back to the car,' he said.

Laura drove back fast while Martin hugged himself into whatever warmth his clothes could garner from his fevered body. His head ached and his limbs throbbed. When they got home he took aspirin and a lot of tea, lying in bed wrapped in heavy sweaters. After a couple of hours the fever came under control, and he seemed to have broken the surface of a mass of turgid water, to be floating in a relieved, peaceful exhaustion.

'I'll take the sodden towels away now,' Laura said. 'The sweating's stopped. Do you feel better?'

'Yes, it's as good as over. It lasts twenty-four hours.'

'What do you mean?'

'I get this every year, sometimes twice in a year. Everybody has an affliction, this is mine. I don't know how I managed when I was on my own. Thanks.'

Laura kissed him and said, 'I love you.'

Head sunk wearily into the pillow, with glowing eyes, Martin said, 'Are you still happy here?'

'Oh yes.' She paused, to let the moment breathe. 'Shall I get you some more dry clothes?'

'Yes, good idea, please.'

'I'll get that book you wanted,' she called from the landing.

She went into Martin's workroom. The day was fading into a red sunset, the kind of mellow light that made the acres of pinkish-brown heather look soft. In the moment Laura gazed out, a far-off movement caught her attention. She took the binoculars from the shelf and focused them on the spot about half a mile away where she had seen something move.

The man had stopped and was crouching on one of the footpaths through the heather. He turned his head and waved, and Laura trained the glasses in that direction. She found another man, also wearing olive drab combat gear and approaching the cottage in stealth.

A frozen incomprehension that had not yet become fear set her face muscles rigid. Then she quickly went back to Martin.

'There are some people outside, creeping about on the moor.'

Martin propped himself up on a pillow. 'Naturalists?'

'I don't think so.'

'There's a car coming.'

As always, his hearing was a second ahead of hers. Now Laura heard it, the confident roar of a powerful engine which hardly decelerated before the brakes were applied.

Martin pushed the bedclothes back, but Laura stopped him.

'Stay there. I'll go.'

Someone knocked brusquely at the door as she went down. Two men in plain clothes looked at her with eyes that contrived to be blank and aggressive at the same time.

'A Mr Martin Ritchie lives here?'

'Yes.'

'We'd like to interview him. We also have a warrant to search this house.'

The voice was a monotone, boredom conveying suspicion. The speaker was a thin, raincoated man, unprepossessing but indifferent to the impression he made. A professional. He flashed a sheet of paper at Laura and grunted the names of himself and his heavier, silent colleague. He also waved an identification pocketbook at her, openly defying her to inspect it before he snapped it away again.

'Might I ask why?' Laura said.

'Can we see Mr Ritchie?'

'He's ill. In bed.'

'Are you his wife?'

'No.'

'I see.'

Laura was suddenly very angry. A whole sneering sexist weaponry opened up between them. She kept her eyes tight on those of the Special Branch man. He could do what he liked with his police procedures, she would outface him on a personal level. Then she turned and went back upstairs to Martin. She refused to offer them a pretence of hospitality. On her way up she wondered why the hell she had not shut the door on them.

'It's the police. They want to search the house.'

'Why?'

Somebody was already moving about downstairs, and Laura could sense people outside. Maybe it was her imagination, but the house felt in a stranglehold. The thin SB man appeared in the bedroom doorway.

'Mr Ritchie?'

The haggard face of illness and the fever itself stripped Martin of any inhibition.

'What are you doing in my house?'

'We have to ask you some questions, sir. And we need to search the property, if you don't mind.'

'For what?'

'May I sit down, sir? I'm sorry to disturb your sickbed.' The apology had all the warmth of a police bulletin.

Martin demanded, 'What's going on downstairs?'

'Just a check, sir. One of my colleagues carrying out his assignment.'

'What bloody assignment have you got here?'

The Branch man was only killing time while the hunt went

88

on elsewhere, and his lack of enthusiasm showed.

'Can we start at the beginning, sir?'

'The beginning of what?'

'The person who was staying here and may still be staying here. Or do you deny that such a person exists?'

'I deny nothing.'

'Do you still have him here?'

'No, he stayed here last night, and this morning he was gone.'

'Gone.'

'Yes.'

'Do you know where?'

'No. What's this all about?'

The Branch man sniffed. 'You've been harbouring a wanted and possibly dangerous man. Your co-operation in helping us find him would be appreciated.'

Two men appeared on the landing, the detective from the front door and one of the marksmen from outside.

'Nothing, sir.'

'The garden?'

'Only a hen-house. We checked – nothing. Downstairs is clear.'

'This floor,' the Branch man said. The men moved off.

'As I told you,' Martin said, 'he left.'

'We wouldn't be doing our job if we didn't look, sir. Now, for the moment I just need a few details from you. And we'll need access to your roof.'

Martin asked Laura wearily, 'Could you show them where the trapdoor is?'

Because of the fever sweat, Martin was in the bed which Ray had occupied. Laura went to the main bedroom. There was some of her underwear, freshly washed and dried, lying on the bedspread. The man who had been silent at the front door looked from the bed to Laura and back again.

'This room seems clear,' he said, then, 'If you're not the wife, who are you?' His eyes dropped to the bed again. 'A friend?'

89

Laura wanted to fight back, to put him down. But something told her not to cross these people, not to give them a reason for returning.

'I'll show you the way into the loft,' she said, and waited till he was ready.

For the senior Branch man Martin was patiently reconstructing the sequence of their meetings with Ray. He simplified where he could, and did not mention the birdwatcher who spoke of an amnesiac brother. Whatever the truth was, for now their best chance was to present themselves as good-natured dupes.

'Why did he leave so abruptly?' the Branch man asked. 'In your opinion?'

'I've no idea,' Martin said, sticking to the curt, categorical manner that was the only way with these people.

'After you'd been so good to him? A bit of an odd way to behave, wasn't it?' The Branch man waited. Always there was the implication of a lie, of some inconsistency hiding a guilty secret.

Martin said flatly, 'As I explained.'

Suddenly, the other side of the room, the ceiling cracked. The two men both flinched. The plasterboard split open and sent a light scatter of flaky dust through the air. A black shoe appeared through the ceiling, protruding at an angle. Muffled obscenities came from the attic. The shoe began to move, but could not retract past the downward-jagged board.

The Branch man looked irritated and forced himself to say, 'I'm sorry about this, sir.'

Martin fought his impulse to laugh. The shoe was wiggling about now, as the body above tried to combine force with care in extracting his foot without smashing the plasterboard or his ankle further.

Laura came to the doorway and saw the truncated foot oscillating through the ceiling. For a moment she stared in disbelief, then looked at Martin's Comédie-Française face, all mock dignity and lurking lampoon, and her face cleared and she burst into a helpless laugh. Within seconds she had to support herself on the door jamb, while Martin rolled around in his bed like a hysterical sea-beast incongruously swaddled in wool.

The Branch man's control snapped once he realised that Laura was not about to leave the room. He went to find the trapdoor and shouted up into the roof, 'Donkin!'

The name started off a fresh scream of laughter. After a terse dialogue, the Branch man returned to the bedroom, and while Martin and Laura failed to smother their hilarity, he got up on a chair and unlaced the shoe to remove it. The stripy sock disappeared into the roof with embarrassed speed, and it was some minutes before the situation regained its formality.

'I'm sorry about this, Mr Ritchie. If you contact your local station they'll put you on to the correct claims procedure.'

'Fine,' Martin said, his dislike of these callers still intact.

They had inquired what name the man they wanted came under, but there was no reaction when Martin said, 'We just called him Ray.' The name was palpably false, and the Branch man only employed it once.

'If this Ray character turns up again, you'll let the local police know immediately. I repeat, he is a dangerous man.'

Martin said, 'Of course.'

Laura watched as they went. There were five of them altogether, two with pump-action shotguns. They didn't know she was watching. Before they got into the car, the two doorstep men looked back up at the cottage and exchanged words that had to be bitter and hard. There was something they wouldn't forgive, and it wasn't just Donkin's striped foot jammed through the ceiling.

That day was still not over. While Martin was having a bath preparatory to changing beds, the phone rang.

'That was Sarah Keeling.'

Martin was towelling himself down. 'Why?'

'She apologised for her approach.'

'What approach?'

'I'll tell you what she said. She said she was crass and

91

manipulative, and she felt she blew what would have been a very interesting conversation.'

'It wasn't all her fault.'

'No – I think she's diplomatically asking for another try.'

'She rattled me,' Martin said. 'I don't know why, but she screwed me up.'

'Maybe you fancied her.'

Martin gave an ironic grimace.

'Or maybe it was the fever coming.'

'Now you're being diplomatic. We both know what it was. She cut me open. I was vulnerable, and she got straight to it. I'm not used to that.'

Laura said, 'You put too high a premium on your serenity. Get dressed before you start shivering again. She wants to come back the day after tomorrow. I said OK.'

Chapter Seven

Salt of the earth, the backbone of England, Harry Teal observed, people who live in cottages and cultivate their gardens. He noted the car, the blue Dyane with the CND sticker, and remembered the blonde woman who owned it. She would probably recall him too. He would have liked it otherwise.

The garden itself had been left to run wild, which for that first moment gave the cottage an abandoned air. Probably people who felt superior about growing rare species of weeds. You couldn't get more artificial than that, Teal thought. Smelly with subversion too, Ban the Bomb and let the weeds run riot. He preferred the well-trimmed lawns and rose-beds of outer London.

'Morning. My name's Teal, T-E-A-L. Could I come in and have a word?'

'Regarding what?' Martin asked. 'We were just going out.'

'It won't take long.'

They were both large men. Teal was younger, podgier, but possessed a self-assurance that usually impressed people he was dealing with. As he knew.

'What was it about?'

'A sort of follow-up to a visit you had yesterday. I heard you were unwell. I hope you've recovered.'

A good night's sleep and the pleasant contrast with the way he felt the day before made Martin resilient. He told himself –

because life was easier if this was true – that the call was about the police officer's foot through the ceiling, although it disturbed him to remember that this was also the man they had passed on the moor the other day. He led him through. When Laura appeared she barely concealed a double take, but Teal showed no previous knowledge of her. His blankness was totally convincing, and for a moment she accepted that she might be mistaken.

Teal wasted no time on small talk. He simply waited for the ceremony of coffee and sitting down to conclude, then said, 'This person who may be known to you as –'

'Just a minute,' Martin said. 'Your identification, please.'

Teal gave the standard-issue answer. 'Let's just say I'm a government employee.'

Surprising, but most people were satisfied by that. It even gave some a little thrill. But there was no pleasing this man Ritchie, who objected:

'Anybody could come here saying that.'

'Of course they could. But they don't, do they? Why should anybody want to, unless it was true? Now, the reason for yesterday's visit was that we had tracked this – Ray – that's not his real name, of course, and the amnesia story was just a corny trick, I'm sure he played the part well – we traced him here, and we hoped to find him at your house. It was bad luck.'

'What's his crime?' Martin asked.

'If I told you that – it wouldn't make sense, would it? Think about it.'

'You want us to help you, and you won't even tell us why,' Martin said. 'Laughable.'

Coolly, Teal said, 'After you've had your laugh, think again.'

Martin said, 'I don't find you persuasive.'

Laura kept out of it deliberately, but it worried her to see the male archetypes squaring up to each other, Teal's sly sense of his own power versus Martin's disdainful rejection.

'If you and Mrs –' He looked at Laura, who wanted to say, I

gave you my name yesterday, but she knew it was a waste of time.

'Sondergard,' Laura said. She could see him thinking, *foreign name*.

'If you wish to be regarded as suspects yourselves, there's no quota, we can accommodate you. On the other hand, if you want to help us, you have to trust us as much as we're prepared to trust you.'

'Which is how far?'

'As far as you're worthy of it.'

'And who decides that?'

'Let's put it like this,' Teal said, playing a favourite card. 'What are your feelings about patriotism?'

'Depends which brand.'

'That already answers the question, doesn't it?'

'Not in my opinion.'

Teal was bluff, disarming. 'A simple choice. Would you ever do something which you believed to be unpatriotic?'

'No. But my patriotism is probably different from yours.'

Teal gave a fleshy-lipped smile and said, 'You juggle the idea to avoid having to make a choice.'

Martin said, 'I haven't done moral philosophy for years, but I don't think you're very good.'

It was Teal's unconcern that was unnerving. Like a hyped-up market researcher, he took everything as an equally valuable response. Blandly he continued, 'About the man you know as Ray. The story you gave yesterday, by the way, checks out. We don't suspect anything in that.' He paused. If they didn't believe him, fine – let them sweat. He continued, 'It's the future we have to make sure of. If he comes back into your lives at all, I want you to ring my colleague Mr Greenwood at this number.'

Teal put a card with the relevant information on the low table. From the corner of his eye he watched Laura, whom he saw as the kind of angular, over-bright feminist who wanted to mess up a world which men had already messed up well enough for themselves. To Laura he was physically unattractive, and everything about him, from the unmatching patterns of his clothes to his emollient manner and the scrawl on the card, spelt *doctor* to her, the kind of doctor whose bald language held power over the rest of your life.

Martin had become passive. Laura waited for one more objection from him, one more show of distaste, but it never came. Something about that bothered her.

Teal stood up and said, 'Thanks for your co-operation. I know we can count on it. If Mr Ray returns, use any trust you've established to keep him sweet, and make the contact I've indicated. If necessary, leave a message just saying something like, we have news of our mutual friend, your name and number, and the wheels will turn.'

He was already speaking to them as if by long-distance phone. Even his sloppy style of giving instructions seemed calculated, condescending and threatening at the same time. After the Volvo had gone, Laura said, 'We've met him before, don't you remember?'

'Yes,' Martin said, 'the day we saw the kite. The last time we saw poor old Vayro.'

'What are we going to do?'

Martin seemed depressed, as if contaminated by Teal's visit. Then he began moving about decisively and noisily. He had decided to shove it all away.

'It's nothing, it'll pass,' he said. 'We've done nothing wrong. And we're not going to be used by anybody.'

Laura looked round and suddenly, unaccountably thought, I love it here. 'Let's hope so,' she said.

She woke up, went to the bathroom, then could not sleep again. It was just past midnight, and a thin strip of white light from the crack between the curtains fell aslant across the bed. Some way out on the moor a fox yelped its tubercular monotone at the full moon.

Laura went downstairs, zipping up the velours robe over her naked body. She put the light on in the kitchen, opened the fridge, poured some milk. She went to pull the blind down. Nothing was so dark as an uncurtained window at night, the glass black and shiny like newly cut coal. The arid moonlight fascinated her, and she bent her head to the window to peer out.

Movement in the garden. Her hand slackened on the draw-string, and the blind scrolled up again. She took a grip on herself and pulled it down. Then she froze, in the same mix of confusion and fear as when she had seen the police marksmen out in the heather. She turned her head and checked that the door latch was on, but it was only a Yale, easy to force. When he was alone here, Martin had never locked up at night, till she had brought her security fears from London.

A trick of the moonlight, she told herself. But she knew it was no trick. They were back again. She went upstairs and tapped Martin awake.

'There's somebody outside.'

He woke easily, always a light sleeper, shaking the sleep off him like a cat. 'Where?'

'Near the kitchen.'

Martin's nude body swung out of bed. He got straight into his clothes.

'Be careful,' Laura said.

'I'll put a bloody stop to this,' he said. Halfway downstairs he called back, 'Stay up there.'

He pulled on shoes and a jacket, then blacked out the kitchen. His eyes adapted to the dark as he slipped out. He knew where a discarded axe-handle, as long as his arm, lay, and stooped down for it. Hugging the moonless side of the cottage, he worked his way round.

He saw and heard nobody. He had not questioned Laura's story, but he did now, as he came round to the moon-bleached front of the house, the lungs tight in his chest.

'Mr Ritchie. It's me – Ray.'

Martin wheeled to the whisper. He saw Ray shrink as he took the axe-handle for a shotgun. He kept his hands half up even after he corrected this impression, in fear and concili-

97

ation as Martin stepped out towards him.

'What the hell are you doing here?'

'There's nowhere else to go.'

'The joke's over. People are hunting you.'

'Help me.'

'What help? We had armed police here. You left because you knew they would be coming. Why are you here now?'

The fox started baying again, nearer now. They both tensed at the rasping cry.

'I'm afraid I lied to you.'

'We'd worked that out.'

'You feel betrayed?'

'I don't give a stuff about being betrayed. But a lot of people want to know where you are, and if you come here I don't have much choice about telling them.'

Laura had heard the voices, and with a coat over her robe now came out into the garden.

'Hello,' Ray said shyly. But he had much more authority now he did not have to play the amnesiac.

Martin quickly intervened to head off a bond which he felt forming. 'I'm sorry, you can't stay.'

'At least hear my story.'

Martin gripped the axe-handle and stared ahead of him. Laura touched his arm and said, 'I'd like to hear it.'

'Wait a minute!' They had not reached the back door. 'Martin!'

Laura beckoned him aside. They withdrew into the dark. She whispered urgently, 'They could have bugged the house.'

Martin was scathing. 'Oh, ridiculous.'

'They went everywhere. We wouldn't know. They must be watching us, or that man Teal wouldn't have come.'

It's not that easy, Martin wanted to say, you can't hide a bug in five minutes, and anyway how would it transmit? But he lacked certainty, he couldn't dismiss the suspicion. It made a hideous sense, squalid and chilling.

He appealed to her. 'What do we do?'

'Go inside, make some coffee, don't speak,' Laura said. 'I'll be twenty minutes.'

'Where are you going?'

'John Vayro's house.'

He realised that mentally Laura was working faster than him, and he submitted to her greater energy. She quickly dressed in daytime clothes and left the house. The Dyane, with only Laura inside, whirred off into the night.

In the kitchen Martin followed instructions and made some coffee. A wave of unfinished sleep hit him from behind and for a few minutes sucked the energy from him. When he recovered he focused on things he wanted to ask Ray when the time came. Ray himself, unchanged except for the pepper of black stubble across his face, sat in the kitchen with the same stillness and self-possession he had used to convey amnesia.

Martin heard the car returning and went to look. Laura's twenty minutes had been a good estimate.

'Why no lights?' he asked.

She put a finger to her lips. Martin shook his head irritably. The bugs game was getting on his nerves. Laura drew his ear to her mouth.

'The moonlight's great. I didn't want to give anybody a light to follow. Just in case.'

Martin looked at her in an agitation that was about to spill over. His face said, look, I'm nearly fifty, a sedate rational man, I can walk over the cliffs for a whole day, but cops-and-robbers at midnight is beyond me.

Laura whispered, 'We have to go. We can't keep him here.'

They locked the house, and Laura navigated the unlit car into the milky-lit, dark-hollowed country. Sporadically, as if to outlast the moon, the fox still bayed.

'I'm going to tape this.'

Martin frowned in surprise when Laura pulled out his pocket recorder. He used it for his own bugging of nature, leaving it running by nests or feeding-sites and boiling the

99

results down later for his radio talks. It jarred with him to see the offhand way Laura had grabbed some spare cassettes without asking.

At the mention of taping a trace of unease passed over Ray's face. Laura said, 'Take it or leave it, that's the deal. We may need something to protect ourselves. We're already taking too much risk.'

Ray silently gestured acquiescence.

'You don't mind?' Laura asked Martin.

'I suppose not.' What else could he say?

'Can you set it up?'

Martin reluctantly put the hand-size machine to one side of the triangle the three of them made.

'It's all yours,' Laura said.

'I came back here to the coast to see if they had followed me, and events confirmed that they had. When I made myself known to you, that was deliberate. I had gradually increased my visibility, to give them a chance to spot me, and I was using you to test whether they were on my trail. I had faked a disappearance, but I left them one clue that would lead here, and I needed to know if they had bought it or not. When I left your house two nights ago, I knew they'd come, I just didn't know when. My plan had been to disappear, and if nothing had followed me out here that's what I would have done. It didn't work out, and my intentions now partly depend on you. First, my story. I'll keep it brief.

'The details of who I am and how I came to be in this situation don't matter. But I'm one of a small team of people who have been training for some time. Training for what, I'll get to in a minute. We were recruited privately, and it was only some way into the training that we found out the real goal we had been selected for. I also began to suspect who my real employers were.

'You're familiar with the flasks of radioactive waste they ship out of nuclear reactors? Our objective was to steal one of those. We weren't told much about why. The pay-offs were

100

mainly financial. Nobody asked questions. But the basic motive was to show that it could be done. I did some homework. I'll give you some details.

'The average flask of spent fuel is an eight-foot cube. It weighs between forty and fifty tonnes, and the shell of the flask is just over a foot of solid steel. Inside the ones that go from Caunder, for example, there are a couple of hundred rods of spent uranium clad in magnox. You may know more about this than I do, so I won't waste too much time. The rods are ninety-nine per cent uranium. The remaining one per cent consists of ruthenium, caesium, strontium and plutonium. A standard flask might contain half a dozen grammes of ruthenium, and if you know that a millionth of a gramme of that element, when inhaled, is lethal, you get some idea of what might happen if one of these flasks let its contents out on to the air. On a wind, or a fire, for example. Apart from the damage to any humans in the vicinity, an area of God knows how many square miles would be uninhabitable for centuries. Project that on to the centre of London, for instance.

'OK, it's a ridiculous idea. And yet, why not? The things can be hijacked. Eight feet cubed, no bigger than a few crates of cigarettes. Fifty tonnes, the right-sized truck could take that without sweating. The problem of lifting – the gear's already there. Caunder has its own railhead, with a gantry to hoist the flask from the truck on to the train. The interception – simple, because the flasks are often left there for a day before the train takes them. The timing – no problem, because the shipments are made once, maybe twice, a week.

'We had to be armed, of course. Not for the snatch, but for later. We had to be fit, know nothing about each other, and have no messy pasts dragging around after us.

'It had to be for real, because nobody outside the team would be collaborating. Nobody would know. We had three plans, and we would only be told the operative one at the last minute. One of them was to hijack the truck that came from the reactor. That eliminated the problem of lifting. We had destinations for the flask, and a programme for later events.

'The first objective was to show that it could be done. It suited a number of people to demonstrate this. Classed as terrorism, of course. Our crew wouldn't be tagged with any particular label, right-wing, left-wing, it would all be the same in the end. The show was for the benefit of the public. The message they had to get was that terrorists could hijack flasks of radioactive waste and threaten to detonate them. It didn't matter where or how – the flasks have lids, which are sealed and bolted, and removing and replacing them is specialised work, but it can be done. Or somebody who felt suicidal and had the right laser equipment could open one up. It wouldn't need to be in a city, because after Chernobyl everybody's scared of invisible radioactive clouds. The point of release would be of secondary importance to the composition of elements that came out of the flask.

'Why should anybody want this to happen? The consequences of our project would have to be extreme. So OK – if you want to create a police state out of a democracy, you have to get people to agree. They've got to want the police state because they figure it protects them. With the prospect of nuclear terrorism, the police state becomes everybody's friend. The reactors are already well policed, but the movement of materials and waste involves a whole society. So our project was designed to achieve that particular objective.

'I said it had to be for real. This meant that before we could release the flask, we had to be – eliminated, in some way. In fact, our escapes were set up in advance. We would disappear overseas, large bank accounts would be waiting for us. There was one exception. One of us would be caught, tried and imprisoned. Later he would be sprung. They wanted to give him credentials for a further infiltration of international terrorist organisations. I wasn't supposed to know that, but I found out. His testimony on trial would deflect attention anywhere but to who our ultimate employers were.

'This is why I left the group. I'd better say first that there was no permission to leave. It was laid on the line from the start that we were in this all the way. But these are the reasons I got out.

'As I learnt more about the job in front of us, it just didn't add up that we would all be neatly spirited away. They could stitch us up and lock us away for twenty years, and control us totally. Our stories could be discredited easily enough. Or they could take us out the tough way, with a few rounds of machine-gun fire that we hadn't been anticipating. Either way I didn't like it. I also began to suspect that our activities with the flask might involve more danger than we had been told, and I didn't want to be burned by a radiation leak.

'I'm trying to get across to you my reasons for wanting out. They weren't ethical. I could try to win myself some favour with you by claiming that I objected to what we were doing on moral grounds, but it wouldn't be true. And if I was that kind of person I would never have survived the recruitment procedure. I'd like that to be understood.

'I faked a death, to see if they'd buy it. That was why when you met me I was in somebody else's clothes. I came out here because I knew I could live for a while on the cliffs, and I was testing their ability to trace me. If they hadn't come, then – OK, move on, it's cool. But within days I knew that something was going down, and it meant that escape was not an option for me. Wherever I went, they would track me. If they catch me now, they'll kill me. So I have to fight them.

'OK, that's it.'

Ray waited. Although his meaning was fluent, his speech had shown difficulty keeping step with his thoughts. He seemed drained by the experience. Laura switched off the machine and slid it into her pocket.

'We'll hang on to this.'

'I don't think it was very good. If you've got questions –'

'Another time,' Martin said, rousing himself. The room had the chill of unlived-in houses, and he was stiff from the tension of listening to Ray's monologue. He wrote down their phone number and gave it to Ray, then shrugged. 'We may be tapped. Perhaps better not.'

Ray immediately said, 'Work out a code.'

'What?'

'You're a naturalist, right? Put down some words or phrases that mean things, so if I call and say, the winter birds will soon be arriving, or something like that, we both know what it really means.'

'Oh, good God, no.' Martin's reaction was dismissive. As every minute went by he appeared increasingly a heavy, middle-aged man, inflexible and self-important, petulant even. It was the caricature effect of dead-of-night exhaustion, but it contained a truth too.

'A good idea, surely,' Laura said.

'Rubbish. Like some second-rate TV movie.'

His eyes were staring and angry. She took his arms and eased him out. To Ray she said, 'We'll contact you.'

'Preposterous. Absolute nonsense.'

Even Martin's language had aged with the strain of that night.

'You don't believe him?'

'Of course not. Do you?'

'Why should he be making it up?'

'That's not my problem.'

'Martin, it's *our* problem.'

'I wish you'd put the bloody headlights on.'

'It's all right, I know the road now.'

The car rocked momentarily on to a bank, as if to mock what Laura said. She corrected it and clenched her teeth, refused to put even dip beams on. The ensuing silence was too much. She said, 'What do you want to do, then?'

'What I'm going to do is phone that policeman Teal and tell him he can have his man.'

Laura said, 'Oh no.'

'Look, I'm just bloody cheesed off with the whole thing. He comes into our life with some damn stupid story about losing his memory, we try to help him, he disappears and comes back again, and now he wants us to take this absurd piece of fiction seriously. As far as I'm concerned, he can take it up

104

with the proper authorities, and let me get on with what I'm interested in. The fact is, I don't believe him, and I refuse to play along with his or anybody else's demented power fantasies.'

'What if it isn't a fantasy?'

'You better hope it is.'

'Why?'

'The people who are really behind it – who do you think he meant?'

'He said he didn't know.'

'You believe that?'

'Why didn't you ask him?'

'I was going to. Or didn't you notice?'

'Yes, but in the middle of the tape –'

'When else?'

'He didn't want to stop at that point.'

'Or he didn't have an answer.'

Martin had tried to interrupt and Ray had silenced him with an upraised hand. After that Martin had sat through the proceeding with badly concealed impatience, and now it was all coming out.

'But if he wants us to believe him I expect serious answers.'

'That's really a *you* word, Martin – "serious" – you mean he was just pissing about? Or is it just the fact that he wouldn't let you control him?'

She was right. Martin ignored it.

Laura continued, 'He actually asked us if we had any questions when he'd finished. Why didn't you –?'

'Because by then he'd constructed a story that nobody could penetrate. Who's behind it – somebody very important. How do you know? Well, something so nasty couldn't be organised by just anybody, could it?'

'But if you wanted a specific answer?'

'He wasn't about to give one. What was the point asking for more hypothetical rubbish?'

'So who do you think is behind it?'

'Who cares? By the end I'd stopped believing the story.'

'Well, I believe it.'

'Then what are you going to do about it?'

'*I* or *we*?'

A grim, fearful silence in the car. 'Whichever you like.'

'And if he's right?'

'I'm still not interested.'

'Before you do anything, can I –?'

Martin's defensiveness, and the stress of being the passenger in an unlit car, pushed his reaction to hysteria pitch.

'First thing in the morning, I'm phoning Teal.'

'I want to play the tape to Sarah Keeling.'

'Oh my God! Why complicate it?'

'I want you to agree. And not ring Teal.'

'And if I don't agree?'

Without hesitation, Laura said, 'I'll leave you.'

The remainder of the night was a dreary interlude of silence, shallow sleep, and fitful, ugly dreams. In the morning, diplomatically, Martin went out for a couple of hours with his camera, and Laura withdrew to her drawing-board. Her last words had not been referred to. Their echo was like a shadow, but what really shook Laura was the ease with which she had spoken them.

Sarah Keeling arrived before Martin returned. The two women got on smoothly, chatted about London, as if there was a complicity between them, a shared bit of humour, circling around the need to soften Martin up. Before the small talk ran out he returned. Unloading his photographic gear and his anorak he seemed in a better mood, back in the timeless relaxation which a few hours on the country always gave him.

Sarah stood up. She was dressed in cords and a Shetland jumper, was less made up, calculating a more appropriate image.

'I came to apologise.'

Martin was generous to the point of sheepishness. 'Yes,

yes, it wasn't necessary. I'm afraid I took something person-ally, and I should have known better. It should be me apologising.'

'Well – can we return to the subject?' Sarah asked. She conspicuously had no notebook with her.

Martin glanced at Laura. As naturally as he could, he said, 'I think Laura has something to talk to you about.'

It was a conciliatory gesture, but a trace of sulkiness lingered. Ray had manipulated him, and Laura had coerced him, and the threat to leave him, even if she didn't mean it, was a dirty shot. He wouldn't forgive it, and this showed in his abnormal composure.

'Don't forget the bugs,' Martin said.

Laura glared at him. She was inclined not to take it seriously any more, but with her eyes she directed Sarah out to the car. They sat in frozen attitudes as Ray's testimony played through. The reproduction gave his voice a metallic timbre which emphasised the halting speech, the broken attempts at clarity. It sounded convincing. Sarah Keeling was impressed and puzzled and excited, all at once and visibly.

'Where did you get this?'

'We taped it last night.'

'You know this person?'

'Are you interested in it?' Laura asked.

Sarah asked, 'Are you offering it to me?'

'Yes, I think I am.'

'You don't think it's a hoax?'

'What would be the point?'

Sarah thought for a moment. 'Can I meet him?'

'I'll have to ask him.'

'He doesn't know you're giving me this?'

'No.'

'What's his angle?'

'I'm not sure.'

They went back into the house.

Sarah said, 'I'm going back to London tonight. Let me talk to one or two people and feel it out. I'll give you my card.

Does it all check out?' she asked as Martin came back into the room.'

'He knows what he's talking about,' Martin said. He pointed to a shelf, to a section of books on nuclear power. 'I looked it up this morning. It all makes horrible sense.'

Very quietly, Laura said, 'Sarah's taking the tape.'

'Fine, fine.'

Sarah made ready to go. 'Can we leave our discussion for another time?'

With an excessive courtliness Martin said, 'Of course.'

Sarah left, and Martin headed for the kitchen. It was a long time since Laura had shared a house with someone and devoted time and energy to avoiding them. She didn't want to reacquire the habit.

'What are you making?'

He was thumping dough. She knew what he was making.

'Pizza.'

The almost emotional significance pizza-making had for Martin was a sort of friendly joke between them. For guests he made nothing else, indifferent to the suggestion that his cooking skills went no further. The pride he took in his springy dough, the glowing, sizzling art-works he lifted from the oven at the end, gave him an endless naïve pleasure.

But now there was something harsh and aggressive in his manner, apart from the fact that tonight they were supposed to be having dinner at Scardale. Martin was reasserting himself. Laura had talked of leaving him, and mentally he was already back on his own. It was just one petty way of showing her that he could handle his life without her.

'Would it be a good idea to have a word with Godfrey Knapp about it tonight?'

Thump, the dough went. Martin growled, 'About what?'

'Tell him about Ray.'

'Out of the question. He's an old friend, and I won't have him lumbered.'

'You don't trust him?'

'Of course I trust him.'

108

'You once said if ever you had a problem he was the man to go to.'

Martin grunted, an unwilling admission.

'So speak to him.'

'No.'

'He's your friend.'

'Precisely.'

'You don't trust him, do you?' She narrowed her eyes. 'Why?'

Refusing to face this, Martin said, 'All right, I'll speak to him.'

Laura said, 'I'd better take Ray some food.'

'If he's still there.'

Martin pounded the dough obsessively, far more than it required. Laura clicked her tongue.

'Are we going to fight over this? Really fight?'

'No. You've already won, haven't you? It's your party. Get on with it.'

So that's it, Laura thought. He feels displaced. Oh well. She took a few items of non-perishable food and left.

The portico at Scardale, a small colonnade of cylindrical brick columns, was modest in itself, but brilliantly set off the rest of the eighteenth-century house, the vintage yellow-grey of its stone, its golden-ratio windows. Even the mauve warmth of the roof-lead, in the autumn evening light, had an air of design about it. Knapp had gutted the house of all the Victorian accretion of his forebears – no dark wood, no damask wallpaper, no ghastly objects brooding in silent rooms – he had created a Palladian interior of space and light, restored the black and white marble floors, sold off the terrible oil portraits of his manic-depressive ancestors. Entering the house, as indeed approaching it up the long curving drive, should have been accompanied by violins and piccolo trumpets.

Martin and Laura had driven there in silence. It was easier to go than to make an excuse and have to face each other all

109

evening. And Laura intended to play the Godfrey Knapp card once more, this time in the man's presence.

There were two other couples – a senior man, so Knapp described him, from Caunder, and a submarine captain who lived in a house at the foot of the Lendra hill-fort. A place the thought of which, he said, together with his Snoopy dog, kept him sane when circumnavigating the earth under total water with a payload of sixteen Polaris missiles. The wives of the two men formed a pallid shadow to their husbands' careers and settled on their coming winter holidays as a backbone of conversation.

The dinner had been prepared by Knapp himself, and he greeted the guests with his flamboyant shirt partly concealed by a striped, discreetly Dior-labelled, butcher's apron. The melancholy and effeminate Harold, with his shiny pointed head and ancient butler's suit, did the fetching and carrying. The funereal silence of Harold, together with Knapp's booming extroversion, Laura found irresistibly funny. She felt that Knapp would share the joke. But the other aspects of the visit kept her from laughing aloud.

She listened in to snatches of dialogue that formed a bizarre descant to the music of cutlery against china.

'. . . your book on Ashcot,' the submarine commander was telling Martin, 'a superb little thing. I took it with me on our last mission, right under the Arctic ice-pack. Wonderful place to have a nice quiet read . . .'

The physicist was saying, 'There's no doubt we'll have a fast-breeder, maybe two, at Caunder ten years from now. And you won't even notice it. That's the beauty of those things, the way they fit into the environment and make no impression whatsoever, just a few cuboids and spheres.'

'The basic shapes of nature, as Cézanne said,' Godfrey Knapp added, and quoted from some remote bank of memory, ' "Let us study nature in the form of the cube, the sphere, the cone . . ." '

'The French love nuclear power,' the physicist said, 'precisely because it's elegant and clean, it has style . . .'

110

And regularly Knapp's eyes turned along the table to gaze at Laura. She knew it, and she was afraid he would bully her into conversation. He would see her reserve as a female reticence which challenged his powers of assault. That old chestnut. But when he met her eye he only smiled, a little sadly even, and the odd remarks he put her way were modest, even his voice was toned down. It was a strange way of coming on to someone, but it all added up to a message.

Knapp fancied a cigar, and the sub commander smoked too, so they all agreed to a twilight stroll in the park. Martin and Laura joined up for the first time since dinner. The semi-darkness made talking easier.

'Will you speak to Godfrey before we go? About Ray?'

Through the meal she had been watching Martin from the corner of her eye. He had relaxed, he was at home with these people, back in his role of local naturalist. She knew what she was doing to him. But a feeling that if she did nothing, she would be crushed, drove her on.

'I said I would.'

'When?' Laura asked. She sensed a stuffy irritation – this isn't the occasion, as guests we have no right. She knew that Martin was not planning to do it this evening.

'If you like, I will.' She said it reasonably, not threatening.

'All right, I'll talk to him,' Martin said. The words were grudging, but he meant it.

Laura gave him a brief hug, but it was the wrong moment. She didn't allow for what Martin had seen going on all through dinner, something which he had known Godfrey Knapp long enough to read instantly and correctly. All the signs of middle-aged infatuation had been there – the abstracted gaze, the almost shy deference, the beaming face when Laura spoke to him. Two birds with one stone, Martin thought, kill this Ray issue once and for all, and head Laura away from Godfrey. Out there in the dark it all made sense.

They had a long and tedious wait for the others to leave. Knapp was in no hurry to return to his solitude. He seemed glad when Martin and Laura were not the first to leave. The physicist and his wife were also in no hurry. Knapp came back in and put more logs on the fire. He had the peculiar loneliness of the dominant. His brashness had modulated into something almost apologetic.

'Everybody stay. Can't say I feel like going to bed.' Knapp could not deny himself another glance at Laura, but kept it under control. 'Have another drink. Whoever's driving, you won't hit much between here and the Moor. Maybe the odd fallow deer. Stick it in the freezer, eh?'

Martin joined Knapp at the drinks cabinet and muttered, 'Could I have a word, Godfrey?'

Knapp looked round, swivel-eyed. Laura was still talking to the physicist's wife.

'The library,' he whispered, and still clutching his glass and the brandy bottle by its neck, headed off through the nearest of the drawing-room's three doors.

On the library shelves the sets of leather-bound volumes had to compete with Knapp's Edgar Wallace first editions and his collection of old-style orange-and-white Penguins.

'Please sit if you wish, but I feel that we may do this better in an upright position. So to speak. How can I help you, Martin?'

After some pondering Martin outlined the bare facts of the story as Ray had told it. Knapp stroked his beard and puffed reflectively at his cigar, his mouth pursed, his eyes half closed.

'And that's it to date?'

'Yes.'

'My advice?'

'Please.'

'Where is this gentleman now?'

'I'd better not say. I'm sorry – that seems as if I don't trust you.'

Knapp refused to be offended. 'Keep him under wraps. He's probably a con man. He might just be somebody with a grudge. Whichever, he's using you. Can you leave it with me for a day or two? Of course, if his story has any truth in it, we should follow it up at the highest level.'

112

He gently slapped Martin's arm. 'And now let's rescue your lovely – *friend* from the clutches of horrible Hilda. You know, I keep wanting to call her your wife. Must be some sort of married look you have about you. Bad sign, that.'

'But what did he say he'd do?'

'I told you, nothing specific. Good God, what do you expect him to say on the spur of the moment?'

'Did you tell it the way it was, Martin?'

'Yes, the whole absurd fantasy.'

'I don't believe it's a fantasy.'

There were many spells of silence on the journey back, as they both privately assessed the possible next moves.

'Why are you obsessed by this man Ray?'

'I'm not obsessed by him, Martin. But he's there. You're not interested in him any more, so you want him to stop existing. Fine. But what if he's for real?'

'I don't want him in Vayro's house much longer. John Vayro was a good friend of mine.'

'Oh Christ, don't be so middle-aged.'

Back at the cottage Laura said, 'I'm just going over to check on him. I said I would.'

'You could phone.'

'We didn't work out a code.'

Martin grunted and slammed the car door as he got out. Laura believed that he had spoken to Knapp in such a way as to close the subject down and shut her up in the process. She drove away, angry. When she came to the junction she steered the Dyane towards Scardale.

Harold was no fool. His impassive face, fine shiny brown skin stretched over an elongated skull, hardly flickered as he asked Laura to step inside. No nonsense about seeing if Mr Knapp was at home. They both knew he was at home and would want to see her.

In pyjamas and a silk dressing gown, Godfrey Knapp joined Laura beside the embers of the drawing-room fire. He extended his hand, and again Laura noted the care with which he took hers, a gentle grip that said he was more than glad to see her and would do anything she wanted.

'I was trying to find a way to console myself for your absence – and here you are again. What pleasure, what torment.'

Laura gave a smile that acknowledged his charm.

'A drink?'

'No, thanks.'

'Well, then –?'

Laura took a breath. 'Martin told you about a man we've met –'

'Yes, yes.'

'I'm sure this is a serious matter.'

'From Martin's outline, I would agree.'

'But Martin doesn't think it's serious.'

'Ah. You mean he doesn't believe this gentleman.'

'That's right.'

'And you do.'

'Yes. He put it all on tape –'

'I see.'

'Martin didn't mention that?'

Knapp paused over his reply, loitering through the exquisite torture of falling in love, an emotion he had lost touch with and given up hope of ever recapturing. Softly, 'No.'

'He – this man, I'm sorry, I can't name him – wants to find someone to accept his story, then he'll be willing to authenticate it further.'

'Where is this tape now?'

'I've given it to – a journalist I know.'

'And what will *he* do with it?'

Knapp placed the gender marker unobtrusively. If Laura wanted to tell him it was Sarah Keeling, fine. If not, she would think he suspected nothing.

'I'm waiting to see.'

'I'll be candid,' Knapp said. 'I like your company very

114

much. I desire no justification for your being here, now or ever. But I'm obliged to ask the next, slightly obtuse question. Why have you come to me?'

Laura had foreseen this and answered promptly. 'To know if I can count on your help if I need it.'

Knapp tasted the pleasure, the potency, of being able to offer himself so generously to a woman who fascinated him. 'It goes without saying.'

'Thank you,' Laura said.

He loved the mix of confidence and diffidence, the hint of fire, the touch of wilfulness, of being her own woman.

'Can I clear up one more thing? Given that Martin – an old and very respected friend – has already approached me, how do I play this? Although I've had a lifetime of difficult positions, I feel that in this one you have to guide me.'

Laura said quietly, 'I don't belong to Martin.'

'No, quite.'

'If you don't object, I'd like to communicate separately with you. If necessary.'

'In confidence?'

'Yes.'

'You are asking a lot.'

'I know. Perhaps I shouldn't have come. I shan't be hurt if you refuse.'

Knapp savoured every moment. Of all the pistols he had ever had pointed at his head, this was the most elegant.

'You have my agreement.'

'Thanks,' Laura said, and he knew that for now that was all he would get.

Laura looked at her watch. 'I have to go.'

Seeing her to her car, Knapp said, 'I shall wait for you to come to me.'

When he went back in, Harold reported a phone call from Mrs Knapp saying that her return to Scardale would be delayed by a few days, and might not even precede Godfrey's planned trip to London. Knapp nodded severely at the news, then smiled to himself and settled down with some Verdi on the hi-fi and a fresh cigar, to think. This evening was getting better all the time.

Chapter Eight

Martin was asleep when Laura returned. She got out of her clothes, put off the corner lamp he had left for her, and slipped into bed next to the humped, silent shape, suspecting that really he was awake, but careful not to put it to the test. She found herself recalling her years of married life. Something about the distance within a shared bed reminded her.

She had married Andy Sondergard because he was the funniest man she had ever met, and she figured that his demented humour would keep all the boredoms and disasters of daily living in their place. Eventually she discovered that the humorist's paramount need is an audience, and that finally no audience can do justice to the jokes without tapping into the melancholy beneath. And the melancholy once exposed, the humorist turns on himself, and the jokes become eruptions of self-hatred. And the audience is blamed. Funny men were difficult to hate, but impossible to love, and that was the end of Andy.

Reminded of him, Laura fell asleep easily. When she woke it was morning, and Martin had brought her fruit juice and a biscuit.

'This is nice,' she said, friendly but defensive.

She pulled the bedclothes up with her, but Martin slid them down again and kissed her nipples. Sex, she thought, orange juice and a Wheatybake as an erotic fanfare, terrific. She tried to stamp out this latest bubble of hypercritical disillusion.

117

But things didn't go that way. Martin rested his thigh against hers till they were both warm.

'I want to ask you something.'

'OK.'

He cleared his throat. 'Let's get married.'

Laura was surprised at how sick the proposal made her feel, not disgusted, but fearful and unaccepting. 'Why?'

'To say something about what we mean to each other.'

'Oh, Martin.'

She wanted to be gentle, and she couldn't. It was always the same, her own instinct for self-preservation had to override the other person's feelings. And the one thing men could not take in a liberated woman was the vein of cold blood they had always exercised themselves.

Martin was trying to keep it practical. 'Why not?'

'No, lover, the question is *why*. I don't have to defend anything.'

Their thighs, warmly together, suddenly felt like the limbs of two other people. Martin got up again, pulling on his clothes like someone in a hurry. Then he said casually, 'Ray seems to be managing quite well.'

Laura went cold. 'What do you mean?'

'When I saw him last night he seemed fine.'

'You saw him last night?'

'I went there just after you. Except that you didn't go there.'

'Oh, you lying bastard, Martin. You self-righteous lying bastard.'

'Are you calling me a liar?' He paused for his moment of moral triumph, liking it in spite of himself. 'I don't want to know where you go. Just don't lie to me. It insults us both.'

He left the room. Laura got up and quickly reached for some clothes. Martin reappeared in the doorway. He knew where she had been last night, he was taunting her to explain herself and apologise. Pride said no chance.

'I have maybe fifteen good years left,' he said, with a grim well-rehearsed conviction. 'I know how I want to spend them.

I'm too old, and too bloody gauche, to play games with people, or to do anything I consider a waste of time. For me, that's the only way to live.'

The marriage idea was a straight piece of manipulation. Yet he must have hoped she would accept.

'You're weird, Martin,' she said, and he took it as a comment on his last statement. Laura let him.

He went out. The Land-Rover revved up and tapered away in the distance. By the time Martin came back, late afternoon, Laura told him, 'I have to go to London for a couple of days.' He said, 'OK.' A minute later she told him she was going that evening, and he remained agreeable, remote, not wasting his or her energy. She would be staying with Sarah Keeling, but that she did not tell him.

Soon after Laura had gone, as she claimed, to see Ray, Martin began to find the loneliness of the cottage, the sudden estrangement, unbearable. He went out and started the Land-Rover. But after the wildness of his initial impulse he realised that if Laura saw headlamps racing after her through the dark she would draw the wrong conclusion. So he drove slowly, giving her time to reach Vayro's house first, and worked on what he was going to say when he got there.

When he pulled in and saw no sign of the Dyane, the perfect script he had devised curled up and evaporated like a sheet of paper in a fire. He skirted the solitary house. One light was on, at the back. He tapped the window, and waited. He heard nothing, but Ray must have come out by the front door, appearing at Martin's side and taking him at a complete disadvantage. It was like revenge for the moment with the axe-handle.

Abashed and uncertain of why he was there, Martin said, 'Oh, I – came to see how things were – is Laura here?'

'No.'

'She hasn't been?'

'No.'

'Ah.'

'How are things at your end?' Ray asked. 'What's happening?'

'Can we go inside?'

'Sure.'

Ray closed the door and said apologetically, 'I've had the fire on. You don't mind?'

'No.' Martin looked round at Vayro's house, the vaguely funereal lair of a lonely man who had rejected comfort. He contemplated the ideas he had had for this place, and what a dead weight it had now become. The pressure on him was too much. He demanded, 'How long are you expecting to be here?'

Ray said coolly, 'It depends what happens.'

'It depends, surely, on you,' Martin said. 'We can't hide you indefinitely.'

'I understand,' Ray said. His eyes rested coldly, almost in mockery, on Martin's strained features.

'We're taking a great risk having you here at all.'

'You want me to go?'

Uncomfortably aware that at any moment Laura might still turn up and catch him there, Martin was now eager to leave.

'I think perhaps a couple more days is all we can manage,' he said. It was a fatuous, arbitrary thing to say, but he needed to assert himself over this place. He had done nothing with Vayro's collection of pornography, and among other things it troubled him that by now Ray had probably found it.

'OK,' Ray said.

'Two days is the absolute maximum,' Martin said, as though repeating made it more rational.

On his way out he asked, 'Have you got enough food?'

Ray answered yes, softly, indifferently.

Another night.

They were splitting, they had a fatal flaw the way all couples do, and it was clear that he had driven a spike right into it. Dozing and waking in front of the small gas fire, Ray reviewed his options.

He had come to the Faul peninsula because he knew it well, and if he was forced on to the country he could use that knowledge, had already used it. As for these people – the woman was a bit up and down, impetuous and not sure what she was getting into, but she might be useful. The man was shrewder and might well be tougher when the crunch came, but was obviously getting loose bowels about something. And meanwhile this house, like all good refuges, was ultimately the perfect trap. A point would come, maybe had come already, where their help would turn into stringing him along. For a moment Ray's gut knotted, and he breathed deep and waited for it to pass. He needed control now, and very fine judgment.

The world he had seen with the marines was not quite the world that most people saw as they went about it. He had done time for activities of a fraudulent character at the expense of HM Government, he had killed on the streets of Belfast, and fetched up in various countries on schemes of an unspecified but dangerous, although often lucrative, nature. But drowsing by the fire in this Wendy-house nestling in deepest England, he reflected, was the trickiest bastard spot he had ever been in.

Godfrey Knapp told Harold to go to bed, wedged one last chunk of pine branch into the dying fire, and with one slippered foot rubbed the head of Tarquin, the wimpish and misnamed spaniel who sprawled in raggy, drooling squalor on the floor beside him.

'Mais qu'est-ce qu'ils cherchent au ciel, ces aveugles?' If Baudelaire had lived now, Knapp would not give him the time of day, and knew it. Yet the Frenchman's lines had echoed down the years of Knapp's life. 'What do they seek in the sky, these blind people?' How many times had this idea struck him when, under cover of business and public relations affairs abroad, he had made contacts, carried information, reported observations, even a few times run people of his own for a while?

The tree of the secret world flourished and grew to great purpose, and at least as much energy was expended on isolating the people in it from each other, as on keeping information from the various 'enemies'. And by the time you were through with the double and triple agents, the buyers and sellers, the unstable cases and the prima donnas, it was unclear who the ultimate enemy was. Godfrey Knapp's motivation had been at different times patriotism, excitement, power, and finally, he admitted, allowing himself a dash of self-knowledge in the warm brandy of his self-appraisal, vanity.

He was out of it now, of course. New brooms, winds of change, yesterday's men, tarred with the Hollis brush, all the clichés organisations use to bury lifetimes of service. Fortunately Knapp had steered away from genteel espionage as a career, being talented and well enough off to play many parts in his time. His finest moment, in his own view, had been in his last year at Cambridge, when he had repelled the blandishments of the Foreign Service and utilised his family connection to get work in the Persian oilfields. Finest moment because at the age of twenty-one he had decided that the dominant factor in his life would be his low capacity for boredom. So, judging every apparent opportunity by its boredom potential, he avoided many possible lifetimes crawling up other men's ladders.

He had been in his time director of many companies, overseas front-man for various interests, property developer, backer of West End shows, patron of the arts, political grey eminence at the regional level. He was fond of saying, 'I still don't know what I want to do when I grow up.' It made people laugh, and he always felt good saying it. He had played at things, elevating play to a level of seriousness which few people brought to work, and for this reason, apart from his irredeemably high profile and periodic need to cut loose, life as a long-term agent would have been unthinkable.

He still saw some of them occasionally, men he had had dealings with in the past, perhaps twenty, thirty years ago, sitting bored and alone in restaurants or clubs. There was still the odd social encounter, when he felt that they were testing him out, still keeping a check that he was sound, wasn't giving anything away, might still be used. A hypothesis Knapp had always played up to. Indeed, he still had the running contact with that Colonel Bramble figure who sometimes phoned for a chat about everything *but* – you know, nod's as good as a wink, old boy. They never really let you go. Maybe they daredn't.

And now? Since he returned from the States they had been in touch again, and this time Colonel Bramble had assured him of how solid they felt he was, and how they would depend on men like Knapp in the difficult days ahead. The Colonel's getting menopausal, Knapp had thought, or pissed, the world view of someone with prostate trouble. But then Martin Ritchie had brought him this story. Probably a fly in a jam jar, no more, not worth speculating over. Yet it had brought Laura to him, and if it turned out to be a dud, she would have no need to come to him again . . .

At that thought his heart felt empty, and his whole life bitter.

'I'll take it in my study,' Knapp snarled as Harold languidly informed the caller that he would ascertain if Mr Knapp was at home.

'Knapp!' he bellowed into the speaker, a noise that communicated nothing but menace, certainly not a name. It had been a shitty night, poor sleep, palpitations and thoughts of death, and too many cigars had made every tube and sinus of his body feel like the Paris sewers.

Why Paris? But where else? He brushed his beard as he waited for the voice to come through. It was the coincidence that was so striking. The Colonel himself, clearly with his Guards tie on already, and this time no farting charade that they were interested in cricket, but a message to transmit, a name to introduce.

It was brief, *comme il faut*, amiable. Just to authenticate

123

our man Mr Teal, who will explain everything. There were never goodbyes. Somehow one just knew the conversation was terminated. Knapp had the *frisson* of knowing that he was being used, but the agreeable sense that it was by a higher intelligence, as if they had waited just long enough to let him see that they were in control of the process that had him about to call them. Without even tossing the usual salad of erudition for a quote, Knapp went upstairs to change from his corduroy-and-denim country wear.

While he alternated between studying himself in the mirror and gazing down at the lake, Knapp found himself taking seriously the story Martin Ritchie had brought him.

The real problem, in Knapp's analysis, the truly enchanting game, was lucidly clear. This paranoid fantasy was an outward expression of the internal rupture of the sacred togetherness between Martin and Laura. Unable to face their incompatibility, they needed a dramatic issue over which to edge their way towards a separation. All couples were the same in the end.

But that was different, that was fun. Civilisation was about private life, not the banal *longueurs* of the public stage. Piss on all that.

Yet if it *was* true, who was the man on the tape? Well, that was not such a hard one. The eighties had thrown up a new breed of adventurer, people no longer satisfied with a lifetime's career of mediocre advancement under the blanket of a 'security' that could be ripped away at any moment by the forces of the so-called market. People with character and muscle and a hunger for money could put themselves out for hire to all kinds of entrepreneurial agencies. It was open season on the law.

That, or the man was undercover himself, an *agent provocateur*. Intriguing possibility, that.

But grant the story was true. Who then was behind it? Which *them* was it being orchestrated by?

The Army? No, no – the Army had all it wanted, a big, powerful but cumbersome machine, not fine-tuned enough for devious operations like this.

The Atomic Energy Authority? As a whole, no. Someone within it? Quite possibly.

The police? The Branch? Somehow not their style. They would come into it, should it happen, in the course of a day's work. Better not to have them behind it from the off.

The government? What the hell were governments anyway? Nobody knew, that was the trouble with politics. The cabinet? No, too baggy, too leaky, cabinets. A power group within the cabinet, though? That was certainly on. The PM? Not necessarily. A minister or two, the Home Secretary? A power group within the government, operating unilaterally? Could be.

The security services? Not as a whole, but they never did anything as a whole, did they? A faction, though – had to be a good bet. Nothing could ever be traced back, of course.

Then, just as the perfect account was about to crystallise, Knapp got bored by it. Spies, spycatchers, plots to overthrow civilisation as we know it, counterplots to rescue same civilisation for all right-thinking people, made him ache from the roots of his teeth right down to his anal nodules.

And as for 'our Mr Teal', he'd better have brought all his marbles with him. Knapp had never given anybody a free lunch in his life, and wasn't about to start now. Still, he reflected, slowly brushing his beard, it was flattering if nothing else. Power is the ultimate aphrodisiac. Kissinger said that, but where the hell did *he* get it from? Politicians never said anything *original*.

Harry Teal was shown into the library. Knapp met him in a chalk-stripe suit, three-piece, and a tie that mimicked the broken subtlety of medieval stained glass, a tie in which you could meet anybody. The studied ordinariness of Teal's self-presentation was something Knapp instantly recognised, the brownish-greenish clothing, the plumpish, pinkish, fairish man inside, not frayed enough to be a schoolteacher or slick enough to sell insurance.

'Too early for a drink?'

'Yes, thanks.' Teal paused. Nothing like a first impression, and he saw in front of him a typical relic of the old brigade, the ones who talked in public-school patois and reminisced over shindigs in Bongo-Bongo Land. Might be worth a look-over, they had said, high commendation. But Teal was hard to impress, and he wanted it to show. 'I was advised to come to you because of valuable services you've given in the past.'

Knapp looked august. 'Quite.'

'I have to be vague about some details, you'll appreciate –'

Knapp swept the apology aside with a cloud of cigar smoke.

'We're on the trail of a man who could be both dangerous and extremely embarrassing – we know he's around here, and we would like to have him in custody before he can damage – it has to be said, the nation.'

'And what do you wish me to do? For the nation?'

'He's been in contact with, and may still be, one Martin Ritchie, who lives not far –'

Knapp interrupted. 'I know him.' Either they had this information already, or they soon would. Better to flaunt it.

'Fine,' Teal said. 'That's useful. Are you willing to do anything you can –?'

Anything? Knapp thought. He despised Mr Teal and his salesman's approach to loyalty. But he had his own reasons. 'Certainly.'

'Is this man Ritchie a personal friend?'

'Hardly that.'

'If you could monitor him – even use him as a bait – he may well know where chummy has gone to ground. Could save us a lot of trouble. But it needs a delicate approach. You're probably the ideal person.'

Knapp gave a smile that was not quite as patient or indulgent as it seemed. Cheeky young tit. It was, also, a dull brief. To liven it up, Knapp asked, 'And how do we feel about Mr Ritchie?'

'I don't follow,' Teal said.

'Is he a witting or an unwitting accomplice to all this?'

'I can't say.'

'You mean you won't say, or you don't know?'

Teal felt that Knapp was looking to capsize the questions, all the time probing for a rotten plank. But he was not going to get to Harry Teal.

'Guilt unproven but suspicion remaining.'

'Ah,' Knapp intoned, 'you quote those words. Of course, Kim was before your time. I actually met him. I found him neither as evil as some have described, nor as brilliant, but a strangely human character.'

The upstaging had no effect. Teal's puffy, uncomplicated eyes remained unmoved.

'I don't know what you're talking about.'

'You quoted the verdict on Philby after his interrogation.'

'I wasn't aware. A coincidence.'

'I see,' Knapp answered, and thought: dismal little shit, where do they dig them up from?

'Your best service at the present time,' Teal continued, 'is probably to impress on Mr Ritchie the serious nature of what he's getting into. He may be under a lot of internal strain, and if you could persuade him to confide in you, he should be easy to run.'

Tiring of the interview, and unable to express his amusement at all its little ironies, Knapp now brimmed with compliant *bonhomie*.

'I'll work on him, never fear. Urgent, of course. How do I report to you?'

'Directly,' Teal said, and took out his pen, a plastic souvenir of the Imperial War Museum.

Knapp spent the day fishing, in his trout-stocked lake, with a friend from the City and an important Arab visitor and the three young female companions they had brought with them in the helicopter which now stood in one of the paddocks of Scardale. Thigh-deep in the water, between the serious fishing and the bouts of personal levity that consumed the day, Knapp scrutinised the idea which had come to him even

127

while that appalling gumshoe Teal had been there. He projected himself into each of the characters involved, seeing events with the limited knowledge they had, till he was satisfied that he knew more than any one of them.

He had hired his favourite chef from the area to cater for them at Scardale that evening. At one point, when the food was over and the sex only in its budding stages, Knapp excused himself and went to his study. He dialled the number given and asked for Mr Greenwood.

Teal's jumped-up provincial grammar-school voice came on. Where do they train them, Knapp thought, in camps with the words 'Mediocrity is Strength' in wrought iron over the gates? He cleared his throat before speaking in measured, slightly contemptuous tones.

'I have one piece of information for you. There is a tape relating to the person you spoke of, and you should perhaps look very closely at the affairs of one Miss Sarah Keeling. A journalist.'

Knapp spelt out the surname and coolly put the receiver down. Then he laughed to himself gently, not the wild guffaw he used in company, but a much more satisfying melody of amusement.

As the signs ticked off the monotonous motorway landscape towards London, Laura admitted to herself that, for all her love of Martin and her need to share a place with him, keeping the London flat had represented a streak of that cool acceptance of eventual failure that typified all her relationships with men. She was starting to feel glad that the flat was still there.

It had been a perfect summer, staying at the Moor, preparing to move there for good. It had felt like her rebirth. But suddenly all that was a temporary space, bracketed off from her real life, the idyll a shattered egg.

She had an arrangement with the friend who had rented her flat about staying there, but rather than make use of this she had phoned Sarah. The coincidence of them living, one on the north, the other on the south side of Clapham Common, made it somehow easy. Sarah was watching as Laura arrived in a sudden shower, and went down to help carry her things in from the street.

Sarah lived alone. She and Laura were instantly at ease together. The ten years' difference in their ages had something to do with it; the competitiveness and aggression had all gone somewhere else. Both achievers, they could accord each other the proper unobtrusive admiration.

After clearing away a lot of other subjects, Sarah said, 'I passed on the tape. I've got one of those machines myself, so I took a copy.'

'Good,' Laura said. She hadn't thought to copy it.

'It's a guy I know who makes independent documentaries. It's no good approaching the big channels. He's coming back to me tomorrow. How long are you staying?'

Laura smiled and said, 'Tough question.'

'You've actually left Martin?'

'No.'

It was a very uncertain negative. 'But I feel as if I've torn up a piece of paper. It didn't exist, but I still feel that I've torn it up.'

Tactfully, Sarah refrained from commenting on her impression of Martin: authoritarian, quietistic, tunnel vision. Better left unspoken till Laura said it.

'Are you going back to Macemoor?'

'Oh yes, I'll go back. But I don't know on what basis we're going to live together now.'

'I was looking at your portfolio while you were in the bath. I hope you don't mind.'

'No. They're for a school history book. It was a good contract to get. Should sell a lot.'

Sarah looked at her with a pretty, conniving smile.

'You're a naughty girl. You put Martin in one of them.'

Laura's face softened, and she laughed.

'He wouldn't enjoy it. I might have to change that.'

The picture in question showed a visit by the Enclosure

129

Commissioners to an eighteenth-century village, overruling the protests of villagers at the loss of their common land. The Enclosure man, the heartless official just obeying orders and doing his job, had the face of Martin. What Sarah did not know was that the leading villager, already being eyed by a redcoat in the background, had the features of Ray.

'You can stay as long as you like,' Sarah said. 'As long as you need to get things sorted out.'

Laura said thanks.

Sarah narrowed her eyes through her glasses and said, 'Tell me about you and men.'

'I like them,' Laura said.

'Is that all?'

'No.'

They both laughed.

'Do you want to talk about it?'

'Not yet,' Laura said. 'But I'd like to know I can talk to you when I want.'

'Please.'

'And what about you?'

'Me?'

'Yes.'

'I guess I – prefer my own sex, when it comes to it.'

'That's what I felt,' Laura said.

'It doesn't bother you?'

'Of course not.'

'Have you ever –?'

'No. But it's – all right.'

Sarah smiled, suddenly much the younger woman. Laura felt that for once being forty was an advantage.

'We'll talk again,' she said.

'Thanks,' Sarah said. 'I feel we've already said a lot.'

Chapter Nine

Hour by hour after Laura had gone, Martin tried to accept that she might come back from this London trip, might continue to live with him, but it could never be the same as before.

They had both deceived each other, trivially perhaps, but it poisoned his idea of what their relationship had been about. Mr and Mrs Country-Cottage they were never going to be, but he realised now that his idea of how they would both live at Macemoor had been too simple, too innocent. It made him burn to admit it. It seemed that everything he had offered Laura had been handed back to him. Even her stylish self-control seemed to taunt him, making him feel old. The competent, independent life he had been leading appeared a sad alienation, the timid self-exile of a broken man.

These fears keyed into thoughts of John Vayro, who had once been a sympathetic model for Martin's older self, the kind of man he might well become. But the store of sado-masochistic male pornography that he had found in Vayro's house had forced him to reevaluate his old friend's life. All that proud self-containment had covered a tortured lone-liness which in years of friendship Martin had never even guessed at. It was a depressing comment on his own powers of perception.

And Vayro's example beckoned further. Between Eleanor's death and the arrival of Laura, Martin had managed with the functional, solitary sexual relief of those whose emotions have migrated elsewhere. But Laura had opened things up in him which Eleanor had never done, and now he could not shake off the desires which regularly stirred in him. Every time he thought of her body, a potent craving that was like rage blew the embers of humiliation back to flame inside him. There was, also, something vulpine and amoral in her sexuality, which Martin felt he had failed to rise to, and this also gnawed at him now, the hurt anger of someone who has been made to feel less than successful.

But if she left him his life could never have any meaning again. All the places around Macemoor were spoored with Laura's trace now. There was nowhere he could escape from her. Fantasies of the sea, of the watery suicide Vayro had always talked of, haunted him and settled into a fatalistic sense that his own future would end like that.

And inside him somewhere, the ghost of a rational man, an inner-directed purposeful man in his right mind, wondered how at the age of forty-eight he could ever have become so pathetic.

Sarah went out, and Laura took a long bath, trying to understand the strange certainty that had sent her to live with Martin – to recapture it, even, because she was willing. But it would not come any more.

As she stepped from the door she was surprised to hear, as she thought, Sarah returning. The bathroom door was ajar. She listened. Then she reached for a towel, in a gesture of defence. It was not the sound of the door being unlocked, and before she wondered any further what it was, she shut the bathroom door and turned the key.

She hardly breathed. Her skin tingled. She heard the apartment door give, the lock maybe wrenched off, the entry forcible and uncompromising. The bathwater made a slight gurgle as it drained away. Laura quickly replaced the plug. She kept checking the lock, which she could see lodged in place between door and jamb. A heavy shoulder could soon smash through it.

She looked round the room for some article of defence. There was nothing heavier than a lotion bottle. She had an idea, took a toothmug and filled it with bleach from a plastic bottle beside the toilet. A faceful of bleach would sting, blind, delay. She gripped a pair of nail scissors. Her clothes were in the bedroom, there was nothing she could do about that. The pulse in her body was like the sea.

Through the door she heard the noises of a flat being hastily and angrily turned over. Only a few minutes, but she had no measure of time. Drawers were being pulled out, things swept aside, furniture pushed over. Carpets muffled some of the effects, but suddenly Laura could feel someone on the other side of the bathroom door. The handle went down, and she was nearly sick as she saw it move. Once, twice, then a flat hand shoving the door. She clutched her improvised weapons, begging herself to be able to use them.

Maybe the intruder realised the bathroom was occupied. Maybe it was not a place worth searching. But there was no more attempt to get in, and no more noise of burglary from the rest of the flat. Perhaps a lure, to get her to ease the door open. But burglars didn't hang about, they were usually scared of being seen – Weren't they?

Laura sat in the wicker chair, her head in her hands. It was half an hour before she came out. By then she was in a state of mild shock, which the blitzed appearance of the flat reinforced.

Still holding her primitive weapons, she went from room to room. She felt guilty on Sarah's account. She wanted to clear it up, but touched nothing. When Sarah returned they hunted for the object of the break-in. Although things had been scattered everywhere, to divert attention or leave an after-taste of terror, not much had gone.

'The tapes,' Sarah said. 'Every bloody cassette.'

'Including the –?' Laura said.

'Shit!' Sarah exclaimed. She looked to the shelf where she had left the copy of Ray's evidence. It was gone. Falling back on propriety, indignation finally surfacing, Laura asked, 'Shouldn't we call the police?'

'No, ducky,' Sarah said. 'I don't think we'll bother.'

They poured a drink and sat down amid the wreckage, tacitly reassuring each other that they could ride this out, at least for the moment.

'Somebody must have followed you here,' Sarah said.

'I guess so.' That creepy bastard Teal, Laura thought. Then, going cold, she thought of Martin. He had known when she left. Was putting them on to her a last revenge? Or even a perverted way of getting her back?

'I saw my producer friend,' Sarah said. 'He's interested in the tape. He wants to know if this guy would be prepared to go on film. It could be a back view, silhouette, but they'd need a lot more hard fact.'

'I'll have to talk to him.'

'Can you reach him by phone?'

'No,' Laura lied.

Indicating the flat, Sarah said, 'Looks like it might be urgent.'

As they tidied up, Laura said, 'There is one phone call I'd like to make.'

She rang Scardale and learned that Knapp would be in London later that day. Harold had been briefed to give his London number if Laura phoned. For a moment she wondered if Knapp had followed her to town as well. After three attempts she found him in. She accepted his surprise as genuine and said, 'I need to talk to you.'

Knapp's fruity voice answered, 'My dear Laura, only say when. How about a late lunch with me here? It's only Fulham, the chichi end of the pseudo-gentrification down-market, but I'd be delighted to entertain you here.'

'Adorable,' Laura said. It was the kind of word Knapp liked, and he almost purred as he fixed up the time.

As she left the Clapham flat Laura did not notice, although he saw her, the unremarkable figure of Harry Teal.

The birdwatcher from Saltmayne. Disoriented, Martin Ritchie tried to place the round-faced man in glasses and angler's hat. The birdwatcher reminded him of where they had met. It was only five days ago, but time and place had got warped since then.

'I didn't realise who you were.' Rotund, boyish, ingratiating, the birdwatcher oozed inoffensiveness. 'Then someone told me who you were – *the* Martin Ritchie – I couldn't believe it. I'm only an amateur myself, just here for a holiday, but I know your name from various journals, the radio – I have one of your books at home –'

'You'd better come in,' Martin said.

Hardly pausing, the birdwatcher continued his apology for being there as he followed Martin into the cottage.

'You probably don't remember, but I was making enquiries about my brother, who'd wandered off with an attack of amnesia. Well, he's turned up in Glasgow, and he's back with the family now, and that's worked out all right.'

Martin tried to place the birdwatcher – 'My name's Giles Pilkington, by the way' – into the scrambled tangram of the last week. The moment when he and Laura had met and suspected the birdwatcher was long gone, and as Pilkington wittered on now Martin found it hard to take him seriously.

He offered a cup of tea, which Pilkington accepted, along with some perfunctory discussion of local bird life. Then, the soul of good manners, Pilkington insisted on leaving, apologising again for having called, but timorously delighted at having met someone he regarded as an outstanding man. He flapped his hands and almost forgot to take his hat.

From Pilkington's point of view it was a good risk. Either Ritchie took him at face value, which was fine, or the visit would make him jumpy, and that could be better. If Ritchie panicked, the whole thing could be sewn up before Teal returned, and that would be super.

135

*

Although the rush hour was officially over, the Kingston bypass was packed with cars, three lanes crawling through the sodium-lit darkness in either direction, the carriageways walled in from the outside world and divided by cast-iron fencing. Harry Teal finally escaped from the jam and accelerated up the slip-road that filtered him off into the winding suburban back-streets of Malden.

The 'For Sale' notice had started to lean in the privet hedge. Teal left the car in the road, unlatched the gate to the narrow front garden, all the time watching the dark house for details. This should be the one place he could approach in a relaxed way, but trade habits didn't keep office hours. No light, no sign of Maureen. He had had the locks changed to prevent her coming back and stripping the house in his absence. Yet he still half-expected her to be there one day, waiting in the porch. He had fleshed out a number of punitive fantasies based on such a return.

He went to the drinks cupboard in what they used to call the breakfast room. The long evening threatened to be endless. Below the hard-cased layer of scorn Teal knew that she had done it for real. Weeks were becoming months now, and Maureen could never do a thing like this as a gesture. She didn't have a gesture in her whole body. After half an hour of angrily tipping Scotch into himself, Teal went out.

The house with its G-Plan furniture and conservative wallpaper seemed to be laughing at him. The streets were dismal, but he felt less pressured out there. A part of him loved these suburban streets, where people led quiet lives behind their neat front gardens. He had grown up in the same section of a provincial town, and for Teal it was for streets such as these that the Union Jack had always flown. Grammar school and red-brick university took him to a three-year commission in the Army, where being unable to match the other officers socially, he had equalled and surpassed them in patriotism. And then, the great moment of his life, the service had chosen him.

Along the street, past the pool of ghostly light thrown out by a petrol station, three young men were jumping on and off a low wall and kicking an empty can between them. The sight of Teal ambling towards them provoked their interest, and one detached himself from the group and strutted forwards, directly in Teal's path. At the last moment he swerved, then bounced against Teal's shoulder. The face was coarse, pimply, with a pig-like ugliness as he shouted abuse at Teal. The other two came up quickly. They all wore leather bumfreezers and calf-height boots, small woollen hats squatting on their cropped heads. Union Jack badges were stitched on their jacket sleeves.

The teenager shoved his fist in Teal's face. 'OK, you cunt, give. Turn your fucking pockets out. Or do you want this?' Saliva flecked his mouth. He trembled his fist an inch away from Teal's nose.

Teal contemplated them. If they had been black it would have been easier. He disliked blacks, and blacks didn't overlap with anything in his world, so anything that involved them could be dismissed. But these people were white, about to rob and beat up a fellow-Englishman. Add the scum like these to the subversives and you had half the population. The shit, Teal thought, the shit we have to live in.

'Come on, cunt, move it.'

The fist shook in his face. Teal grabbed the arm, twisted it. The skinhead spun round with a yell. His friends tensed but were reluctant to act. Teal screwed the arm tight behind the skinhead's back, pulled him in close and jerked one knee up into the small of his back. Then he half-turned him and drove his right fist into the boy's belly, and before dumping him on the pavement he chopped his nose, not to break it but enough to make the blood gush down his agonised, piggish face.

The other two ran off. The boy on the ground curled himself against the anticipated kicking, hysterical at the feel of his own sticky blood soaking everywhere. When he looked out from behind his arm, Teal had gone.

*

137

That was the woman from Macemoor. My God, Teal thought, as Laura disappeared along the street, what a connection. Physical contact, the efficient beating he had given the skinhead the night before, had sharpened his taste for really rich blood. And after he had taken care of business, he would get even with Maureen. First things first.

'Miss Sarah Keeling?'

Her eyes were wary, and she had one of those smart know-it-all looks that he hated. But this was his game now. From a position of strength she could not even guess at, Teal kept his sneers internal and made his play calm and amicable.

'Who are you?' Sarah asked.

'My name is Teal.'

He spelt it by letter, as if it was important. He wasn't giving any more away, and he sure wasn't selling double glazing. Sarah was worried. When these creeps volunteered their names to a journalist, they felt very secure indeed.

'There are a few things I have to ask you.'

Sarah countered, 'Your identification?'

Teal was not feeling too friendly towards women. 'The questions I ask identify me.'

Sarah turned her back and walked into the flat. Teal carefully closed the door behind him and followed her. He helped himself to a chair.

'You know my flat was burgled this morning?'

'How should I know that?'

'It wouldn't be anything to do with you?'

Teal ignored this. 'You've contacted the police?'

'Just get it over with,' Sarah said. 'Whatever you're here for.'

'You're getting into something very dangerous.'

Sarah watched his expression. There weren't many human puzzles she couldn't crack. He had the tape, that was certain. The timing, the space between the break-in and Teal's appearance, was masterly. But – she spelt it out mono-syllabically in her mind – *there's one copy of the tape he doesn't know about*. That was her only trick.

'Of course, you could be an innocent party. Certain people may be using you. In which case, take this as a warning in good faith.'

'A warning to do what?'

'You could help me.'

Stony-faced, Sarah said, 'Excuse my mirth.'

'And I could harm you,' Teal replied. 'If I need to, I will harm you. But that's a remote possibility. What I'm here to do is stop you committing professional suicide.'

'Big of you.'

'Well, for a start you could be privy to offences under the Official Secrets Act. And you may be dealing with a felon as defined by the Prevention of Terrorism Act –'

'It's all a closed book to me,' Sarah said sweetly. 'You could tell me anything, I'd believe you.'

Placidly Teal said, 'You're lucky. You're dealing with me. I'm not a gorilla. I'm doing my job, and I'm giving you a little advice about yours. Let me ask you a question. Do you believe there's such a thing as traitors?'

Sarah said, 'Don't play silly verbal games with me.'

'You can't avoid it,' Teal said. 'No answer is an answer. I'll tell you why I ask. The man whose voice you taped is as much of a traitor as it's possible to be. A man who would destroy this country – its values, its security – a man who needs to deceive others into being his friends. But being a traitor, he has no stake in what happens to them after he's used them.' A deep vein of bourgeois indignation ran through Teal's bland reasonableness. 'Am I making myself clear?'

'Not in the least,' Sarah said. She resisted the impulse to argue with him. He reminded her of a large mollusc.

'It remains to be seen,' Teal said, 'whether you're breaking the law. In that case others will deal with you. But you know whether you're breaking the law, don't you? Whether you're acting against the interests of the nation. That's the real law, isn't it? You know where this man is hiding. I have to ask you to give me that information.'

Sarah said, 'I don't know.'

'You can find out.'

'Not necessarily.'

'Sure you can. You're a well-known journalist. They haven't contacted you for nothing. If you give us this man it could make your career.'

'I've made my career, thanks.'

Teal was impassive. 'If you don't co-operate, the investigation has to branch out – people who know you, who employ you. Instead of assisting with the enquiry, you become an object of the enquiry. And there are no second chances.'

Sarah asked, 'Are you giving me time to think about this?'

'To think, but not to stall. Or do anything clever. You can get me between six and seven tonight at this number. After that –'

Teal gave a shrug of lazy contempt.

'Think about it,' he said at the door. On the landing he reached inside his jacket and switched off his Sony pocket recorder. It was so light he sometimes forgot. It was amazing what rubbish he sometimes picked up.

Then he was gone, silently and effortlessly as a slug. Sarah felt the trail of slime, inexpungable, glistening and viscous across the face of her life.

'I thought you said Fulham.'

'Oh,' Godfrey Knapp answered, 'the Fulham Road's out there somewhere. It's just a pleasant little backwater, nice for a quiet elderly gent on his own.'

His whole face twinkled. Laura walked past him, and her ironic amusement mirrored his as their eyes met.

'What a lovely flat!' It had space, subtle colours, and suddenly the crowded acres of London were obliterated. Knapp insisted on showing her the jacuzzi in the bathroom, and in the sitting-room Laura started at the sight of a number of books, laid out on a polished walnut table, in which she had been involved as illustrator. She knew how much energy it had taken to put them there. Knapp's theory had been right. He had touched her ego in the one spot where it had no resistance.

140

'I'm collecting your work,' he said. 'I hope to become an authority. They are very good.'

Laura said, 'You certainly know how to flatter.'

'I simply know how to express my fascination.'

Skilled movers in the sexual dance, they bantered for a while, always keeping the bodily dimension at bay. The door was knocked, and a covered tray of cold food which Knapp had ordered from a place 'just along the street' brought in. With the wine, which he conspicuously refused to show off or be knowledgeable about, the atmosphere changed and he remarked:

'You needed to talk to me.'

'Yes.' Laura had rehearsed what she would say, but it changed all the time, and there was no easy formula. 'You remember what I told you about a man we had met – Martin and I had met –?'

'And a tape, I recall.'

'I'm staying with a friend, and her flat was broken into this morning. All her cassettes were taken, including the tape we're talking about. It can't be a coincidence.'

'But how would anybody know?' Knapp asked.

'Did I tell you that Martin and I were questioned by Special Branch? At the cottage. They came and searched the place.'

With the wine, and the summoning up of excitement and fear, a flush had appeared along Laura's cheekbones. Knapp's insides quivered with erotic need. He looked grave and shook his head.

'Doesn't it prove that I'm right?'

'It certainly suggests,' Knapp said, 'that the man you're talking about is very important to certain people.' One hand massaged his neatly trimmed beard. 'The problem we have . . .'

He left the words in the air. Laura, uneasy, asked, 'Which problem?'

'Is your friend a goodie or a baddie? Isn't that it?'

A misgiving, a foretaste of disappointment, slackened Laura's facial muscles a little, but decisively. Knapp realised he had dealt her a blow, and paused compassionately.

'We have to accept, my very dear Laura, that the people who oversee our so-called security may be a loathsome bunch, but they are not always wrong. You have considered that possibility?'

There was a depth of worldly experience and cynical detachment about Knapp which Laura had to defer to.

'Not really.'

'We should consider it.'

'I know I'm right,' Laura said.

Knapp smiled indulgently and took her to see the view from the back balcony, a panorama of inaccessible, well-tended gardens. As they stood there, he placed his hands on her shoulders.

'Right or wrong,' he said, 'I will always help you.'

'You're very sweet,' Laura said. She kissed his bristly cheek. They both knew that was the limit for today, and Knapp sought no more. But he judged the moment right for candour, a small raising of the stakes.

'There are two things you should know about me,' he said. 'One, I have no aspirations to be a sugar daddy. Two, I have no intention of being a father figure.' Then he thought of a third. 'I also – forgive the chauvinistic tone of this – am perfectly capable of stealing another man's woman, and to hell with the consequences.'

Laura smiled in acknowledgement. Inside the ogre there was a layer of charm, and the charm imprisoned a man who had never found himself. That was his appeal. She forced herself back to the subject.

'What am I going to do?'

'About your refugee?'

'Yes. Would you talk to him?'

Knapp looked doubtful but said, 'If you think it a good thing, certainly.'

Sarah told Laura nothing of Teal's visit. An instinct that was part of her professional success made her hold on to anything which kept her one jump ahead. Ahead of somebody, no matter who. But to get counterweight from another quarter she phoned the producer who had the copy of Ray's tape. She kept quiet about the burglary. The producer was matter-of-fact, and she left him that way.

'We'll need him on film,' he repeated, regarding this as one of a number of options bidding for his time, 'and we want names and places that we can follow through. Personally I think he's a phoney, no disrespect, Sarah sweetie.'

Sarah would never know if she had really already concluded that herself, or if this conversation tipped her over. But in spite of it she told Laura, 'I've got some work to finish here. I'll drive down tomorrow, first thing in the morning. Can you fix up for me to meet him?'

Laura said, 'I'll try.'

'I'm not optimistic.'

'What about?'

'I'm just not sure if the guy's genuine.'

'Then why does everybody want him so badly?'

'I didn't say he's not a wanted man.'

'So,' Laura said defensively, 'there must be a story in there somewhere.'

'Oh sure,' Sarah answered. 'But what's it going to cost us to get it?'

A dreary rainswept night and the prospect of a cross-London drive through miles of commuter traffic, a dark sludge punctuated by rain-refracted headlamp beams, followed by hours of black countryside, made Laura reluctant to leave. But another night at Sarah's could get complicated, and she sensed that Sarah preferred her to go. But equally the thought of the first night back with Martin, especially after a long journey, made her heart sink.

The solution was simple. She drove the few streets to the other side of the Common, to her own flat. She had never used the easy-going arrangement before, but it paid off now, and she spent the night there on a futon in the tiny second bedroom. For one night, at least, it answered all the dilemmas.

She got up with the light, had a quick session in bathroom and kitchen, avoided too many personal awakenings in her old home, left a thank-you note for her sleeping tenant, and drove off through the melancholy silver of the deserted early-morning city.

Martin had heard the car and opened the cottage door. She was glad he did it, dreading the moment of letting herself in and finding him angry or ignoring her. He looked his old self, a little remote but friendly and tolerant, and she relaxed immediately. They kissed gently, a kiss neither defiant nor spoiled by remorse.

'Sorry I didn't phone,' Laura said.

Martin said, 'It's a nice surprise.'

'Are you sure?'

He smiled. 'I was just going after the mushrooms.'

Martin had always promised to show her those edible wild fungi that made the pallid things in shops taste like rubber bands. In a book he had shown her the agarics, the parasols, the family of Russulas, large meaty toadstools coloured from pale brown through gold to purply-red, and described his mental map of their cropping territories, unchanging year by year. No greater pleasure, he said, than wandering the stretches of woodland and discovering clusters of fungi glowing in decomposing corners.

'Come on, let's go.'

Laura suspected Martin of a ploy designed to wrongfoot her. But he seemed to be saying, let's have a happy interlude before those other things pile up on us again. 'Yes,' she said, and gave him a brief hug as they went out.

Their bags were soon full. The few acres of neglected, wooded hillside, mainly beech and scrawny oak, were new to Laura. Martin steered her to particular spots, then let her find the firm, convex, voluptuous-to-handle fungi. He had a precise knowledge of where different types grew, which were

144

toxic and which worth eating. It was a good outing, and they both took it on the simple level where it could succeed.

In the fifteen years between the two phases of their relationship, Laura had thought of Martin as an intellectual, too intellectual, man, and she now realised how he needed projects, a practical focus for his life. Ideas made him uncomfortable, he was a micro-, not a macro-man, and one small plot of earth could yield up all he wanted to know about the universe. She envied it, it was a rare kind of fulfilment, and yet she wondered how she could have misunderstood him.

Returning with a gorgeous russet-capped fungus the size of her hand, Laura bent her head to dodge a low branch, then almost stumbled at the realisation that somebody else was there. She gasped and her hand went involuntarily to her chest, and even with empty lungs her body shuddered and found more air to push out.

She stared at the man who leered back from behind a tree, on a slope choked with undergrowth, some feet above her. The snarling grin on his face and the malign blankness of his eyes were frightening and simultaneously ridiculous because his glasses had slipped to one side and hung diagonally across his face. He was leaning awkwardly over a slender branch that bowed under his weight. His head was bare, and the strands of hair normally brushed across the baldness drooped out-wards above one ear like part of a bizarre tippet. The expression on his face, and the rising admission that she was looking at a dead man, froze out of Laura's mind the recognition that she had met him before.

She backed away from the birdwatcher and his deranged eyes, unseeing yet inescapable as a blind man's. Becoming aware of the clammy red flesh of the Lactarius in her hand, she threw it back into the bushes in a sudden repelled association of its feel with the body sprawled on the ash sapling in front of her.

Her voice would not function, her legs refused to move.

Paralysed on the sandy path she heard Martin calling as he approached.

'Laura – Laura!'

Her skin went cold at the sound.

Chapter Ten

'His name was Giles Pilkington.'

The Land-Rover smelt of fungoid earth, mushroomy and warm. They had gone straight back there from their discovery of the birdwatcher's corpse. Although still numb, Laura showed surprise. 'You knew him?'

'He called at the house when you were in London.'

'Why?'

'He'd found out who I was, wanted to – you know – discuss birdwatching, something like that –'

'Who was he really?'

'Christ knows.'

'Just an ornithologist?'

Martin groaned despondently. 'I think when he came to see me he was letting me know that he wasn't just a – that was the feeling I got, that he wanted me to know. He was evidently worth murdering.'

'He was looking for Ray, wasn't he? All that rubbish about his brother –'

'He said they'd found his brother.'

'Absolute crap, Martin. Couldn't you tell he was lying?'

'I always assume people are not lying. Why should I care?'

'You better not be so sniffy now.'

'Why? I've done nothing.'

'The police – oh God –!'

'What?'

'We have to keep away from Ray. They'll want a complete account of our movements. Let's not do anything we don't want them looking into.'

Martin said, 'Let's just ignore it.'

Laura looked at him in almost comic disbelief. He meant it. She loved but was infuriated by this streak in him that could disregard anything, however important, that failed to fit in with his schemes.

'You're not serious?'

'Look,' Martin protested, 'we came here to hunt mushrooms. A yard to the left or right, you wouldn't have seen him. All right, you *didn't* see him. *Finito.*' That quasi-Gallic shrug again.

Laura laughed. He was serious, and it was comic.

'Martin,' she said, 'how many people come here?'

'Hard to say. Not many.'

'The poor man could hang on that tree for weeks while the rats and crows come and eat him. I don't want to wake up every night and think of that. Anyway, we've left footprints all over the place.'

Martin conceded, but grudgingly. In his opinion his footprints were his business. Even as they drove away, towards the nearest village with a police house, the nearest actual station being in Barnbrook, Martin searched for loopholes.

'We don't have to say that we'd met him. Look – we found the body, we make a statement, we're not involved any further.'

'And the police go through his effects,' Laura said, 'find a diary or something describing how he visited his favourite naturalist, Martin Ritchie, who then becomes a prime suspect because of his gratuitous lying.'

'You think we should tell everything?' Martin demanded. 'They've turned over our house, that man Teal came and said he knew we'd been helping Ray and it was some kind of treason – Jesus Christ. I haven't done anything wrong, and I feel guilty as hell. I don't want to add to it.'

The stress was becoming competitive, and Laura was about to say, that's nothing, they stole the tape from Sarah's flat – But she stopped herself.

'Look,' she said, 'it could be a straightforward murder.'

Martin grunted ironically. 'Like what?'

'Pilkington might have come across something – there was a policeman once who, off duty, happened on two men having sex in a wood. They blew his head off with a shotgun. I lived next door to the policeman's family when I was a girl.'

'Nice and straightforward,' Martin observed sardonically.

'I mean not connected with us.'

For Martin the line between humour and outrage was wavering.

'Of course it's not bloody connected with us. You didn't kill him, I didn't kill him – I only met the bloody man twice, I had a job even remembering his name –'

'What are we scared of, then?' Laura asked.

'I'm not scared of anything,' Martin said. 'I'm just scared.'

They led the police to Pilkington's body, and the rest of day hung over them like a pall of smoke. The police took a statement and told them to go home but remain available for further questioning. Martin and Laura went to lie down together, clothed, their bodies close for comfort, their minds elsewhere. Mid-morning a car approached, then there were police at the door. They required Martin in Barnbrook to help with their enquiries.

Unnaturally detached, Martin got ready. He was still in the old clothes he wore for expeditions, and he had not shaved for two days. Against the brace of young constables, featureless behind their caps and silver buttons, he suddenly looked exactly the part of a seedy misfit on whom they could hang any crime they wanted. And then it struck Laura that he might in fact be Pilkington's killer, and she had to avert her eyes.

But his bearing was untroubled, and when Laura spoke of going with him he said, 'No, you stay here and take care of things.'

149

He came near for a kiss, and his eyes looked significantly into hers. Laura refused to watch him being taken away. The message in his eyes had been forceful but not clear. She could only act on her own interpretation.

The autumn landscape was easy to hide in. The big illuminated skies of the summer coastal light had gone for another year, and now contours, landmarks, people, blended back into a blurred expanse of muted colour. The islands of gorse or stunted bushes, the occasional coppice, provided good vantages for observation of what might be coming or going. The field glasses which Ray had found in the house served him well in his main activity of confirming that his isolation remained intact.

He trusted that couple as far as he had to. The man was getting jumpy and wanted to see the back of him, the woman he couldn't be sure about but at least she brought tins of food and had stocked the freezer. He had been uncomfortably aware that since he made the tape they had been walking around with a hell of a weapon against him. A weapon regardless of their good intentions, because once they did anything with it events would fly out of their control. Admittedly to provoke events was precisely his reason for taping the story. But since then he had lived on the edge of his nerves, on years of trained powers and animal cunning alert to whatever might be coming at his back. So every day was a victory.

It was the woman. From the concealed rise above the house he watched the Dyane switchback into and out of sight as it got nearer. He played a little hide-and-seek, but the woman was no match, and he easily got within a few paces of her. She held her body rigid, and there was agitation in her repeated knocking at the door.

Quietly he said, 'Hello.'

She jumped, turned quickly, then steadied herself against the porch. 'Don't do that,' she said.

Ray apologised. 'I was out there and saw you arrive.'

'Let's go in,' Laura said. He was already opening the door.

She wasted no time. 'There's been a murder. The police are questioning Martin at this moment.'

'A murder?' Ray gave nothing away, and Laura knew there was no point in studying him. He had her beat for that every time.

'A birdwatcher called Pilkington.'

Ray shrugged. 'Why have they got Martin?'

'We found the body.'

This seemed to give Ray no trouble. He asked, 'What else is new?'

Telescoping facts, Laura said, 'I took the tape to London. Somebody stole it. And obviously knew what they were stealing. No, I've no idea how they could have known, but you'd better get away from here.'

'Yes,' Ray said, 'I've been thinking that.'

Hiding her relief, Laura said, 'We could let you have some money.'

'You've been very good to me,' Ray said.

There was a blend of the deferential and the impersonal about him that for the first time prompted Laura to think, you've been a soldier. It suggested a sort of surface integrity, but she knew she would never completely trust him.

'We'd like to help you,' she said, 'only we're not sure now – what do we do, what do you want?'

Playing her carefully, avoiding panic by lowering the stake, Ray said, 'It's all right. I've got a plan. You don't need to be involved, I'll just vanish. Some money would help.'

Laura asked how much, and he said, 'Anything you can spare is useful.'

She smiled nervously and went to get some food from the car. Sarah Keeling's suspicion of Ray was eating away at her, along with the memory of Pilkington's snarling dead face peering at her from the undergrowth. She had not recovered from that. She found being with Ray an eerie experience, and she was twitching to get out of the place. His deliberate elusiveness, and the still silence of Vayro's house, bled into

151

that image of woodland death with a ruthless insistence. She had to stamp it out before her body succumbed to a wave of open-mouthed terror.

She channelled her hysteria into practical detail – when to get money, although they normally got cash from a building society in Barnbrook, and, she could not see far enough ahead to believe she would ever do this, where to leave it if Ray was not in the house. But below the surface something was already yelling at her to escape from this house, this man, before she began to sob and gibber. Before she let him see that she knew who had killed Pilkington.

Ray stayed inside, and already as she turned the ignition key Laura's hands were shaking in a tremor that originated in her spine. Proper breathing only returned when she had left Vayro's house a mile behind.

The birdwatcher had got too clever, made no allowance for Ray having noticed him when he was still living out on the cliffs. How he had tracked him to the house Ray would never know, or care now. Maybe following the woman – she would probably never have noticed. Or by luck, combing a tract of land, he had made a sighting and followed it through. Less intelligent had been to call at the house.

No doubt he had an innocent cover story and that Browning automatic inside his coat. Ray had watched from upstairs as the birdwatcher, binocular case bumping against his stomach, casually surveyed the exterior. Then the stumpy-legged figure in the wax-finish parka had ambled back along the lane to whatever concealed spot gave him a secure view of the house.

Slipping out by the back way, after an interval, Ray had gambled on the birdwatcher picking him up and pursuing. He made infrequent checks, but you learnt to intuit a tail from the vibrations of your own nervous system. He gave the birdwatcher an easy stalk, leading him to a small wood which he had scouted days earlier. Once there he hid, and waited till his tracker, obligingly noisy on those stout legs, came warily along a glade down which beech leaves idly drifted.

That he might be armed, Ray had considered briefly, then disregarded. It seemed unlikely. He emerged into the clearing, fifty yards behind the birdwatcher, and got him to turn by snapping his foot down on a rotten branch.

The birdwatcher began walking towards Ray, his genial face and friendly manner bespeaking a stranger who had perhaps lost his way. At twenty yards, Ray, who had not moved, stepped back into the trees. The birdwatcher was faster than he looked, and when he entered the undergrowth he had the pistol ready to fire. The pretence was over.

Ray had still not registered the gun when he let the birdwatcher see him again. Having proved his point, he would take him barehanded. A cool efficient death. The sight of the pistol stopped him short, and at eight yards the birdwatcher brought it up two-handed for a shot.

When Ray heard the crack he was already on the ground, barrelling through the rusty bracken. He was a dead man, Pilkington had shot for a kill. It was not personal. The birdwatcher was just carrying out orders. As he rolled through the undergrowth Ray seized a length of hardwood, an offcut of a branch left from some tree felling. As he asked himself how he could get close to the birdwatcher without a bullet cutting him down first, he remembered an old trick from the marines.

You cannot aim a gun if some other object is moving at great speed towards your face. Momentarily Pilkington had lost track of him, but Ray heard his footsteps, some thirty degrees off course, coming in that direction. He raised his eyes through the bracken. He had a second on the birdwatcher.

As he scrambled up, the birdwatcher wheeled to the right. Ray's arm scythed through the air, and the chunk of beechwood flew and axed the side of Pilkington's head. The protective reflex of his raised arm had ruined the chance of a shot.

Before he could recover, Ray charged at him and chopped

his neck with the side of his hand. An accident of posture must have helped the blow. The birdwatcher spun round, over-balancing down a short bank, and spreadeagled into a clump of saplings, hanging there, no life in him.

Ray pocketed the automatic, retrieved from the bracken. He left the body propped where it fell. There was no time to search Pilkington's clothes, nothing there to interest him. The spinney was small, self-contained. He satisfied himself that nobody had witnessed this, then found a hiding place till the daylight faded enough for an unidentifiable return to the house.

Harry Teal's first act, from the Roebuck Hotel, was to phone Pilkington's lodging out in the peninsula. He did it in some excitement, having just opened and read the message which Pilkington had left for him the day before. A good man after all, Pilkington, a countryman, a terrier who would never take his jaws off the quarry till he had worried it to death. Why had he left this note? The good field man at work, Teal acknowledged, simple and efficient, ensuring that one vital fact became available to those who needed it.

He had verified the bolt-hole, and was going to dig the vermin out. Would terminate only if necessary. As instructed. Affirmative, Teal thought, bloody affirmative, the sooner we can close this show down the better, for the country, and for me. He waited for Pilkington's landlady to answer. She had been slow on the occasions he had rung before.

Shock also, this time. She reported what had been told her by the police, who had found the local phone number in the dead man's bird-spotting notebook. Teal listened no longer than he had to, said thanks and hung up.

A superlative field man. With his tersely worded note Pilkington had enclosed a sketch plan of the solitary, inaccessible house's location. Not even blinking with emotion, Teal fingered the dial, to raise his Special Branch colleagues for the final sweep.

154

'Come, my dears, come.'

Godfrey Knapp was careful to include Martin in the telephoned verbal embrace. Laura had phoned him after the police took Martin away. He joked about their yo-yo-like trips to London, and Laura knew he had only come back to Scardale because of her return. She told him about the murder. Knapp of course knew the chief constable, and would intercede on Martin's behalf for all his testimony of good character was worth.

'And if they haven't let him go by this afternoon, call me again, and I will apply a little heat to these provincial coppers. I'll expect you both up here for dinner at eight, and you can tell me about it then.'

Martin called in the early afternoon. They were releasing him, and he wanted Laura to drive to Barnbrook and collect him. By this time she had seen Ray, and it was also a chance to go to the bank for money.

On the way back to Macemoor, above the roadside half a mile ahead, a bright blue light suddenly danced into view. Laura, driving, just said, 'Police.'

Two officers flagged the car down. The Dyane whined to a halt. One of the constables came to the side window. Martin stared grimly into the middle distance while Laura slid the panel back.

'Step outside please.'

Laura asked, 'What's the problem?'

'No problem.'

'Then why do I have to get out of the car?'

The policeman looked over to his colleague, who supported him by taking a couple of steps forward. Then Martin pushed his door open and got out, still bridling from those hours of questioning when, for want of evidence, two detectives had made him account for practically every detail of his life.

His voice was loud but cold. 'What the hell do you want?'

'Your car, sir?'

'No.'

'Whose car, then?'

The officer was about thirty. Martin looked at him with the contempt of age. The policeman stared back at him with the contempt of youth.

Laura got out. 'It's my car. So what?'

'Open it up please. We need to search it.'

'For what?'

'Oi, Dave.' The second policeman drew attention to the rear window, the CND sticker.

'Oh, right.' They exchanged knowing glances. 'We're looking for a man on the run. But in a car like this it could be anything, couldn't it?'

'Are you from round here?' Martin said. 'I don't recognise you.'

'We don't recognise *you*, chum.'

'No, but this is where I live, and I ought to be able to drive home without harassment.'

The police had scented blood. 'Harassment, is it? You want to make an official complaint?'

'We just want to go home.'

'Open the car.'

Wearily Laura raised the tailgate. They made her remove the false floor of the boot and they made a derisive play of looking under the seats. The police car radio squawked into life, and while one of them answered it, the other officer silently watched Martin and Laura, drumming two fingers on the stiff fabric of his uniform.

Laura asked, 'Can we go now?'

'Wait.' He cocked his head towards the police car.

Trying not to offer them anger as a soft target, Martin said, 'Wait for what?'

But they were all distracted by the distant clatter of a helicopter, conducting a low, tacking reconnaissance over the moorland. The rotors stuttered like machine-gun fire as the Wasp combed its way towards them. Veering away to a new sector, it passed close enough to buffet them with a cone of cold air. The policemen both waved as the chopper swung overhead and away.

'Who are you looking for?' Laura asked.

'A dangerous man. If you see any dangerous men, be sure and let us know. We're counting on the co-operation of all right-minded citizens like yourselves.'

'Thin jobs, these cars,' the other policeman said. Inspecting the symbol in the rear window again, he lifted his boot against the flimsy red and white plastic of the tail-light. 'Breaks dead easy, that. And then you can't drive it.' He tapped his boot against the plastic.

Another car appeared on the crest of the moorland road. The police got ready to intercept.

'I should stay in tonight if I were you.'

The police turned their backs, dismissive, awaiting the oncoming car, indifferent to the Dyane with the CND sticker as it puttered away down the lonely road.

'Bastards,' Martin fumed. 'Power-crazy, pathetic little bastards!'

Laura put a hand on his thigh. 'Forget it. It could have got nasty, and it didn't, so that's all right. Let's go and get pissed with Godfrey.'

'I'm not going out tonight. Not to Godfrey's, anyway.'

'Martin,' Laura said, 'I'm trying to be cheerful to help you. How the bloody hell do you think I feel? You know what all this is about, don't you – roadblocks, helicopters – they've probably got him already. I don't think we even know what we've got outselves into. I just wanted to have a few laughs to try and fight it all off. Us, together. And all you want to do is your bloody King Lear act.'

'My King Lear act?'

'You want to disappear in the middle of all *that*' – she gestured at the darkening landscape – 'and pretend that all the things you don't like don't exist.'

Martin was furious, out of control. 'Is that how you see me?'

'It's how you are.'

Laura glanced from the corner of her eye, but could not see anything more than the brooding figure in the passenger seat. She had to keep her vision on the narrow twists of the road.

'Stop the car!'

It was a yell like someone in an animal trap, panic and pain clenching their teeth on each other. Affronted, but shaking from Martin's scream, Laura brought the car to a stop. Before she could even finish braking he had the door open.

He staggered down into a gorse-covered hollow crossed by sandy paths which were hidden by banked verges of dead heather. After a moment of white-faced, tight-jawed anger, Laura got out and ran after him.

Martin had come to a stop. The trackways all fed into each other, labyrinthine, mocking the direction-seeker. As much out of practicality as sympathy, Laura decided she had to get him home. She turned him to face her. He looked tired, old suddenly, empty of cunning or resilience. Events were battering him, leaving a middle-aged man, unsure of himself, his fight all gone.

'It'll soon be over now,' she said. 'Let's go home.'

Docile, like a stroke victim, Martin followed her back to the car. They continued their journey in a drained silence.

Not half a mile from the cottage Martin started from his blank trance and said, this time quietly and rationally, 'Pull in a minute. Off the road.'

Out of patience, Laura said, 'I'd like to get home.'

'Pull in. Please.'

The car rocked on its wheels as Laura drove on to the roadside. 'What?' she said.

'Just stay here.'

He's cracking up, she thought. Then she felt guilty, that she had betrayed him, driven him into something which had to end by humiliating him. She forced herself not to look in the rear-view mirror.

Martin came back and got in the car.

'Police. They're here as well.'

Laura said, 'This road hardly goes anywhere but the cottage.'

'That's right.' He paused, he had recovered his self-control. 'I noticed a car, parked off the road half out of sight, back there. Empty.'

'They're watching the house.'

'I expect so.'

Laura sighed heavily, tapping the steering wheel. 'They think we're some kind of bait, that he'll come here because of us –'

'They'll be armed,' Martin said.

'I'm sorry,' Laura said. 'I feel that I've brought all this on you. I really loved it here when I first came. I still love it. And now we daren't even go back to the bloody place. So what do we do?'

'A while back,' Martin said, 'you used the words, it'll soon be over now. What did you mean?'

'Ray, the whole thing with Ray. They're bound to catch him now.'

'He killed Pilkington. You know that, don't you?'

'I don't care. I feel we let him down.'

'We don't even know who he was.'

'*Was*, that's right. Do you think he'll get out of all this alive? I don't care who he was, the more I see of all this, the more I wish we'd helped him.'

Martin was about to protest that surely they *had* helped Ray, but thought better of it. A grim silence in the car wrapped the subject up.

'I don't want to be part of a trap,' Laura said. 'and I don't want to see what happens. I'm not going back to the cottage.'

Martin thought and said, 'I know a road they won't have blocked. Let me drive.'

159

Chapter Eleven

The moon rose slowly. Martin snaked the Dyane through lanes and gated dirt-tracks until they were well out of any zone the police were likely to have sealed off. Then miles more of back roads, while the white gibbous moon solidified and glowed over a bleached, papery landscape. Then, 'We're here,' and they stopped.

No longer caring about food and drink, time or purpose, Laura zipped her coat and followed him. From a narrow tarmac road they crossed a stile, then another, and the footpath began to climb. Then they saw it. Laura said, 'Jesus,' under her breath, in reverence as much as profanity.

Martin looked at her in a slightly mad enchantment, his face large and pale and clown-like in the moonlight. 'You know where you are?'

'Lendra,' she said.

'Yes.'

They had always intended to come, and never made it, and now suddenly they were here. Under the moonwashed night the unfarmed grass of the ancient hill-fort seemed to fill the landscape ahead of them, on one hand the mounded centre still rising, on the other the steep hill-edge moulded into ramparts whose brows seemed like waves crested with a foam of moonlight.

They walked on, all the time ascending to the plateau that had once underlaid a town, their steps silent on the short, dry grass. The irregular contours of the great hill rippled away, every few yards throwing up a topological dreamscape of mounds and hollows, summits that melted away, remains of old pathways that one moment offered visual dominance for miles around, then led into a hillside oubliette overshadowed by converging ramparts.

From some viewpoints the fort resembled a gigantic dead animal, its flesh dried and its pelt crisply preserved, twisted haunches sprawling across the hill which had supported its death. Elsewhere it rounded and softened into the feminine languor of some giant earth-goddess whose slumbering form stretched out over all the miles of milky distance.

The sheep that cropped the fort lay huddled in its declivities and sometimes, as Martin and Laura approached, rose in a ghostly mass and trotted a few paces away to browse in the uncanny flood of moonlight. As always the wind scoured the top of Lendra, a wind that came from many sea-miles, the upper-air wind that carried seabirds beyond the range of vision. But unlike the cloud-pummelling winds of daylight, the air moved now with a night-time stealth, an elegant sharpness that matched the cool brightness of the moon, shaking the dry grass and the patches of dead harebells underfoot.

To historicise or sentimentalise the place, the diurnal impulse to repopulate the fort with its past dwellers, the herdsmen and fighters, the women turning their backs to the wind, the skin-clad children, was superfluous, because on a night like this anyone walking the slopes of Lendra sensed already their own ghost coming to meet them, as if time was reversed and they were visiting the future that would exist after their own deaths.

Martin and Laura walked every corner of the great earthwork. Although they avoided touching physically, there was a feeling of softening, of growing closer again, old pain washed away in the transcendent lunar stillness. To talk was irrelevant. Lendra was a place which had never known much speech, and somehow overawed it.

161

Then Laura struck her forehead and exclaimed, 'Oh Christ! Godfrey!'

Reluctantly, Martin recalled what she meant. He had genuinely forgotten about their date, but he had been glad to forget.

'Godfrey survives,' he said.

Laura said, 'I feel terrible. What can we do?'

'Look, he'll phone, we're not in, maybe we've been detained somewhere –'

'Without calling him?'

'He'll put it down to our uncouth manners. Don't worry about it.'

There was a note of, *Godfrey's my friend, I'll answer for him.* Which, Laura thought, might have been true once, but certainly wasn't now.

'Anything could have happened,' she said.

'Godfrey's larger than life, he won't bother. He'll just get on with things.'

'You think he doesn't care if we turn up or not?'

'Well yes, from one point of view –'

'He was very concerned about your bad experience with the police –'

'Godfrey doesn't care a shit about me. He's in love with you. Don't you know that?'

Laura replied coldly, 'Is he?'

'Perhaps you don't see it.'

'I'm not interested in love. Once people say they love each other, it just becomes an excuse for ripping each other off. Love means always having to say you're sorry. Keep it.'

They walked on, both suppressed by this outburst, its venom, its chill. Laura felt harsh, and wanted to modify and soften the violence. But it said what she felt. She refused to take it back.

'Whatever happens between us,' she said, 'however we stay together, let's do it without the word "love". Feel it, maybe. But not the word. It's just a stone round our necks.'

Martin didn't answer. She was not surprised. Without

162

mentioning it, they were now definitely heading back to the car. As they crossed one of the stiles, he surprised her in the way he still could sometimes. As he gave her a hand down he said, 'You really are an exceptional woman. A smashing lady.'

Laura smiled, trying to keep back guilt, and said, 'Let's go home.'

She reached out to him, and they held hands all the way back along the dark tarmac road.

*

A neat, snug study on a winter's night,
A book, friend, single lady, or a glass
Of claret, sandwich, and an appetite
Are things which make an English evening pass.

The lines recurred, more mocking each time, as Godfrey Knapp rang the cottage and listened to the emptiness of the house in which his call went unanswered. There were three extension phones at Scardale, and in the end he had used them all, wandering the house and avoiding Harold who was about to start asking awkward questions about dinner.

Contingency plans, as they always did, thrust themselves forward for Knapp's approval. Never get caught with a bum steer. The restlessness in him, which had once needed half the world to cater for it, was now afflicted by a sort of Parkinsonian hesitancy. Tiredness, fear of disablement, the stroke, the coronary, the runaway paunch, the useless jelly-like prick, and the suspicion that some desires would outlive him, remain unsatisfied even when he died, paralysed his every move.

There was a yacht party off Marbella. He could be there at this moment, but he had made his excuses. In London there were the girls the agency sent round, but the last one, the soixante-neuf expert, so clinically sexual, had left him depressed to the extent that he found himself in a blind, half-drunk rage, after she went, hurling crockery at the floor of his *bijou* kitchen. Out here he had access to a whole hinterland, in theory, thousands of women drying up for lack of excitement.

But in the end it was either ghastly young provincial tarts or their equivalents a few steps up the social echelon, younger versions of Dorothy, who couldn't jack themselves off without seeing a fox killed first.

Une oasis d'horreur dans un désert d'ennui.

And yet – Images drifted through Knapp's mind like dhows along the Nile, lazy, ephemeral, mystically powerful, images of French lingerie and Laura's body, of a different sensuality, sex as open-ended and laughing, a raft of flickering desire from which they could observe, admire and deride the distant world. *'Luxe, calme et volupté'*, the Frenchman had it dead right.

> I pass my evenings in long galleries solely,
> And that's the reason I'm so melancholy.

He sank more Scotch, pointlessly, since he wasn't enjoying it. But it kept something at bay while he waited for the phone to ring and deferred the moment when he would call again. It worked him up, and he felt again the need to smash something, to bleed the demon from his tormented mind. It got so he could not make himself hang up, but sat there with his ear getting hot and his brain stupefying at the beeping down the line.

Telephones had once been emblems of power, a leash on the world and its savage glamour. Now they confirmed helplessness, rubbed it in, like trying to crank up a hard-on when the brain refused to co-operate. He tried one more time, and this would be the final attempt.

No answer. The police had let Martin go, Knapp had checked that. Where the hell were they? Laura, Laura – *'Je n'ai pas oublié, voisine de la ville'* –

'Harold, I'm going out. Supper won't be necessary.'

'Very good, sir.'

Harold waited calmly for the Jaguar to screech away into the night. Knowing the ropes, he had prepared no more food than was necessary in advance, and now it would fit in nicely with the little meal he was planning for his own friend who was driving over from Saltmayne to eat with him in the kitchen.

Headlights swivelling as he oversteered, Knapp hurtled the Jaguar out of the Scardale estate and across country in the direction of the Moor. It was a drive without purpose, and he knew it, but the drink and the speed made this dash to nowhere seem urgent. The moon glared from the sky, and occasionally on shadowed roads his car lights picked out the eyes of a fox or the flash of a rabbit's scut.

The lights ahead hove into view faster than he could deal with them. As Knapp thumped his foot at the floor the wheels bit the road and slewed the car. He gripped the wheel in a long moment of icy panic. The Jaguar was more powerful than his reflexes, and he was still twenty yards from the roadblock when the car lurched to a stop. Collecting himself, he got into gear and rolled forward as the police officer advanced, brusquely waving him in.

Knapp buzzed the window down. 'Damn stupid place to stop. What's your game, officer?' He barked domineeringly, knowing he had to counteract the smell of the booze. At a pinch he could stick it to them with the name of his good friend the chief constable.

'You always drive like that, sir?'

'From up there this patch of road is half-unsighted. By the time I saw you it was almost too late.'

The policeman called to his partner, 'Tim, we've got a stroppy bugger. Bring the breathalyser.'

Beneath the greying beard that spread up to his cheekbones, Knapp felt himself paling.

'I was talking to your chief constable earlier today. Perhaps you'd care to –'

'Are you trying to subvert the law, sir?'

Shit and derision, Knapp thought, navy-blue incorruptibles. Keep them talking. He got out of the car and drew himself up to his full barrel-chested height, imposing in the well-tailored sheepskin coat.

'Which station are you from, officer?'

The constable happened to be a sociology graduate, still in his first year on the streets. He hoped to cancel Knapp's mixture of *bonhomie* and intimidation by saying, 'We're not from round here.'

Knapp seized the point. 'What's going on, then? Police out of area, roadblocks –? Somebody got loose? Can I help?'

The second policeman was walking across with the breathalyser. The really absurd thing, Knapp thought, was as soon as they dangled one of these things at you, how bloody sober you became. Sobriety, or a desperate need to get out of this cow-turd, pushed him to play his one advantage.

'I've got it! This operation must be concerned with the murder over near Macemoor.' He paused and fixed the young copper's eye. 'Yes, I know it's not public knowledge yet. But as I say, you check me out with the chief constable. Hope you find your man. Better search my car, eh?'

Holding the breathalyser like an overfull surgical bottle, the policeman shone a torch into the Jaguar and gave it a perfunctory look-over. Before they could tell Knapp to drive on there was action on the car radio, a choked garble after which one of them called to the other, 'Back to base. All over.'

Knapp confronted them. 'The hunt's concluded, then?'

'Make sure you drive carefully, sir,' the sociology graduate answered, and returned to his car. Before anything else could go wrong, Knapp drove away. He was stony sober now, his sense of urgency had gone. Once he was out of range of the police car he pulled in, killed the lights, and lit a cigar.

Not caring for hypotheses or intangibles, he had given no further thought to the man Laura had described to him three days before. He gave him thought now.

People who moved from big cities, Knapp had observed a number of times, were often destabilised by what came their way in the country, forced to have dealings with the sort of person they would calmly step over in the streets of the West End, and making the predictable misjudgments. The man

166

Laura had taken up was either a liar, conning his way with juicy tales, or a kosher villain whose speedy exit from her life would be the most satisfactory conclusion.

The murder, the roadblocks, the story she had told him, couldn't all be coincidence. But it sounded as if the law had mopped it up, and now maybe things would settle down and give him an even run at his target. He heeled the car round, and within an hour was greeting old friends in the bar of the Faulston Conservative Club. A bunch of raving cadavers, he thought, chuckling his way in. But a few had their bored-looking wives with them, and to Knapp a bored woman was always a challenge.

In the course of that day Laura had driven back from London, got a grip on herself for the confrontation with Martin, found Pilkington's body in the wood, seen Martin taken away by the police, had what must be her last meeting with Ray, then the police roadblock, the awful scene with Martin, the moonlit walk across Lendra. When she finally put her head down on the pillow, she had no idea if Martin was there, awake or asleep, the lamp on or off. Her mind plunged into sleep, but her body had got there first.

Early morning, half-dark, the phone ringing. Laura ran downstairs naked and gasped a tired hello into the receiver. It was Sarah.

'Where are you? Are you –?'

'No. Listen, put the TV on, BBC1. Don't talk, just do it.'

The phone dead, the half-dark stillness, her heartbeat.

167

Chapter Twelve

The breakfast-time news report showed film of a gantry crane straddling a railhead, sinister in an empty landscape, the image echoing both a triumphal arch and the gateway of a camp whose single railway track would channel unending truckloads of victims to their deaths. Above the gantry was a control cabin, and into the rectangular gap beneath it the lifting gear dangled, limp and disjointed like a loose suspender. In the breeze it moved slowly, stiffly.

The voice-over was explaining the system of flask removal. From within the reactor plant itself the flask would be hoisted on to a heavy-duty trailer and driven to the railhead, where it would be transferred to a rail wagon, half a mile beyond the perimeter fence, to await pick-up by freight train and the long journey across Britain to the reprocessing plant at Sellafield.

Martin and Laura caught the end of the item and had to wait for the quarter-hourly rerun. But they heard the word 'Caunder', and met each other's eyes, and fought against but understood everything. Huddled in their dressing-gowns, while the TV glowed in the dark corner, they numbly prepared themselves for what they knew was coming.

With successive repeats the story gained substance. How many of the 'unknown factors' were strategic devices to avoid mass panic only the broadcast controllers knew. But the story itself could no more be contained than a radioactive cloud, and was soon dominating the entire transmission. Even the guest interviewees, brought in to talk about poodle culture or their most embarrassing experience, found themselves being asked for instant opinions on what had happened.

What had happened, as the BBC told it, was this.

The flask had been taken to the railhead late in the afternoon, for a connection that same night. Most nuclear waste was transported through its country-wide web by night. The flask was lifted from the trailer, and the driver watched idly, expecting it to be lowered as normal on to the rolling stock on the single track.

Interviewed on TV, the driver now claimed to have noticed something out of the ordinary in the movement of the flask as it swung through the air, something unlike the smoothness of the regular crane operator's technique. It was also normal for the gantry man to wave from his cab, but although his van was parked in its usual place, this time he didn't salute from the cab window. The trailer driver thought no more of it and returned to the plant once the flask was eased down on to the rail wagon. He also claimed now that as he drove away he glanced in his rear-view mirror and could almost swear that the clamps had not come off the flask, but the more the interviewer pressed him on this, the more he insisted it was only an impression. The light was failing, and he couldn't say for sure, but something had struck him as suspicious.

The railhead itself came in for examination. Every time the flask item interrupted the flow of breakfast-time television they screened a graphic of the general lay-out of the area. The terminal lay at the extremity of what had once been a large siding with a maintenance workshop, shut down years ago. To connect with the line to Barnbrook, and through there to the Inter-City network, the Caunder track covered two miles of cuttings through barren wasteland or little-visited pasture, a paradigm of the middle of nowhere.

The points were operated from a central box somewhere up the line, and inspection was carried out by random sorties along the sleepy track. A defensive British Rail spokesperson declined to be drawn on the frequency of such inspections, trying to deflect any implied fault by stating several times in a variety of wordings that their concern was with the operational efficiency of the rail service, which was not in question here.

An equally defensive spokesperson for the Atomic Energy Authority argued that the only way to prevent hijackings, whether of aeroplanes or nuclear waste, was to have a full-scale police state – his actual words included the phrase 'a nation on permanent security alert' – and it was a sad day if the production of peaceful energy should lead to any such thing, but the people of Britain might now be faced with a terrible choice.

The crane man had been found in his cabin on the gantry. He knew nothing of what had happened. The last thing he remembered was getting out of his van. He had dropped his keys, and he distinctly recollected bending down to pick them up. If someone had come at him from behind, they were silent and had given no warning of their presence. The TV camera panned over an area of grassland which could have hidden the attacker. The crane operator had woken up in the cabin, jerked out of unconsciousness by the ringing of the security phone. The nylon cord round his wrists and the sticking plaster over his mouth forced him to wait until one of the reactor police drove up. By then it was dark and upwards of an hour had elapsed since the flask was unloaded.

The TV cameras, excluded from the plant itself, paid a lot of attention to the half-mile of narrow tarmac road between perimeter fence and railhead. They also showed the direction in which the stealers of the flask must have gone. Assuming a heavy truck, there was only one possible route, since only one made-up road led off the half-mile devoted to radioactive traffic.

But from there? A police spokesman admitted that no firm trail had been identified, but assured the viewing public that a number of people had come forward with possible leads as to events of the night, all of which were being followed up. Meanwhile a full-scale search of the entire region was being conducted – film clips of spotter planes and helicopters, roadblocks in operation since dawn.

And finally the Home Secretary felt sufficiently briefed to make a statement. Instead of mounting a rearguard action against the critics who were lining up out there, taking their separate beads on the government, he fought to win. Cold-blooded and thin-lipped, he enunciated the conclusions which he had already discussed with the Prime Minister.

They were simple. What everyone had feared might happen, although all prayed it would not, and many found so unthinkable they flinched away from it, finally had happened. Terrorism had worked its way up the technological ladder to the complex apparatus of the nuclear state. The big questions now had to be faced. He was sure that the people of Britain would join him in thinking no measure too costly or extreme, providing it eliminated once and for all the vulnerability of the nation to acts of wanton terrorism, striking at the heart of our future prosperity, indeed, survival, namely the nuclear . . .

For hours Martin and Laura stayed with the TV set, one remaining if the other went out of the room. They watched the item repeated so many times that they had to deaden their minds against the banal dramadoc style and the commentary which they now knew by heart. They found it hard to speak to each other. Events had submerged them, and it seemed all they could do to focus their eyes and make themselves go on breathing.

Laura rang Sarah back, but there was no reply. She tried a number of times, but still no reply. There was no one else she could talk to first.

Then, one last time, the phone rang while her hand was still on the receiver. It was Knapp.

'Hello. Godfrey – oh look, I'm so sorry –'

'Laura, my dear, are you well? Something must have happened –'

'It's complicated – we're all right. You must be furious.'

'Not in the least. Only concerned about you. As a matter of fact I was under the weather last night, turned in with a few favourite books –'

'Godfrey, listen. Have you seen TV this morning?'

'Morning television? Is there such a thing?'

'Go and switch it on now. Please.'

'Laura my love, why should –?'

'Godfrey, please. I'll talk to you later.'

She put the phone down. Martin was calling, 'Laura, come and see this. Quick.'

She went back to the TV. An aerial shot of a country town scrolled across the screen, accompanied by a commentary which was concluding '. . . for evacuation of the surrounding area are already under way'. The plane dipped low enough for the camera to pick up movement on the roads. In one shot cars were jammed bumper to bumper, and elsewhere thousands of people on foot, their slowness exaggerated by the height of the camera, straggled out into the countryside. Although the commentator's account emphasised that the emergency plans drawn up as soon as the threat had arisen were being implemented swiftly and smoothly, it was clear even from the discreet height of the TV aircraft that something like chaos had already gripped those narrow roads. The pictures, for the time being, displayed no more.

'It's Faulston,' Martin said. 'They've got the flask in Faulston.'

From a summer visit Laura remembered the market town with its rambling medieval centre, lost amid recent housing estates that were pushing out into the farmland. It was forty miles from Macemoor.

Quietly and intensely she said, 'He was right.' She was drained by a sort of inarticulate shame. 'He was bloody well right, and we didn't believe him.' Her words stamped the air in angry emphasis.

Martin was avoiding her gaze. He blustered slightly. 'How do we know what he said was the truth – oh yes, obviously he was involved in something, they don't organise manhunts like that for nobody. Perhaps I was wrong not to trust him, I don't know. But what could we have done? About this?'

He waved an arm at the TV screen, then jumped up and grabbed Laura's shoulders. 'We're not in this league, you and me. My God, terrorists, dead bodies, radioactive waste held over the heads of innocent people – I don't want any part of that. And as for your friend Ray, he was using us, and whatever the truth behind it was, I know I wouldn't like it. I've spent my life in opposition to all that, the paranoia, the madness that rules people's lives – And what do you want? You blame me for this?'

He waved his hand at the screen again. Laura's eyes watched him coldly, narrowing slightly as they always did when he ranted. She hated her own sense of guilt. But the unforgiving light in her eyes said that she somehow blamed the guilt on him.

'You're a small man, Martin,' she said.

The words were an instant epitaph, a block of stone between them. He repeated, 'A small man,' neutrally, totally composed, almost as if he accepted it. 'That's all I'm worth, to be called a small man.'

Laura regretted the words. But her eyes were wandering past him to the screen, and the moment of apology and possible reconciliation vanished. Even the gash of bitterness was temporarily sealed by the latest item of news.

A talking head, accompanied by the slick graphics that were nowadays *de rigueur* even for emergency programmes, had begun to explain the likely effects of damage to the flask.

If the total waste content was released, an area of radius twelve miles would have to be evacuated for two hundred years. If only ten per cent of the waste escaped, depending on a variety of factors, several square miles around the site of the leak would be uninhabitable for anything from five to five hundred years. The surreal arithmetic thudded out of the screen, the statistics banging like nails into the public consciousness.

173

The talking head now turned his attention to the flask itself. Something approximating an eight-foot cube, it had a shell of steel 14 inches thick. It was built to resist fire at 800° Celsius for half an hour. The weak point was the seal between the flask body and the seven-tonne lid. Although the lid was clamped down by a stitch-line of securing bolts, which the expert stressed could only be fastened and removed by special equipment, the join between lid and flask was the one inevitable crack in the structure. Should that be exploited, or any other damage done to the flask, by impact or explosion, the probable sequence of ensuing disaster would be: leakage of the radioactive cooling water, the heat radiated by the waste melting the cladding on the spent fuel rods, followed by a fire which would pump the caesium, strontium, ruthenium and plutonium directly into the atmosphere.

Anyone deliberately creating such an accident (the word 'accident' was used without logic, perhaps to trade on the reassuring Act of God idea that accidents will happen) would be exposed to the densest concentration of radioactivity, and the effects would be fatal. On the other hand, detonation from a distance might persuade the terrorists that they could get away unscathed. So, the interviewer chipped in, they don't have to be kamikazes, it is a real threat. It was, the talking head conceded, a very real threat.

So far, nobody had any idea why. The police were withholding details of the terrorists' demands. The news-flashes reiterated the story, although for now there was nothing to add.

Shortly before dawn a truck, a Mercedes cab with a heavy trailer, loaded with the fifty-tonne flask, had driven into the country town of Faulston. Where the stolen flask had been hidden since its theft the night before was not known. A meticulous plan was obviously being carried out, and thousands of square miles of diverse countryside, night-blanketed, had sheltered the deadly haul. In Faulston the terrorists had crashed the truck through the wooden gates of the town's comprehensive school – deserted apart from the caretaker, who was still asleep in his bungalow in sight of but a hundred yards away from the gate.

Woken by the smashing of the barrier, the caretaker was the link with the world outside. Instructed to inform the police of what had happened, he was then directed to leave the site, driving away with his wife and three papillon dogs. Later, as the TV cameras made an instant celebrity of the caretaker, the papillons gradually stole the show, until all Britain knew that their names were Candy, Shandy and Randy, and thousands of families had discovered a deep-felt need to own a papillon for themselves.

The terrorists' request was simple. They wanted a million, sterling, and a light aircraft, which would land on the playing fields at the back of the school, the plane to have pilot and co-pilot, who would serve as hostages. There were five terrorists, all hooded and armed with enough plastic explosive and timed charges to scatter the contents of the flask to the winds. (The TV weather analysts were already providing regular updates of the wind patterns around Faulston, monitoring changes in direction and velocity, while other experts hypothesised on the possible size and content of the fallout plume.)

The terrorists were also armed with sub-machine guns. They requested that one police officer should make himself known to them via the school telephone, and then act as the sole mediator between them and the agencies who might wish to negotiate.

As the night greyed into opaque autumn daylight, the only life in the streets of Faulston was the milk floats slowly humming along on their rounds. The milkmen rapidly became aware of unusual activity, police cars – white with a red stripe, known locally as jam sandwiches – driving at speed through the centre of town. One or two, whose homes were near, abandoned their deliveries and steered the floats to their houses, to wake sleeping families in the fear that something was up.

175

The police had no specific plan for this contingency. The general reaction to crisis was to head off outbreaks of civilian panic, and that meant primarily restriction of traffic flow, on the assumption that panic could best be controlled by separating people from their automobiles. So as the rooftops of Faulston gained definition in the raw morning light, roadblocks were already in force. The three major and five minor roads out of the town were cordoned, as were all important junctions in the town itself.

The police officers themselves were not told any more than they needed to know about the hazards of the situation they had been ordered to control. Word was that the Army would be brought in later, and it was a holding operation till then. Once they were away from the town, coaches and trucks could be provided to move large numbers of people in good order. But nobody had seen a plan that specified how this transport fleet would be organised or where it would be told to deliver its vast human cargo. Meanwhile the population were to be directed, on foot, out of the town by the two roads which ran most nearly to the south-west. The wind that morning was blowing from the south-west.

It was a work-day. People were waking uneasily, some already up, preparing for the morning, although the radio and TV on in most homes gave as yet no news of what had happened in Faulston. The routines were shattered by the grating voice of police loudhailers as cars crawled from street to street directing the sixty thousand population how to behave in a crisis of which, so far, they knew nothing.

'This is the police. Please leave your homes. Do not panic. Please leave your homes as quickly as possible. Bring warm clothing and food and drink only. Do not take personal belongings. This is an emergency. Your co-operation is vital. Please ensure your own safety by following instructions. Do not use motor vehicles. Make your way on foot to the Barnbrook Road. Follow all signposts to Barnbrook. This operation must be carried out quickly. Please leave whatever you are doing and bring your families outside. The town must be evacuated as quickly as possible. This is the police . . .'

As the jam sandwiches vacated a district, they left behind them a wake of what seemed like badly rehearsed street theatre. Slowly, resentfully, people emerged from their houses, not with intent to leave them, but to react angrily to this disruption of their lives. Neighbours consulted, seeking from each other reassurance that there was no problem, it was a mistake, it referred to something local – a gas leak or a burst water main – which couldn't apply to them because there was no visible evidence of threat to their lives. Seeking, but not finding.

Not finding, because the people, mostly the men of the families, whose instinct was to stand firm and wait things out, saw others along the street taking flight as the best form of salvation – ignoring the police directives, urgently cramming their cars with food, valuables, and driving furiously away from the street.

The knock-on effect was rapid. At the sight of other families taking to their cars, few people were able to set off as ordered – disoriented and afraid, with upset or complaining children – on foot. Cars meant speed, the chance of salvation from this unnamed disaster. Cars also had radios, and information was strength. And wherever they might end that day, cars offered shelter.

The first vehicles to encounter the police were angrily flagged down. It was noticed that some of the police had side-arms which they were making no effort to hide. The tailbacks soon grew, and a short spell of delay worked fast on Faulston's population of self-savers. They became frightened, docile, suddenly eager for instruction again, gladly accepting the company of other shocked families who carefully locked their cars and dragged themselves after many similar hunched figures along an endless road, overseen by the baleful gaze of a uniformed policeman.

It was difficult for people to panic on foot. Too dependent on the easy speed of cars, as pedestrians they had no way of expressing their anxiety, their determination to escape, their fear that there *was* no escape. Some asked policemen for information, reassurance as to where they would be assembled, the arrangements that were being made for them. You'll be told further along, was the standard answer, and then everybody knew. There were no arrangements. They were human rubble that had to be cleared off the streets of Faulston, and after that they were on their own.

Some were haunted by the flickering images of refugees that had washed across their TV screens year after year, the hecatombs of victims, the starving, the persecuted, the captive, human beings robbed of hope. Was this different? For many the strain of treading the country as part of a silent, depressed, helpless rabble of displaced humanity became unbearable, and cracking early rather than later they climbed gates or fences and struck off across the fields. If nothing else, it regained them some illusion of control over what was happening to them.

But what was happening? Rumours were muttered through the crowds. After Chernobyl anybody living within twenty miles of a nuclear reactor had known this day must come – the day on which they would be herded away, perhaps lethally irradiated already, handed assurances, lied to and left to die degraded, premature, meaningless deaths. Even now a miasma of radiation could be drifting over them, and the dread of its imperceptible contamination was perhaps what, more than any other factor, kept people submissive, hoping that at least by following what they took for orders would bring them through to safety in the end.

There were other rumours. The story of terrorists taking over the comprehensive school was dismissed as a blind, exactly the way they would cover up a leak from Caunder. And then there were people who, bringing up the rear of the evacuees, had seen the police suddenly desert their posts and get the hell out of Faulston – along roads which they had kept empty of traffic, and in the opposite direction to that in which they had sent the ordinary citizens. The police had no friends that day.

In fact, whether or not the police had abandoned the town, there had been one exception to the conduct of the passive foot-army now trailing aimlessly out into the countryside.

Some people had refused to surrender their cars. Driving on pavements, crossing any obstacle they could navigate, they had reached the outskirts of Faulston, picking up similarly aggressive drivers as they went, till one of the main police roadblocks barred them from going further. A troop of enraged men approached the pair of constables on duty and demanded that they open up the road. If not, they would shift the police car themselves. The policemen argued back briefly, then got into the jam sandwich and drove away. All the police families had been evacuated right at the start, and would be fifty miles away by now. Maybe it was time to join them.

At the first junction the police car turned off and took a narrower, quieter route. On the road behind, many of its members still ignorant of what they were fleeing from, a frantic caravan of automobiles – three wide and horns yelping as any car jostled or slowed for a second – took flight across the country.

Chapter Thirteen

On the phone this time Godfrey Knapp sounded like a ghost. The resonance of his voice now suggested cavernous rooms, a drained stillness. He spoke in a measured indirect way, like someone who knew he was dying but had no idea how to tell anyone else. Glad to escape from the horror and guilt that pinned them before their TV screen, Martin and Laura drove to Scardale.

It was a sombre, tight-lipped journey, as if a death hung over them. For all they knew Ray *was* dead now. Their failure to save him in turn killed off any discussion of what might have happened, who he was, what course events would now take in Faulston. The stolen flask was like a symbol of a kind of madness that had entered their own relationship, and they sped through the brooding countryside with pursed lips and whirling, confused minds.

As Knapp waited for them, pacing the terrace of Scardale, he tried to separate the sickness in his stomach from his wider physical need to see Laura again.

He was in a bad way. Even the clothes she wore had left an indelible print on his mind, every garment from every meeting meant something to him, the colour schemes she dressed in snared him in an obsessive, abject delight. It was an abnormal state for Knapp to be in, and he was getting worried. De Clerambault's syndrome, the condition of falling in love to the point of psychopathic delusion, did not only afflict women or the sexually timid. Yet his guts told him he was right, this woman was unique, a star among women, a constellation among mere stars. And Knapp's guts were the only thing in life he knew would never lie to him.

To more immediate matters. A cigar, he thought, but try to inhale less. Go to meet them, allow for their trauma. Without condescension, put them at their ease before delivering this next blow, which they are not expecting, and which could shatter them irreparably.

Ushering them through the marble of Scardale's entrance hall Knapp placed an arm on the shoulder of each of them and said, 'I have something to show you.'

He took them into his study. Surrounded by the jumbled shelves of a man who constantly used his books, and the stylish furnishing, the good taste of the artist *manqué*, he pressed a few buttons on a video recorder.

'This came up a few minutes ago. You'll have been on the road at the time. Fortunately I've been taping all morning, so I caught it.'

Martin and Laura sat down as invited and watched footage they had already seen a dozen times, long shots of the school and the flood of evacuees. Twice Knapp rapped the machine impatiently and whizzed the tape forward.

'News has come in that the police are seeking a man believed to be a member of the terrorist faction, although not with the group at the Faulston comprehensive school. His present whereabouts are uncertain, but known to be some-where between Barnbrook and the Faul peninsula . . .'

Ray's picture suddenly appeared on the screen. Martin and Laura flashed a look at each other, then the screen drew their eyes back again.

'. . . last known alias was Peter English, but this is certain not to be the name he is using now . . .'

Godfrey Knapp had his own secrets to keep, and acted with all the control of sixty years' gamesmanship. He waited for his two visitors to show signs of despair or even collapse. But they jumped out of their chairs, faces alight, and hugged each other.

181

Laura cried, 'They didn't get him!' Even Martin, for all his caution, could not resist Laura's jubilation and relief.

Knapp's face fell slightly as he froze the screen. It was a picture taken unawares, not the vacant mugshot of prison or army, but snapped deliberately by a concealed camera and stored for official use. It captured an expression which did not match the word 'terrorist'. Something reflective in the eyes which did not know they were being photographed and had no space for camouflage. A thin, dark face, intelligent but cold.

Knapp recalled Harry Teal's interest in this man, the secrecy of it all. And now here he was splashed across the TV sets of a whole country. So where did that leave Harry Teal? Up shit creek, Knapp thought, with a flicker of sadistic hope.

Well, the scheduled fifty-mile drive to a board meeting, the evening reception to announce the regional Arts Council awards, were off now. Today looked like being a different animal altogether. But why were these two so elated? A discreet bullet through this stray terrorist's head would have removed their problem. As it was, the radar of Knapp's intestinal system said, their problems were only just beginning.

'Shall we watch the rest of the item?'

The commentary warned people that the man whose face they had just seen was armed, dangerous, would kill without hesitation, and must in no circumstances be approached. A police number was given for anyone sighting the terrorist to contact.

Knapp stopped the video.

'It appears your friend was telling a certain amount of truth.'

Laura said, 'I always believed him.'

'Martin?'

Ritchie looked at Godfrey Knapp, uncertain what he wanted. A void had developed between the two men which made moments like this very tricky.

Knapp added, 'You seemed more sceptical, I recall.'

'Yes. I was wrong.'

'How do you feel now? If your man was right, which he has been so far, then we all know what's going to happen next. Do we not? Laura?'

The momentary excitement of knowing that Ray had escaped the dragnet had vanished. Laura said, 'I don't know any more.'

'According to your account, the terrorists will be killed, the flask will be recovered, the danger will pass, the consequences will follow. Christ, my friends, you realise the privileged position we occupy? While the whole bloody country holds its breath and awaits nuclear catastrophe, we've already had a sneak preview, and we know it won't happen. We few, we happy few.' He paused, and added sardonically, 'We band of brothers.'

'Please don't joke, Godfrey,' Laura said. 'What are we going to do?'

'There was a tape. Stolen from the flat in London, you told me.'

Knapp saw Martin's face twitch at this detail, which was clearly new to him. Pique, jealousy, was part of it. Knapp knew the score instantly. What a bore the man was, so earnest, so hurt about things. A woman like Laura was wasted on him.

Laura herself tried to stifle embarrassment. 'That's right. But there's a copy.' Except that only Sarah Keeling knew where the copy was, and there was no telling what had happened to it by now.

'Of course, the tape without the man is worthless. Anybody could have made it. Outstripped by events. The man.' Knapp tapped a thumbnail with his cigar-cutter, then leaned forward to the video and replayed the item about Ray.

'Wouldn't you rather forget,' he asked, 'that you had anything to do with this character? You've already come under some suspicion. But at least you could plead – what? – lack of information, simple human charity being exploited. Now, however, whatever you get into, you'll be deemed fully aware of its nature, and the next time the authorities come your way, my guess is they'll be a lot less understanding.'

Knapp looked benignly from Laura to Martin and back again. In the end he was right, it had been a trauma for them. But he was confident now that he could steer them to the right answer.

It was a good day for the burglars in Faulston, and a bad day for Harry Teal. For him it had started the previous night, with a phone message from London notifying him that the case of the man known as Peter English was now transferred completely to police hands. The murder of Pilkington, and the failure of the manhunt, meant that things could not be kept under wraps any longer. Teal was complimented on his running of the operation, told to take two days' leave and then report to his London base.

And that was it. They didn't frig around with conversation's politer forms. Teal spent hours analysing his own conduct of the assignment, a job he had never wanted, stuck in this godawful countryside which swallowed people and places whole.

But it didn't matter how often he told himself he was glad to be returning to London, or reassured himself that nobody could have done more than he had done. Pilkington had gone in too close, had got horny – Pilkington the old field man who knew it all – and he had blown it. And paid the price of an unceremonious death for it. Less fairly, Teal had seen snatched away a case which would have made him, and it smarted. All the leads he had been following hung loose and painful like broken fingernails, snagging wherever his mind turned.

A few hours of congested sleep, then grey daylight and a pair of jays screeching outside his hotel window, drove Teal from his bed. It was too early to get any coffee downstairs. He drank tap-water from the *en suite* bathroom, shaved and dressed, and left the hotel. Blunt insoluble anger made him hate the day in advance. He drove blindly into that country whose endless inconstancy he had tried to master but which still eluded him.

A couple of hours later, heading for Faulston with a plate of sausage and bacon in mind, Teal first noticed the helicopters. Four, maybe five, swooping around in the middle distance. Buzzards over a corpse, or enraged hornets – Teal ignored their dramatic effect, but knew something bad when he saw it.

Then, round a long curve in the road, a car went past him, heading away from Faulston, doing minimum sixty and skidding across the road, barely missing the front wing of Teal's Volvo. It was drizzling slightly. He switched the periodic wipers on. The road straightened out, long and visible under autumnal trees. Still muttering at the car which had nearly ditched him, Teal could not believe what he saw now. Along both lanes, all racing towards him, cars jammed the minor road.

Reacting fast, he swung the Volvo round on to a muddy strip of verge beside a gate. The full lock pulled the car in a tight arc across the road. It went half up the opposite bank, but he managed to get it back at speed on to the tarmac just in time to escape this unbelievable onrush of traffic.

Teal put his foot down to keep ahead of them. There was no mistake, he watched them in his rear mirror, mile after mile, bearing down on him. If he slowed they would crash him into the roadside ditch. Yet he felt strangely exhilarated. Whatever it was all about, this had cleared his mood, just as his fight with the skinheads had relieved the gall of his wife walking out on him. The speed of his reflexes pleased him. They could never write off a man with reflexes like that.

The question was, how far to go? Whenever he slowed to fifty or lower for sharp bends, the leading cars almost caught up, and in his mirror Teal could see drawn, panicky faces that underscored the extended shrieking of the horns – *move, or we'll blast you off the road*. He was down on petrol, he had planned to fill the car in Faulston, and now he was burning his tank off because these out-of-control bastards were stampeding him.

The road diverged three ways. Teal took another instant decision and pulled into the narrowest branch of the fork. They had made him run, and suddenly it revolted him to have to run from anybody. He stopped the car half on the road, half off, beside a tree, where nobody could either pass on his inside or shoulder him off the tarmac altogether. Now let the bastards come.

But nobody followed. The collective madness went in a straight line. No driver dared quit the road. They were all aiming as far away from Faulston as possible, scared they would never be able to re-enter the stream of traffic once out of it. Teal felt contempt for them. He left his car unlocked and found a way through a crumbled stone wall. Ignoring the wetness of the grass, he strode up a steep meadow. The drizzle had stopped, and a warm sunlight lit up the misty air. The noise of the unseen traffic was staggering as he climbed to the peak of the down.

He had never known, or wanted to know, why he was hunting the man he knew as Peter English. For Harry Teal the word 'terrorist' defined everything. And the word 'suspected' held no trace of innocence; it meant dangerous, subversive, traitor. Teal had no doubt that this mass panic was tied to the failure to catch English. That wasn't what bothered him. In fact, that didn't bother him at all.

No, Harry Teal thought, as he came in sight of the road now a hundred feet below him, the real lesson was what these events taught you about your fellow-countrymen. If ever you saw all the reasons why people needed to be governed, policed, kept under constant watch, it was at moments like this. The authorities spent years drawing up plans for crisis contingencies, control plans designed to help threatened populations, and at the first sign of threat the people involved went berserk and in the rush to save themselves were willing to destroy everybody. God, how he despised them, their lack of control, their total absence of order.

A mile past the junction – Teal did not know this, but he was already watching the result – a farm tractor was driving towards the onrushing frenzy of traffic. The tractor took up slightly more than half the road width. Its driver had been out since daylight, and the only human contact he had in that time was the Barry Manilow cassettes with which he padded out the lonely boredom of farm labour. As the rapid magma of cars rounded a curve and poured into the stretch ahead, the tractor driver could only brake. There was no space to move on to the roadside. The oncoming cars had to hit their brakes and skid into the narrow gap the tractor offered. A few cars, rebounding off each other, forced a way through, but created an instant bottleneck which the hundreds of vehicles immediately behind could not see and only learnt about when they crashed into its tailback.

By the time Teal was looking down on it, the road had become a blockage, several miles long, of overheated, mutilated metal. In impotent frightened anger people pounded their horns at the wall of immobile cars in front. Eventually, with a last sob of despair, the hooting died away.

Where cars had stopped too late and smashed into others, people were being helped or dragged on to the grass verges. Passengers emerging from the bottled-up cars began to shout, frustration pumping up a pressure which they had to release. In more than one case within Teal's narrow view of the road, men were yelling at each other about the damage to their cars. Others were urging their families out of the vehicles and finding what passageway they could along the car-choked road.

These were the ones who had broken through the police blockade of Faulston. Instant refugees, they took with them whatever few things they had been able to salvage when the police loudspeakers ranged along the streets and ordered them out of their homes. Now they dragged their way along the country road, where soon they would reach the head of the crazy-paving of congested traffic, tired and bewildered people yelling to get a way through the quarter-mile cemetery of buckled and useless automotive metal. Like a scrapyard, Teal thought, and that was what it deserved to be. A scrapyard of patriotism.

187

The tractor driver had switched off his Walkman, disengaged and turned the tractor, and trundled away again, fearing the lynch-mob anger of some of the motorists. Most people were in shock from the long chain of the pile-up, some were injured, a few seriously, but there was no one to care. People were breaking down openly, and the noise of car horns and engines gave way to a widespread dissonance of human upset, from hysterical shrieking to the helpless wailing of the instantly dispossessed. Women sat in the wet roadside grass and cried, and when anger was exhausted, men roared with grief, helplessness, fear. Children, dressed for school, some still in nightclothes, clutching soft toys, cried hopelessly because the grown-ups were crying, or stood with blank wide-eyed faces, pale, uncomprehending, afraid to speak to parents because harmless questions received shouts of punishing rage.

A sad army began to form, as people abandoned cars and made what way they could ahead to the open road. Anything, so long as it took them away from Faulston and the radioactive cloud which even now might be filling the air with its imperceptible deathliness. And in sullen uniformity the inhabitants of the cosy rural town threaded their way down the miles of empty road, some sick with dread, some already feeling hunger and thirst, all silently praying to be spared. Whatever it was, to be spared it.

Harry Teal lifted his head and with narrowed eyes and a pout of non-involvement watched a helicopter track the route of the car-jammed road, then peel off again cross country. There would be a plan, there were always plans, often damned good ones, and they could never work because of *people*, stupid useless people whose salvation depended precisely on the plan working.

They deserved all they got, he thought, those who panicked and ran, the whingers, the morons who put their own safety before that of the nation. The debris of cars and humanity on the road below gave him a grim satisfaction. Stripped of his wife and the chance of a coup in his career, Teal felt a self-sufficient dignity, alone on this hilltop, indifferent to the crisis whose outer ripple he had just witnessed.

He walked back to his car, curious now to find out more about what was going on. Keeping to the minor road, referring to his map from time to time, he found he could weave a route through to Scardale without trouble. The traffic movement he encountered now was still hysterical, but more thinly scattered, and he was able to keep moving.

It was only a chance, but Godfrey Knapp, if he was at home, was a man who would know about these things at the local level. Since the phone call targeting Sarah Keeling, Knapp had been silent, and Teal had a mind to stir him up again.

As he approached the unostentatious entrance to the Scardale estate, another car left the gateway and turned down the road away from Teal's direction. It was gone in seconds, but Teal recognised the blue Dyane with the CND sticker in the window.

He slowed down and pulled off the road for ten minutes. The pause was calculated to avoid any suggestion in Knapp's mind that he, Teal, knew that these people had been at Scardale before him.

Chapter Fourteen

In designer jeans, Viyella shirt and doeskin waistcoat, his normal relaxation uniform when at home, Godfrey Knapp was finishing off a petit corona and luxuriating in the aftermath of another hour in Laura's company.

He felt the raised heartbeat and the lightness of a major decision taken. There was no way back. He was going to fall in love with this woman, he was already in love with her, and he would go all the way with it now. And bugger what happened.

The prize always went to the one who wanted it most badly. So fine, he would want Laura till it hurt, really hurt. And long before it became unbearable, he would have her.

After all, fuck it, what else could raise you from your declining body at the age of sixty, make your flesh sing and your spirit soar? The glorious aquamarine of her eyes, her intensity and wistfulness, hit him like a wind at a dying bonfire. His body trembled as in an ecstasy of sparks.

As for her relationship with Martin Ritchie, Knapp couldn't put his finger on it, but fences had definitely been erected somewhere. The man seemed out of his depth in some way, as if life was making too many demands on him. It was Ritchie's typically old-womanish suggestion that they should head back for Macemoor, in view of the evacuation, in case the panic spread and empty houses were commandeered for evacuees in their owners' absence. No, Ritchie was a man who needed things to be simple, but from now on nothing was going to be simple. And it was just too bad.

Before he could return to the TV, Harold came to announce that a Mr Teal was at the house.

'Damned strange time to call.'

'I'm sorry it's so early.'

'I meant the day, not the time.'

Teal said, 'The day?'

'Where have you been for the last six hours? And don't tell me your visit was nothing to do with all that.'

'It has everything to do with it.'

'Sit down,' Knapp said, minimally polite to the point of rudeness.

'I came to thank you for your most useful lead on the reporter Keeling. Invaluable.'

Knapp quietly cleared his throat. His frosty grey eyes never moved from Teal's face.

'The other people we discussed – Martin Ritchie and his lady friend – have you –?'

'Very little contact,' Knapp rasped. 'Been busy lately – hardly ever here – business interests, cultural pursuits, social obligations in town. You know how it is.'

Teal didn't know how it was, and Knapp was openly enjoying the fact.

'You haven't seen them lately?'

Knapp answered wearily, 'No. Now, you wanted to speak with me about today's events?'

'Yes,' Teal said. 'How much do you know?'

'Same as everyone else, what I've seen on telly. Surely you didn't come here to ask me for information?' Knapp's mind spun round a few times. This tedious shit, this overgrown school prefect, knew less than he did. He added, 'You've seen the programmes this morning?'

'No.' Teal said, 'I've seen the real thing.'

Knapp was elated. '*Television*, my dear Teal, *is* the real thing.' He chuckled and gleefully rewound the video tape, cutting into it at random.

191

'You'll excuse me a moment. This is what our masters choose to let us know. And for people like you and me, what other truth is there?'

He sniffed and abruptly left the study, striding off along a corridor towards one of Scardale's sequestered lavatories, where he roared with laughter and, no mean feat, pissed accurately at the same time.

Amazing. This slithery bastard Teal knew nothing, was just looking for a leg-up. Good God, the man probably went back to whatever ghoulish place he inhabited and typed out laborious reports in which he, Knapp – suitably coded for security, of course, something like PANK or PNAK – was playing a cryptic game that only really existed in Teal's constipated imagination. What Mr Teal needed was a good boot up the bollocks.

In the study Harry Teal sat through a miserable twenty minutes, in which he saw a summary of the incident at Faulston, now two hours old. He also caught the moment when the face of the terrorist Peter English was broadcast. He had begun to notice how long he had been alone in the room, but he was glad not to have his humiliation observed.

A depleted, bitter man, he suddenly realised how small and disposable his dedication was, against this backdrop of nightmare. The incident itself he did not care about, he could rationalise it quite easily – if people wanted security, they had to pay the price. That said it all. What stung Teal was the lack of protocol concerning him. He had not only missed a chance of promotion. All this might even go down on his record as a failure. And he had not failed, not failed . . .

When the door opened it was Harold who stood there.

'Mr Knapp sends his apologies, sir, but he's rather indisposed at the moment and wondered if before you leave I could offer you some refreshment.'

Trying not to make the mistake of showing feelings in front of a servant, Teal left immediately. Hatred of Godfrey Knapp was spreading like a cancer deep inside him. If he couldn't pick the man's brains, he would make sure that one day, one day, he would pick his goddamn bones.

*

In her Clapham flat Sarah Keeling watched the TV account of events in Faulston. Outside, from her view of the common, she saw the trees changing colour, almost as she watched, and beyond them the usual swirl of traffic. Life would not stop because of a terrorist threat in some remote country town. Especially when it came shrink- and gift-wrapped by television.

Yet if the contents of the flask were launched to the winds, nobody could believe themself safe. Before long the whole population would be calculating its degree of risk on the basis of radius from the site of the flask. People would be trying to repel their mutual fears, media authorities expounding soft statistics to make the danger seem negligible, trying to damp down panic.

But in the area of Faulston thousands had been evacuated. In an orderly manner, according to the report, although Sarah made her own interpretation of that. The only way to have an orderly evacuation, as at Chernobyl, was to tell people nothing until the last possible moment. In individualistic, news-hungry Britain, there could be no such thing as a peaceful evacuation.

She watched with mixed feelings. Excitement and guilt alternated, clashing and displacing each other. It was only two days since her flat had been burgled and the man named Teal had called, but things were now fitting together with a neat but fearful inevitability. She rang Laura again, but there was no answer. Suddenly relieved, she put the phone down quickly.

She felt alone, but powerful because she knew something which millions didn't. What scared her was her uncertainty what to do with that knowledge. For a start she had to get her copy of the tape back. Apart from anything else, now that Ray had been plastered over every screen in the country as a wanted and dangerous man, she was potentially involved in a criminal concealment. But she was also less inclined now to dismiss the tape as the product of a madman. Hoping to prompt a further decision, she rang the TV producer.

He sounded hungover and dozy.

'Alan, hi, it's Sarah.' She tried not to sound urgent or nervous, not to alert him.

'Hello, darling, you're early. What can I do for you?'

She could tell he had the phone crooked in his shoulder and was either stroking someone's body or fixing himself a drink.

'That cassette I gave you –'

'Oh yeah – right.'

'Could I borrow it back briefly? I'll tell you why – by the way, I meant to tell you, I thought your drug programme was terrific.'

'Thanks – that tape –'

'You have still got it?'

'Sure. Any progress with the guy?'

'Still trying. Can I come round?'

'Yeah, it's right here.'

'Sorry if I woke you.'

'You can wake me any time, sweetie.'

Sarah put the phone down. Relief made her want to throw up. Alan could always make a crafty copy anyway, but he seemed to have a lot of work, so maybe he wasn't interested.

He was either drunk or in love, because when Sarah arrived he still oozed bedroom, and had not yet switched on the radio or TV. She didn't enlighten him. Within fifteen minutes of her call, the tape was safely back in her hands. But she still had no idea what to do. The events on television sucked her back like a magnet.

'That man is so bloody patronising,' Martin said.

Laura said, 'It's only his manner.'

'You mean that really he's a warm-hearted human being, sensitive to the concerns of others?'

Sarcasm was always a good sign in Martin, so Laura took this exchange lightly.

'No, but he's much more vulnerable than he seems.'

'He's a big fat cat, and his morality says that whatever

keeps him from being bored is fine. That's all.' A stretch of country road went by in a blur. 'What do you really feel about him?'

'Oh God, Martin, do we have to? Today?'

'He's turned you into a fantasy figure.'

'Didn't you?'

'He's a man who wants to sell his soul, but he's never found a worthy buyer.'

'Nice epigram. But is it true?'

'He's corrupt.'

'So am I, Martin. Somewhere deep inside me, maybe deeper than you care to look.'

'You think you're in control of what's happening?'

'No. Do you?'

'He likes you because you make him feel young and attractive. That's your use to him.'

'I know that,' Laura said. And thought, why not, it makes me feel good too.

Martin's directness had the brutality of someone who was scared. But Laura began to wonder if in fact she did know what she was getting into. For the moment the events of the day made it seem academic.

Back at the cottage they watched TV again. But there was no development, only the unending flow of speculation and statistics and an iron silence about official reaction to the terrorists' demands. On the road back from Scardale they had seen no trace of the evacuation. Yet it hung over their minds as surely as if, from that small town the other side of the horizon, a mushroom cloud had spread up across the sky.

A terrible weariness began to sap them. They could not bear to watch or discuss any more. For a long time they lay on the bed, hardly touching, in a depressed emptiness. Finally Laura muttered that she was going to ring Sarah, and five minutes later she forced herself up from the bed.

Sarah explained about the tape. She was still glad to have retrieved what was after all criminal evidence. She could feel Laura's lack of excitement.

'I thought you'd be pleased.'

'Yes, I'm sorry, I am,' Laura said. 'But what difference does it make now?'

'What do you mean?'

'You're not going to use it, are you?'

'Of course not.'

There was silence.

'Laura, love, how can we use it? Didn't you see his face all over the telly this morning? That is the same man, isn't it? Your man?'

Laura confirmed that Peter English was Ray. Then she said, 'So why be cheerful about getting the tape back?'

Sarah was incredulous. 'So we can't be *linked* with him. Laura, don't you realise what you're up against? He's wanted for murder. When you first brought me the tape it was an interesting story. But now it's a can of worms, and I think we should wash our hands of it. Fast.' After a moment of cynical reflection she added, 'Of course, when it's all blown over, the tape might have much more impact – wait till the skeleton's well and truly in the cupboard, *then* expose it.'

Laura was crying at the other end of the line. Sarah listened in faint embarrassment, then revulsion. Other people's tears always froze her up.

'Listen, Laura, sweetheart, isn't it time for a little de-involvement?'

Laura burst out, 'But what if he's right? What if everything he says is true? This isn't just another story, a bit of soap opera, it's about what's being done to this bloody country –'

'Sure,' Sarah murmured, 'sure, but –'

'The tape is mine,' Laura said. Her tears had stopped.

'Yes. Right.'

'Will you let me have it back? If I can't use it with you, I'll take it somewhere else.'

Affronted, Sarah said, 'Fine, I'll mail it. Bye,' and hung up.

They walked across Macemoor to the sea. It was not the sort of rhythmic, effortless walking they enjoyed, but a reluctant, dragging pace which expressed the fact that all they were doing was stay out of the house, away from the screen, away from the horror. They only spoke once.

Laura said, 'Assuming we know –'

Martin understood, and said, 'We know.'

'If we didn't – if we only knew what we've seen on TV –'

'What are you saying?' Martin asked.

'We wouldn't be walking around here. We'd have studied the wind, and we'd be driving the fuck in the opposite direction.'

Martin looked haggard and guilty, stayed silent, unable to find an answer. They were grateful for each other's company, but it was a false experience to walk these places simply for escape. Laura's point even covered that – the moorland only offered a refuge because they knew the human shock wave would not come this far. The last thing people wanted in their path was the sea.

Depressed and weary, they returned to the cottage. After a bath they sat over a drink, downstairs, furtively eyeing the dead TV set as the time of the next news programme approached. All the personal constraints built up earlier that day were forgotten. Occasionally they exchanged weak smiles that conveyed an abiding friendliness, whatever came now. The smiles brought apology too, apology because for once they could not offer each other a sanctuary.

Martin switched on as the title sequence was rolling. He sat beside Laura, and they attempted a cuddle, but soon broke away again at what followed, stiffening and sitting upright, jolted into separateness.

The headline stunned them. The terrorist alert at Faulston was over.

Over. They watched. A confident voice reported that the flask remained undamaged, and was at that moment being transported back to the safe custody of the nuclear power authorities. The terrorists had been taken by surprise in a brilliant manoeuvre by the SAS, and killed. Nobody else was injured, and the people of Faulston and the surrounding area

197

were moving peacefully back through the night to their homes.

The video showed the lamplit outskirts of Faulston, with motor traffic slowly trailing into the town, and people on foot straggling along the streets. The voice-over said '. . . and so the little town of Faulston, which earlier today seemed destined to join the macabre roll-call of the nuclear age, Hiroshima, Nagasaki, Three Mile Island, Chernobyl, becomes once again a sleepy country town which for one day, unforgettable to its inhabitants, was brushed by the wing of nuclear nightmare . . .'

'Oh Christ!' Martin said, and switched off.

In the end the terrorists, for all the plan which Ray had claimed they were part of, trusted nobody. Neither did the organisers of the plan trust the terrorists. And neither side expected the other to be motivated by trust.

Waiting out the hours at the comprehensive school, the terrorists quarrelled over how to move things their way. The agreement was that one of them would be captured and tried, to provide credentials for further terrorist infiltration after the prison break which would be organised for him. But the man selected for the arrest had changed his mind. After a lot of shouting they had compromised on a plan to hijack the plane which they had been promised in advance of the operation. They would take the pilot hostage and make him fly to a different destination from the one he had been given.

The plane came down on time, and for a few minutes it seemed that everything was going to be straight. All armed with sub-machine guns, the terrorists waited for the money to be brought from the plane. By this time it was getting dark. The lights of the empty school and the street lamps of the adjacent housing estate were the only illumination. Muffled coughs in the cold air, the running of the light aircraft engine, the lonely thunk of boots on tarmac, were the only sounds to punctuate the tense twilight.

The man in civilian dress who brought the money threw the

two leather bags on to the school playground. One hooded figure ordered him to open them first. This was done. Armalite aimed at the unarmed civilian, the hooded terrorist stepped forward and kicked the cases behind him.

Two other hooded men crouched down with a bag each. They flicked the catches open again and tore back the flaps at the same moment. Each money bag instantly transmuted into a giant firework-red glare. It ripped the men apart, killing one outright and leaving the other screaming among the netball lines painted on the hard-top. At the same moment the school lights and the street lamps went out.

A third member of the six terrorists was also caught by the blast. Without the use of his legs he had to drag himself away as his companions ran for it. As the cases exploded by remote-controlled detonation, a hollow coughing from the aircraft announced the trajectory of gas canisters. Before they could gun down the man who had brought the cash bags, he had disappeared through the cloud of toxic smoke and was inside the plane, which was already veering away over the school playing fields.

Fired from behind the school's perimeter fence, stun grenades blasted holes in the tear gas. The smoking spaces of the schoolyard were raked with machine-gun fire. The slaughter of the terrorists was accomplished quickly. As the gas drifted away, another group of hooded men came forward, guns at the ready, to inspect the mangled bodies that littered the playground.

Thickening trails of blood mingled with splintered glass. The terrorists lay broken and still as more men in mottled combat gear and hoods, unspeaking, rifles poised, moved silently in to take possession of the school grounds and the squat, mundane-looking flask which, against a background of Portakabin classrooms, resembled nothing more than a rubbish skip awaiting collection.

Helicopters with loudspeakers flew at once over the countryside, in which many thousands of people were sullenly preparing for the night, to announce that the alert was over

199

and request that they practised restraint in returning to their homes. The population of Faulston and its surrounding area began a long, exhausted trek back along the unlit, congested roads.

Later in the night other vehicles were driving away from the town. As they regained their homes, the relief of thousands of families was darkened by the discovery that during the evacuation, coolly, casually, of everything that had any value, houses, shops, workplaces had been stripped clean. In Faulston it had been a good day for burglars.

Chapter Fifteen

Gouts of dark water leaked down the rusty walls and dampened the floor of the narrow cave, the human-sized rathole where Ray was lying. For the first time since he had made his run he gave way to despair. It was dark in there, dank with a heavy decayed wetness that no air or sun could ever reach. The sea-wind hurled breakers at the cliff, and the black throat of the cave drank the spray then dribbled it out again down the face of the fractured limestone. Tins, all empty now, littered the further recess, and the smell of wet stone and centuries of saline accretion were overlaid by the stink of his own shit, which since he returned here had become a semiliquid stench on the cave floor. Ray had nearly cracked, and getting back here had been the only thing he could do. And even now, while he tortured himself for a next move, he heard a motor patrol boat out on the sea.

To Martin Ritchie the words 'You're a small man', after some of the insult wore off, seemed affirmative, like a metaphor for the rest of his life. Laura had inadvertently done him a favour. Her words had somehow given him back to himself. Yes, he decided, he was a small man, his concerns were small, but he believed in them. He was desperate to get back to his microcosmic field studies, his lifetime of painstaking observations, the knowledge that the whole of creation did not have to be measured by human failure.

And equally, although he had not stopped loving Laura, he no longer wished to give his life value by whether or not she loved him. This felt like a real freedom. He felt bleak inside, but it was survivable, and in the meantime there was work to be done. He had begun the year by finding Laura, and as it approached its end he had found himself. And for Laura too, the same process.

Or maybe that was too neat. But the limestone crags, the merciless infinity of the sea, the unageing pathos of the grass bowed by the wind, freshened him again and moved his spirit so that his veins chilled with feeling. It was the country of his blood.

Ray knew that he had been seen three times, maybe more. He had made it to near the naval base, past the promontory of Saltmayne, one step ahead of the search. The open terrain and waning daylight were on his side, and he had the Browning automatic which he had taken from Pilkington.

But a lack of purpose slowed him down. He recognised it as a by-product of pain and physical weakness – not only the hunger, which he had paced himself for, but the diarrhoea which cleaned him out and then reamed his insides of a squirty, putrid juice and left him almost unable to climb back out of whatever ditch he had crouched in.

Once someone passed him in the dusk. He had been totally unaware of their approach, and they flicked a torch on, directly into his face. He had refused conversation and stumbled away into the darkness. Later, a car got him in its beam and pulled in to offer a lift before he could take cover.

Ray knew he looked suspicious, and it was only a matter of time before somebody reported their suspicion to the police. And the sightings, if timed, would tie him to an area and a direction. They would track him as surely as a gardener plotting the path of a mole from a few freshly dug mounds.

Before his nerve failed completely, Ray headed back to familiar territory. He knew it sent him straight into the jaws of the manhunt, but the night would have thwarted them, and by daybreak he would be back in the caves, and there he could rest.

The motor patrol boat bucked through the swirling offshore race, dipping into the muscular grey waves and rearing back out of them with the crowns of angry foam. Martin watched through his glasses. Marines. He saw one of them also training binoculars along the coastline. In a gesture of distaste, laced with fear, he lowered his own glasses on to his chest. He had submitted, he did not want to draw the marines' attention by appearing to be watching them.

A prickle of inadequacy reawoke in his nervous system and the depths of his mind. They hunted the Rays of this world like animals, whereas he, Martin Ritchie, was a known, respected, well-liked figure in this entire region, receiving co-operation and support from the nuclear industry and the military, and he was all these things because he threatened nobody, opposed and questioned nobody. The people who owned this land, who could buy and sell it, rape and destroy it, would never refer to him. He hid behind scientific detachment. He was a small man.

Stretched on his belly on the clammy floor of the cave, Ray dragged himself near enough its mouth to get a view of the patrol boat. When he saw the green berets of the marines he knew they were there because of him. The boat was tacking closer in, as near as they could bring it without smashing on to the submerged rocks.

Then a *phut*, hardly audible through the shrieking of wind and wave. Then another, and more. Ray guessed what the sound was, and a sudden clank confirmed it, as a canister hit the cliff and bounced back down into the waters below. There were a number of caves along here, mostly inaccessible, and they were gassing them. Of the three choices in front of him, two were as good as death, and for the third he had to move immediately and not even think about what might happen as he picked his way back along the cliff-face.

Martin had come here for peace, to put himself back together again. For weeks he had neglected his field research, leaving a disastrous gap in his records and a depressed indifference about going on. He had to recover the taste for it, and he had come out here to meet his old self in an act of conciliation.

But there was no peace now. He looked at the sea as the marines in their boat carved up and down the breakers, firing things at the cliffs. At first he thought they were just having fun, but before he could get sore about it he realised that they were not playing. Traces of the CS gas plumed up into the air briefly before the wind dispersed them. And suddenly, while one marine struggled to keep the boat pivoted in the water, the shouts of the others revealed action somewhere out of Martin's view.

Through his glasses he saw one marine speaking into a radiophone. The boat spun as the propeller beat against the waves. The marines watched through binoculars something happening on the cliff-face. As clearly as a hammer-blow between the shoulders, Martin knew what it was. He scrambled down on to the stiff grass, unsighted now from the patrol boat out on the sea.

Ray crept out on to the ledge, proceeding as if the marines were not there. One moment of haste could send him bouncing down on to the jagged sea-washed rocks a hundred feet below. If they had guns, he was gambling that they would not use them. They would not have orders to kill. Yet every second, as the ledge narrowed into the broken teeth of rock which only a practised climber could negotiate, as he inched his way along Ray felt the bullet in his back. And the one that killed you, you never felt. So he let his mind rest on the bullet while his body crawled gently across the cliff-face. The path once reached, he scrambled up and out of the marines' view. But he knew they would not leave it there.

He ran. Relief at being out of that limestone trap, the adrenalin blasting through his body, overcame all the calorie-scoured exhaustion of the last twelve hours. He ran through the familiar reverse-slope of scrappy gorse and uneven barren ground between clusters of rock, yielding to pasture and the odd arable field which had been clawed out between the sea and the dark distant expanse of heathland. But his running soon slowed, as the power seeped from his legs and his blood strained for glycogen which his body had long since bled out. And through the pounding in his ears he heard a helicopter, a long way out in the sky, but eating up miles faster than he could cover yards.

'Ray!'

Martin Ritchie was also running, obliquely across the rutted turf. The helicopter was in the sky behind him. As he caught Ray's attention he waved, indicating a direction. At the end of a stone-chip track Ray saw the Land-Rover. The automatic, zipped into the lining of his jacket, bumped against his ribs as he changed direction towards the jeep.

Ritchie, tall and cumbersome but stronger, beat him there and got the motor started while Ray was still pulling himself into the cab. The ridged tyres scattered stones as they hit forty along the crude road. Breathless, they still had to shout above the engine and the noise of the helicopter which was bearing down on them from the white sky.

Ray yelled 'Thanks!' His gratitude was almost violent.

'I'll get you out of this,' Martin shouted. 'I can't make any other promises. They've put your face on television.'

A pinched reflectiveness deepened the hunted thinness of Ray's face. The dark rings were back around the eyes, the heavy black stubble, the underfed pallor. He said nothing.

Martin drove towards a small wood, one of the meagre coppices that overspread the more fertile patches of the landscape. It gave maybe a hundred yards of concealed road.

He called out, 'I'll slow down, and you'll have to jump. Stay in this wood. I'll come back for you. It may be an hour, or more. But stay here.'

He took the Land-Rover down to ten. Ray tumbled

perfectly on to the roadside bank, rolling to lessen the impact. Rubbing his ribs and shoulders from where the tree roots had smacked them, he watched the jeep accelerate out of the trees. He had never been able to understand this man Ritchie, and still couldn't. But the guy had just provided him with a heart, leg and lung transplant, all in one. Ray whistled softly and patted the automatic zipped into his jacket, fondly almost, and took cover.

Martin carried on into the open moorland. The helicopter used the space to buzz low at him. He drove without even looking up, then slowed and stopped a couple of miles away from the wood. The helicopter banked away then circled back over him as he calmly got out of the Land-Rover and stooped down to examine something on the ground. Martin ignored them as they sought out a clear section of heath to bring the chopper down. Two men in combat gear raced across to him. They were not armed, at least not visibly. Martin was inspecting some clumps of round-leafed sundew.

One of the men shouted, 'Is this your jeep?'

'What if it is?'

'Quick, search the fucker!'

And then Martin saw one of them unslinging a light-metal rifle from his back. They prowled about the jeep, both of them young, jumpy men, unsure what to do if a mad killer suddenly pumped an automatic at them from the depths of the Land-Rover.

Except that the jeep had no depths. One glance told them they would find nobody.

'You have somebody in here with you?'

'No.'

'You're lying, we saw him get in.'

'Somebody ran past me, but he didn't get in.'

From here the acre of trees was out of view. The soldiers did not remember it from their dizzying pursuit of the Land-Rover. They exchanged glances. They had better get back up there.

'We'll need your name.'

'You have no right to demand my name.'

'Take his fucking car number.'

There was a moment of comedy in which neither of them had anything to write with.

'You come our way again, mate, you fucking watch out.'

They ran back to the helicopter and got airborne. Martin waited ten minutes while they etched a menacing spiral in the sky, hunting the sour heathland where nothing stood out, where only the patient observer who could humble his vision would find the diverse magic of infinite life. He drove a few miles to make sure they were not tailing him, then tracked back by a dirt road that ran between high banks towards the patch of woodland. As he drove, for the first time in many days, he found himself smiling.

He left the Land-Rover half-hidden and jogged to the cover of the trees. Ray soon picked up his presence and showed himself. Martin signalled him to go. The helicopter was still up there somewhere, but its sound was that of a tired insect beating its way aimlessly along a pane of glass. Even if they had radioed for help, the chances were momentarily good.

They made it to the Land-Rover unspotted, and hit the dirt road back towards Macemoor. On the way Martin told Ray everything about the previous day. When they arrived at the cottage Laura opened the door. Martin grinned ruefully and said, 'Guess who's coming to dinner.'

Chapter Sixteen

The Home Secretary was an accountant by background, a small gritty man generally regarded as lacking charisma. Of Scottish ancestry, he saw himself as a dour, tough fighter with an immense moral superiority to the flabby south which he witnessed in decay all around him.

But he had not reduced crime, there was less respect for public order by the year, and the drugs market now almost qualified for its own GNP rating. So his days as Home Secretary were reckoned to be numbered.

Faulston changed all that. In an Emergency Debate of a packed House of Commons, the Home Secretary made the chamber swell with a unison it had not known since the Falklands War. Opposition members who attempted to quarrel with items in his package of measures were repelled with curt, dismissive taunts from the Home Secretary and massed howls of hostility from the banks of members behind him.

Later, in his memoirs, he would write, '. . . I hardly slept that night, realising that destiny had called me to answer in the hour of Britain's need. I prayed to the stern god of my forefathers that I should not be found wanting. The chickens, as I would tell the nation, had come home to roost, and the days of cloud-cuckoo-land were over. Two stark choices lay before us – to renounce nuclear power and degenerate rapidly into (to use my phrase which was much quoted over the next few days) a banana republic without the bananas, or to forge ahead along mankind's hard technological road, keeping faith with the scientific pioneers, and constructing a responsible society in which all could enjoy the fruits of that science free from threat or subversion from the disaffected. I therefore, with the full backing of Cabinet, proposed . . .'

On every TV set in Britain, two days after the incident at Faulston, the Home Secretary expounded a list of proposals which were already as good as on the statute book.

Point One. All trains or other transport carrying flasks of radioactive waste or any other dangerous nuclear-power-related substance would from now on have armed guards. Whether these guards were to come from the nuclear industry's own police force, or the civil police, awaited decision, but the nuclear industry, and indeed the government, was not prepared to offer any more free handouts to terrorists.

Point Two. All workers in the nuclear area, civil or military, would now have to accept open, intensive and ongoing vetting of a political nature. 'To some extent, of course, this already goes on. But we would like now to make the process systematic and wide-ranging. I have much evidence to suggest that employees in this field would welcome such a move. They, after all, will be its main beneficiaries. Nuclear power is the great shining hope of our economy, our prosperity and our civilisation. It is the heart of our future, and here above all we must fight the forces of darkness whose menace grows ever closer.'

Point Three. The setting up of 'Nuclear Security Zones'. In these zones, any areas around nuclear complexes, civil or military, and the transport network through which nuclear materials might travel, any unauthorised person would be subject to arrest and detention under the charge of 'intent to behave contrary to the public good in proximity to a nuclear installation'.

Point Four. It would be necessary to direct a far greater proportion of public spending to improving nuclear security.

This money could only be found from the finite sum of public funds at any given time, and there was no doubt that other recipients of public finance would have to moderate their demands in the face of this new and overwhelming threat.

Point Five. A specific programme for schools would be developed in the educational sector, to explain to children of the nuclear age the opportunities and risks of the world which would one day be theirs. The nature of terrorism was also something which many schools had not done enough to point out to children. 'Good citizenship begins in childhood. And from now on, the good citizen must above all be vigilant, because our enemies are among us, and they take for their weapons sources of power which are our own life's blood. I would venture to say that never stood any society under such threat as that which we face now. And if we are to defeat that threat, it is in the schools that battle must be joined.'

Point Six. There must be a tightening up on people of suspect political character, especially when occupying positions of public responsibility. 'We are not talking of spies and traitors now, but something more insidious, those who for reasons best known to themselves wish to undermine our society from within, to hinder progress, to limit the advance of others to their own often bizarre objectives, to turn a man against his brother. We are not proposing a witch-hunt, but the onus should now be on the individual, where there is doubt, to demonstrate his attachment to the society which has raised and sheltered him. And for those who manifest hostility to their society, all I have to offer is that the same enmity will be extended to them.'

Point Seven. There would be, not proscription or active interference with, but open and intensive surveillance of all anti-nuclear and so-called peace groups. 'Clearly, as a tolerant society, we do not wish to ban the expression of opinion. But let me make it clear to the organisations I have just referred to, that the easy ride is over. Where we suspect subversion, we shall root it out, and where we find the diseased mentality that leads to terrorism, we shall expose it to the nation, and I dedicate myself now to its removal.'

Point Eight. 'Demonstrations are an integral part of any free society. But for many years we have seen how peaceful, reasonable expressions of opinion have been infiltrated by militants and turned to their own distorted and often violent purposes. We propose that from now on all demonstrations be licensed, and that people intending to appear at a given demonstration should first apply to the police for a permit. Any person at a demonstration who, when challenged, is unable to show his permit, will be deemed to be an agitator, and held to await charges. In this way yet another umbrella for the actual or potential terrorist will have been eliminated.'

Point Nine. All British subjects, during the coming year, would be issued with identity papers. These would be carried at all times, and failure to produce them on request by the police would result in immediate arrest.

The Home Secretary took pains to make clear his realisation that this measure cut across much of the ancient concern for individual liberty that had made Britain the envy of the world. But he had to say that when freedom of the individual also fostered freedom for the terrorist, then it was time to reconsider priorities. 'For if the terrorist is free, the rest of society is forced to live in perpetual fear. His freedom imprisons us. Any measure which robs the terrorist of his freedom improves life for the rest of society. The issuing of identity papers is, I believe, just such a measure.'

'In the world of shopping malls and multi-storey car parks, it makes no difference,' Sarah Keeling said.

She handed another front page to Laura and Martin. The *Sun* proclaimed in big black capitals, 'THE 9 COMMAND-MENTS! THANK GOD!' The atmosphere in the cottage at Macemoor was gloomy. Martin had thrown himself back into work on a book called *The Ecology of a Path*, which was being reissued in a revised paperback edition. He had asked Laura to illustrate it, but events had buried that discussion. Laura herself was talking vaguely of going to live abroad. To each their own migration. But Sarah found it a strange time to have come back to Macemoor. After these events maybe any time would have been strange.

The remark had come from her editor. 'It makes fuck all difference,' he had actually said. Sarah had repeated the sentence to herself so many times that it now belonged to her. It seemed to encapsulate the ease with which a whole country had been politically lobotomised. Freedom was like a ripple of brain tissue that could be neatly sliced away, leaving all other organs to function outwardly as they had before. The beauty of it was that the difference would not be noticed by the victim.

'Get back out there,' the editor had said. '*Living With the Nukes* went down good. Get to those people in Faulston and see how they like it now. But don't slag off the new laws, right? I know what you probably feel, I probably feel the same. But papers can't fight government on this one. The way people feel right now, we'd be burnt on the streets.'

And there was talk of a new paper starting up, people splintering from various other dinosaurs of Fleet Street and creating a new daily, and Sarah wanted to keep the options open.

One option, an idea she had several times a day and kept repressing, was to resurrect the Ray story. She had mailed Laura's cassette back and not even bothered to make another copy. It was obsolete now, outstripped by events. Yet somewhere in it all there must be mileage. Something about it still made her tingle. If only Ray had not been publicised as a wanted man. Career-wise a tangle with the police, a moment's error of judgment, could destroy her.

First she had to make her peace with Laura. She was glad of the Faulston assignment, because apart from being relatively easy journalism – she had the contacts, the story turned her on – it gave her a neutral excuse for breaking the journey at Macemoor. On the phone Laura was friendly but remote, a little flaky. Yet talking to her made Sarah feel warm and upbeat again, in the jet of energy which she always got from contact with Laura.

The atmosphere at the cottage was difficult. Sarah felt no aftertaste of violence or hysteria, but equally she did not have that slight sense of being an intruder that one usually did with together couples. It was relaxed, nice really, and yet unnerving.

Martin was in his work-room, and Laura cradled a mug of coffee, her eyes distant, then read another front-page acceptance of the government's Nine Points. The press were not seeking a fight. Too many people had been scared, and the government had grasped the public mood correctly. The papers saw no future in kicking against that.

'You don't think it's important?' Laura said.

Sarah answered, 'Important? Listen, there's so much shit on the fan, it's stopped turning.'

But for once macho cynicism had lost its power.

Laura said, 'We could have prevented it.'

Sarah shook her head, sympathetic but final.

Laura insisted, 'If we'd pushed the story, they'd never have gone through with it.'

Sarah thought quickly and as sensitively as she could. She wanted to avoid a case of 'tough newswoman puts down naïve idealist'. Just the peculiar affection she felt for Laura made her want to do that.

'I think it was a loser, love.'

'You never believed him, did you?'

It had been a long drive. Sarah took refuge in tiredness. Her eyes glazed, and she sighed.

'Perhaps if I'd met him –'

Without a word Laura left the room. Her voice came from upstairs, talking presumably to Martin. Then the footsteps on the stair again. Laura's face was pale and uncompromising. Sarah became aware of someone behind her, just beyond the doorway.

'We just call him Ray.'

He stepped into the room, a thin dark man whose haggardness was offset by the benefits of a bath and a decent place to sleep. He was hesitant, and Sarah knew instantly that the only person he trusted was Laura.

'He knows who you are.'

Sarah stood up and offered her hand. Adrenalin pumped her heart and tightened her chest, but she knew how to hide all that. Ray's eyes, hunted but powerful, drilled into her. In her own less direct way, Sarah had all her senses alert for the giveaway, the smallest hint of scam. At first sight she had to admit he was convincing, but in her presence he would be, they always were. Yet everything in her prayed for him to be what Laura claimed.

A few days earlier, back from a morning shooting rabbits in a far covert of the estate, freshly showered and almost sick with growing desire for female flesh, Godfrey Knapp had an hour between Laura's phone call and her arrival at Scardale in which to prepare for the realisation of a fantasy. He dedicated a fresh cigar to its contemplation, but he was troubled by a nervous unease which he could not shake off.

Simply from her voice on the phone he knew why she was coming there. She wanted something from him, and she was prepared to offer herself to get it. The subliminal sexual pursuit which had advanced a stage every time they met was now over.

Knapp restrained his ebullience, and was controlled, almost grave, as he met her at the door and showed her through to his study. It was still morning, and he gave her a sharp concoction of lemon and elderflower made by Harold from trees on the estate. He tried not to ogle her beauty, but his heart nearly stopped at the thought of the candid submission in her voice when she had called him. Always prepared to be a genial rapist, believing that women needed to be forced into admitting their desire, he was unsure how to behave with this upfront approach.

'Tell me how I can help,' he said.

Laura had thought it all through on the way, how much she would ask, how little, what the bounds of possibility were.

'Can you hide somebody for me?'

Knapp had also worked out the reason, the only conceivable reason, for the urgent call. As with his sexual chase, the whole thing took place beyond the region of words.

'You realise what you're asking me to do?'

'Yes.'

'You know I don't have it in me to refuse you anything.'

'I know that, Godfrey, I need to feel that somebody's helping me. I'm scared.'

With a surprising agility Knapp moved from his chair to kneel beside Laura. His dressing-gown parted slightly over the grey hairs of his muscular chest and the gold chain that always hung there. He stroked Laura's blonde hair and stared, hiding nothing now, into the lucid aquamarine eyes. He kissed her lips, and felt that her hunger did not match his. But it was too late to change anything.

Knapp's hands finally on her body did nothing to melt Laura's detachment. A need for romantic love had been reawakened in her by Martin. But with Martin things were always straight, earnest, nobody got ripped off. And romance, in the end, needed its element of swindle. With Godfrey there was no danger, you would get cheated every time. He was cheating himself, and loving it. Laura even felt sorry for him in anticipation of the moment when he would have to face the truth. But for now it was experienced man, experienced woman, and everything to play for.

In Knapp's bedroom, with its view over the lake, Laura recognised the same light, Italianate decorative style as in his London flat. She gazed from the window for a minute, thinking.

Although she could handle what was about to happen, she had expected to be aroused more. As she got older the masculine male excited her less, and Knapp's probing, cigar-flavoured tongue and his big blunt fingers groping her while they were still downstairs, were depressingly predictable. Why were experienced, original men so often like wind-up toys when it came to sex? She let the question go and turned to face him.

Knapp drew her towards the bed, and Laura complied with

the guidance of his forceful hands. She had bare legs, and had put on pretty clothes that were easy to remove, guessing that he would want to strip her. More than that, he wanted to make love to every garment he removed. Laura lay passive but willing as Knapp opened his robe, under which the bulge had long been evident, to display a thick, stubby cock and a rather sparse growth of grey hair. Ignoring the fact that she had to dress again to go home, Knapp slid himself deliriously in and out of her clothes as each piece was removed.

Finally he had her down to her underwear. Laura watched him from a pleasant state halfway between shared sensuality and ironic detachment. As he came to her real body he seemed, under the mania of desire, almost abashed. He bared her breasts and made greedy play with them, his hands, his face, his penis, all zeroing in and pushing them to the limits of their malleability. As he straddled her, Laura stroked his body, to compensate somehow for the fact that he would not meet her eye. At first she thought it was the tunnel vision of lust, but as he worked away at her body Laura felt something else coming over him.

Desperate, as if unable to gratify his own need, Knapp mauled her chest. Laura was fond of her tits. Although one week out of four they ached a lot, they also gave her much pleasure, and her real orgasms always began at the nipple. Yet always she had had to school men in what to do with them, in the fact that when they toyed with her there they were not playing handball or kneading dough. Leaving small smears of genital sap on her pale breast skin, Knapp finally moved down. Laura wondered if he had been making himself defer this moment. She also began to wonder if he was faltering, and if she should take over.

He slid her knickers down her legs, and once they were off rubbed his face and his cock eagerly into them. Then he came to her exposed cunt with its silky blonde hair. He parted her and stared, his eyes beginning to bulge, then went down to smell and taste her, but Laura had to restrain his finger and tongue and ease herself away from the scratch of his beard.

216

Knapp turned her over and examined her from behind. Laura felt a rush of alienation as he nuzzled her and began to claw at her flesh. Why was the average male lover always a cross between a gynaecologist and a rugby full-back? She had had enough, and spun over, raising her knees away from him.

Knapp, fully nude now, paused and instantly knew that he would find it hard to get started again from this break in the onrush of his lust. Staring down at Laura's fair-skinned body, he boomed, 'My God you're the most beautiful creature I've ever seen.'

The word 'creature' did it, although the whole statement sounded trite. But worse was Knapp's appearance. His eyes were bulbous and dilated, his cheeks above the beard were engorged by a purple flush, and his chest heaved in a staccato sequence of gasping breaths. Laura found this episode freaky enough without him cardiac-arresting on her. And she was tired of being on a slab, elegant though the luxurious bed was.

She murmured, 'Come and lie down with me.' Among other things there was the small matter of the climax, how, when and where. Best not left to Godfrey's unbridled passion.

Knapp stretched himself out alongside her. His face was a caricature mask of male carnality, avid, trance-like, devoid of humour or warmth. His hands went to her tits again, then massaged hungrily between her thighs. But the strained breathing became calm and his body relaxed as the pulse stabilised. Even his hands became, if not gentle, at least less frantic. But also, starved by the tired circulatory system, his penis, obviously and humiliatingly and rapidly, wilted. Laura felt it shrivel into comfortable softness against her thigh.

Knapp's eyes closed, in a moment's rest, blurring into shame. Laura felt chilled. She didn't hate him, indeed on one level she still found him fascinating, and although she was disappointed by his commonplace approach to the female body, she had no wish to see him like this, fat and impotent and ludicrous.

She pretended it hadn't happened, and tried to revive him. But nothing came from her except technique, no vibes, no pheromones, her lips did not part or her body ooze for him, and Knapp knew it.

Masterful to the end, he decided to call quits. He kissed her on both cheeks, and some trace of gentleman reasserted itself in him as he retrieved the discarded clothing from the floor and handed it to her.

'I offer no excuse,' he said gruffly, and staggered slightly as he left the room.

Laura weakly said, 'Godfrey –' But he had already gone, a roll of fat shaking above his hips as he walked. He had left his robe on the floor, and Laura realised that he was giving her privacy in which to dress. She got into her clothes, then began smoothing the bed, and it was suddenly furtive, a stolen interval in somebody else's room.

Knapp returned, dressed. His face was dignified, stony, but a disturbed redness still discoloured the skin, and his eyes were dilated and anxious. Still, breeding shone through, and he was so determined not to make Laura feel bad that his own failure was stoically ignored.

Laura insisted on hugging him before she got into her car. Knapp accepted the embrace for a moment, then firmly separated himself from her.

His voice was sepulchral, almost tremulous. 'Whoever you love,' he said, 'if such a person exists, he or she is very lucky.'

Laura smiled. This was the Godfrey she would always like. It was an odd thought, but he would be great on his deathbed. 'Can I call you tomorrow?'

'I'll be away for a couple of days. Let me ring you. I know what you want, and I'll come up with something.'

He stood there dutifully as she moved the car out, too delicate to offer thanks or self-justification, grimly isolated in his own flopped performance.

Laura felt sorry for him. A few miles along the road she almost turned back. A bit further on she thought how dreary the male ego was, and Godfrey Knapp had probably had that coming for a long time. But she knew he would keep his word and help her. Sexually the incident had not touched her. She wished it had.

Chapter Seventeen

Before Knapp got in touch again, Sarah had come to Macemoor and met the man behind the voice on the tape.

'If everything you say is right,' she told Ray, 'and we can make it stick, what do you want?'

His face said, this is obvious. 'Money.'

'I can't guarantee that anybody will buy your story.'

'Find somebody that will.'

'The situation you're in, I don't think they're the sort of people you want to know right now.'

Ray glanced at Laura, who reacted with a noncommittal gesture. They had sat there a long time, eventually joined by Martin, while Ray answered whatever Sarah put to him. At the end of it she was convinced. But the tough questions still lay ahead.

'You don't deny killing this man?'

'I told you, he was going to kill me.'

'You killed him in a wood. Surely you could have escaped?'

'It wasn't like that. I'm not a murderer.'

'How *would* you describe yourself?'

Ray flexed his thin, hard body inside his shirt. Not that he disliked the pert, smooth journalist, he felt nothing for her one way or the other. But facing someone else who held all the cards made the hairs on his neck rise.

'There are a lot of people like me. Just like there are a lot of people like you. It's just the labels don't come so easy.'

A faint smile touched Sarah's glossed lips. She always respected an ability to put the boot in. She tapped a pen on her neat, white teeth, then bit it.

'I've got to get you to London.'

Ray looked to Laura again. She nodded her head.

Sarah continued, 'I might be able to put some money together, but don't count on much. If you stay here I'd say you were dead. All of you.'

She looked at Martin, who all this time had said nothing. 'Don't you agree?'

It surprised her, but Martin said, 'Totally.' He thought for a moment. 'This story has to come out. I no longer care what personal risk it entails for me.'

Sarah looked from Martin to Laura and Ray. She guessed they had all talked this over. Nobody seemed fazed by anything. And she found herself drawn to Ray in one respect. The mercenary and the journalist were close, in their mentality, the forces that drove them. And in the way she handled this story, she would be giving her answer to the question, what is journalism about? In the end it had to be about more than just packaging 'the news', selling people things they already knew.

'OK,' she said. 'Let me make a couple of phone calls. Then I suggest we get the hell out of here. If they're not watching you now, they'll surely be back soon.'

'I'll go with her,' Ray said, indicating Laura.

Sarah promptly nodded agreement. Laura looked to Martin, who smiled and said, 'Yes, you have to go.'

They drove separately, Ray travelling with Laura in the Dyane. The arrangement was that he would stay in Sarah's flat. Laura delivered him there. 'The person living in my flat isn't in on all this, so Sarah's is the best place. If there's any trouble, just disappear and leave a message for me at this number. Otherwise I'll be in touch in the morning.'

Laura then crossed half a mile of Clapham to her own flat. From there she rang Martin.

'You've been very good about everything. Thanks.'

'I've learnt a lot from you.' He said it with warmth, not ironically. 'I hope Sarah can make something of this. Come back to me soon.'

Laura sighed gently at the receiver. She had an impulse to say 'I love you' to him, but it was the wrong moment. At the other end Martin was having the same experience. All they could give each other was a sweet silence. And somehow they both knew that was how it was.

Alone again, Martin drove out to Saltmayne and walked for miles along the cliffs, above the gigantic scree of limestone spoil which convict labourers had once tipped from the now exhausted quarries. The sea wind was cruel and at the same time exhilarating.

He loved this place. He loved this landscape perhaps more than he could ever love another human being. If that denoted some deep flaw in his psyche, he at least no longer felt guilty about it. As fifty approached he could accept such a fact about himself as a badge of humanity.

For that matter, it was only humans that loved country. For the creatures that lived here, it was a place to breed and eat, the backdrop to a short life in which the smallest waning in health made them food for others. He could love it because he was not at the mercy of it, and for all the creation that rose to life and swiftly re-entered eternal death on the face of these rocks, he had to love it.

Martin returned to the spot on the clifftop from which, earlier in the year, he had watched a peregrine kill and a nuclear submarine slip undersea, while he spent, as he thought, his last day alone here. He contemplated the way the year had worked out. He knew he was losing Laura. He was now even going along with the process. Apart from the intrusion of Ray into their lives, the Faulston incident and the changes in the world around them that now threatened to follow from that, he could admit that Laura's move here had been far more experimental than either of them thought at the time.

They had both needed to recharge their lives, revisit that part of their youth which time had not allowed them to forget. But ultimately they both had lives they did not wish to abandon, and now the pull was back to the way they had lived before. The attractions of living together – the abolition of loneliness, the sex, the sharing of thoughts – had their negative side for people who were both loners in their way, insistent on their right to be exhausted or uncommunicative, to withdraw into their respective privacies. And they respected this in each other, even while suffering from its consequences.

As Martin saw it now, they would live apart and see each other intermittently. Laura had never mentioned this, but he felt her moving towards such a break. He knew he could live with it. Maybe he was hardening himself in anticipation, but he was sure it was only a matter of time before Laura moved back to London. Then, he felt, paradoxically they would be more in touch than they were now. They were both people who needed distance in order to love. And he loved her more than ever, with the humbling, terrifying love that goes with not possessing.

'You can sleep in here. The door locks. Perhaps you'd like to go over the flat?'

Dourly, with no show of gratitude, Ray went through the rooms of what was a converted floor of an old house, two bedrooms, living-room, small kitchen, and an unusual triangular bathroom that had been carved out of the over-spacious landing. Sarah followed him, enjoying the *frisson* of watching the hunted animal at close quarters, studying him as he plotted his own survival.

She kept thinking, I have to get some of this down. Her hands itched for the word-processor, but she was not yet ready to shape the words. Instead she took her pocket recorder into the bathroom, pulled the seat cover down, and for ten minutes whispered into the hand-size machine, unloading random details of memory for eventual write-up.

Although she had not used it, she flushed the toilet as a precaution. But as she opened the door Ray was barring her way. She tensed, suddenly fearing a rape. His hands came at her, quickly brushing down her body. But he was clearly not interested in her flesh. He found the pocket with the recorder and ripped it out.

Ray's eyes were long and almost lidless, grey with small pupils that emitted hostility. These eyes fixed Sarah while he rewound the tape, then snapped it into play, and continued to fix her while she was forced to listen to her disjointed, breathless words. She was embarrassed at how naïve they sounded, and at being caught.

'You fucking stupid cow,' he said. 'Rub it off. And don't do that again.'

While she wiped the tape blank on Record, Sarah began to explain, but Ray pointed to the machine and shook his head. She shrugged and sat down, waiting. She lit a rare cigarette, one of the half dozen a week she allowed herself. She looked sideways at Ray with a cynical respect.

He had been listening at the bathroom door. It was funny, really, her sitting on the can whispering into a tape about him, him the other side listening for what she was doing in there. They were two of a kind, really, that was why he would never trust her. He had turned to Laura and Martin because they would never behave like him. But he would never trust her. Sarah almost liked the feeling.

'I think it's finished,' she said. He was taut, not sure whether to let go of his temper and teach her a lesson. Sarah added, 'It's all right, I won't do it any more. I think we're going to get on. Gin, Scotch or vodka?'

Dorothy's handwriting was an unusual sight, especially on a letter. It couldn't be anything good. With a scowl of resentment Knapp put one of the last Beethoven quartets on the quadraphonic hi-fi before knifing open the envelope.

                                        Quoins
                                        Chindale Magna
                                        Uppingham
                                        Leics

My dear Godfrey,

You will shortly be hearing from Clark and Northover, but I wanted to write to you myself rather than leave the whole matter to lawyers.

No doubt you have noticed that my absences from Scardale have been growing longer. I am sure that this never disturbed your life there. I never felt at home there, and you did little to help me in this respect. I know you hate me for many things, but I will never forgive you for the contempt with which you have treated me. I know I was never the woman you wanted, but did you need to punish me so vindictively for it?

The song of thanksgiving of a sick man to his creator shaded unheard into a passage of that unearthly dance music which at better moments Knapp relished as the high point of late Beethoven. But the mental echo of the words in front of him jammed out all other sound.

We have no child, and I am not content to think that I might die and leave all I have to you. I know how much Scardale has meant in your family, but at this stage in my life I feel no abiding personal connection with the place, and I have not regarded it as my home for some time. I wish to live out the rest of my life near members of my family whom you have treated, if that were possible, with more indifference than you have me.

Clark and Northover will be writing to you in pursuance of divorce proceedings. I should tell you that they have evidence of several adulteries committed by you during the last few years, and I have instructed them to act on this evidence without delay. They have also drawn up a proposed financial settlement. I realise that this means that Scardale will probably leave your family, but I no longer regard this as my responsibility. All correspondence between us should now be through the solicitors. Good-bye, Godfrey.

 Yours,

 Dorothy

The needle clicked quietly, every other second, in the dead groove at the end of the record. Knapp was deaf to it, lost in a sudden polar night of hate and confusion. The room seemed to be drifting away from him like a shattering ice-pack. The letter lay stiffly, frozen, in his hand.

When Sarah played back her answering machine, although she had only been away a day, there were a number of dead calls, five in fact, people who had listened to the message, waited for the tone, then hung up. It seemed a lot. Friends were used to it by now, and other people who wanted to talk to a journalist were not usually shy to leave their numbers. Somebody had called repeatedly but not wanted to leave a message. Why?

During the night she planned how she would move the next morning. In the small spare room, the door locked, Ray passed his usual night of sleeping no more than two hours at a stretch, waking fully and checking everything around him before settling down again for another spell of instant shallow unconsciousness.

He was up early, ate, washed, shaved, and packed everything into the one nylon bag he had brought with him. There must be no trace of his presence in the flat. Sarah Keeling had not yet emerged from her room. He fancied her, smart women were his scene when he was loaded, but not now.

The doorbell rang, from street level. Ray moved back into his room and locked the door. He listened as Sarah hurried out to answer the doorphone. He heard her reluctantly let someone in.

Harry Teal's eyes were underlined by crescents of tired, puffy flesh, but otherwise he looked plump and healthy, although a sour lack of humour increasingly curved his shapeless mouth downwards. He wore a brown showerproof overcoat, which he did not remove as Sarah, still in her robe, grudgingly invited him to sit down.

'It seems like a long time since I was here before,' Teal said. 'Actually, it's only –'

Sarah looked at her watch and said, 'Skip the small talk.'

Teal drew a ponderous breath. 'I admired your articles about the impact of nuclear power on people's lives.'

Sarah said, 'I bet.'

'And I believe you're going back to do a follow-up on what happened at Faulston.'

'So?'

'You could help me.'

'No chance.'

'I could help you.'

'Highly unlikely.'

Teal pressed on. 'We're both in positions of, let's say, public responsibility. Especially with these new laws that are coming in, security's going to be a minefield. We'll all need help to find our way through it.'

Sarah wished he would stop snatching glances at bits of tit or leg that her nightclothes failed to cover. She said, 'I thought you were the people who write the law.'

'It's a straight offer,' Teal said. 'Work for me. A lot of journalists act as eyes and ears for us. The pay-offs are considerable. You don't have to sign the Act or anything, it stays unofficial. You feed me, and I feed you.'

'You're running me,' Sarah said. 'That's the word, isn't it?'

'We're not talking about spy stories,' Teal said. 'We're talking about a job of work. There's one thing in particular –'

His words died on the air. Their heads swung in the same direction, towards the noise that had come from outside. The living-room window looked over the front, towards the common. The crashing of dustbins and the shouting had come from the rear of the house.

Teal jumped up and threw himself at the one door which

led that way. It was locked. The force of his action bounced him back. He kicked the door and started rattling the knob.

Sarah ran into her own bedroom. Already she was re-iterating, silent through clenched teeth, the words 'Oh fuck!' over and over. Panic gripped her stomach. She rushed to the window.

In a space in one of the long, densely cultivated gardens, a man was rolling on the ground, clutching his lower body, either the belly or groin. It was not Ray, there was no sign of Ray.

Sarah filled out the picture for herself. Before he had turned in the night before, he had told her not to worry if she heard a noise, he would be trying the wall. 'Trying the wall' meant scaling from his bedroom via window-ledges and a fat cast-iron waste-pipe to the ground. She guessed that was what he had done now, taking no chances on who Teal was or who he might have brought with him.

Teal was beside her now, shoving her aside and craning his thick pink neck for a better view. His hand reached for the latch, but the double glazing seemed to defeat him. He was furious, and seemed to feel foolish on top of it.

He demanded, 'Why is that door locked?'

Sarah's brains never failed her when she needed them. 'I always lock all the doors when I go out. I must have left it locked last night.' She added sweetly, 'It's the spare room.'

'Unlock it now.'

'Get stuffed.'

Teal's lips twitched inarticulate threats.

'How do you explain that?'

Sarah ignored him and opened the window. She called down to the elderly man, who was dragging himself to his feet, 'Are you all right?'

'Bloody burglar,' the man called back hoarsely. 'Tried to stop him.' He shook his head sadly and brushed at his clothes.

Sarah looked into Teal's contorted face and said, 'You see?'

Chapter Eighteen

The woman had put together £100, which Ray kept zipped into the lining of his jacket, the opposite side from the automatic which he still carried over his heart. He had brought all his things away from Sarah Keeling's flat in the nylon bag which soon after his escape he got rid of by leaving it in the public area of Waterloo Station. They would put it on a left luggage shelf, and it could stay there indefinitely. Nothing in it could identify him. He had left no sign of occupancy in the room.

Only the gun in his pocket linked him to Pilkington, and he would junk the gun when he felt safe enough. That would not be yet. He had jumped the house because a night's reflection had sharpened up his idea of where he wanted to go now. That, and the dialogue he had overheard this morning, which made this yuppie hiding place suddenly much too crowded.

He could live on the streets for a while. The weather was against him, but the season was over and people were already going with their heads down, bad-tempered and hunched against the gritty bleakness of another London winter. Nobody wanted to look too close at human flotsam on the street. There was too much of it, human garbage staking out public places, pathetic and sometimes menacing. People lowered their faces from it and hurried on their way.

Out on the cliffs it had been different. Ray had lived like a hunted animal without benefit of natural camouflage. To blend in here it was only necessary to resemble trash. At nights the street people wrapped themselves up in paper and cardboard, even sometimes insulated themselves with rubbish sacks or crowded the pavements near warm cellar-vents. That was the way to hide in the big city, to become garbage. Then nobody wanted to look.

For a day, maybe two, he would feel things out, then call the number Laura had given him. She was a nice woman, a little woolly in the head, and she would do what he wanted. The Keeling chick he would steer away from, she was bad news. It was ironic, because it was mainly staying in her flat that had made up his mind.

Sarah Keeling was the type of smooth, sharp tart Ray liked. On the Costa del Sol you could get them with big brown tits, women who when you asked them to fuck would grab your horn and slide it in for you. During the night, suddenly desperate for Keeling's bed, he had nearly snapped. And she would love it, he suspected, especially if he went to her with a knife in one hand. But he had heard the bolt click on her door, and anyway coolness and fear combined to pull him out of it. So instead he masturbated, for the first time in nearly a month. The stiffened Kleenex was still in the bag on Waterloo Station. With that flushing out of physical tension, he suddenly knew exactly what he was going to do from here on.

He would try it on Keeling when she woke up. He was no longer interested in playing along with these people and their social consciences. What really happened at Faulston he no longer gave a fuck about. Those poor – no, stupid – bastards they had shot down, they were not mates of his, he never even knew their real names. And after he had slipped away, putting them under threat, he knew they would gladly have kicked him to a pulp given the chance. But then you weren't in these things to win friends.

So Faulston was a carve-up. He had guessed right. The wider implications didn't bother him. For Ray, aka Peter English, alias a few other names too, the only complicated thing in the world was *him*. Everything else had to be kept very simple indeed. Laura and her nature-lover friend had done very well by him, but in return they wanted him to spill beans, which for reasons of his own he had been willing to do. Now, equally for reasons of his own, he had changed his mind.

Being with Sarah Keeling had done that for him. She was the works, the real thing. Ray could feel from the start how she was going to take him over and truss him up for the media to roast alive. She couldn't go for a piss without gabbing into a cassette about him. And in the end, if her career was at stake, she would throw him to whichever wolves were nearest. All that was fair enough. But her aura of style, the chic apartment and the fashionable clothes, made him long for the sun again, for all those tanned people on the make, the neat sportswear, the stink of patchouli, the adrenalin-soaked company of the ruthless.

And that was it. Goodbye, folks. If it killed him, he would get back there. That was the only thought that kept him going now. The number Laura gave didn't answer. It wasn't her home any more, maybe she had written it down wrong.

So he kept on the move, snatching sleep by day as much as by night, resting up in greasy burger bars and the sort of urban-decay rubbish places where nobody asked questions. Then he let the streets swallow him again, not even staying in one district long in case some eagle-eyed bastard took too long a look at him. He hated this bloody city, hated it more every time he came to it. He liked to see the big money swan around and flaunt itself in the sun, not buttoned-up and tight-arsed like it was here. Uptight people clinging to their uptight lives, and everywhere the floating scum of human failures, while the buildings ran with grime and the streets had all the charm of open sewers. They could nuke the fucking lot, for all he cared. Just let him get out of it first.

Sarah turned to Harry Teal and said, 'Would you mind getting out of my bedroom?'

Teal's face, all clenched teeth and bulging eyes, looked

round in sudden awareness of where he was. The turned-back duvet, the underwear on the floor, Sarah Keeling in her flimsy robe, a woman he had done things with in masturbatory fantasies which he never had with any woman in real life, was all too much to take. Teal's nose picked up an acrid odour rising from his own armpits. Sarah watched him with an ease and detachment that bordered on malice, this soulless, cock-knotted authority figure.

'If you don't mind,' she repeated, and insisted on waiting for him to quit the room first.

Teal stalked out. The smell of her bedroom, the sense of untouchable intimacy, had destroyed his temper for the rest of the day.

'I'll be watching every move you make,' he said.

Sarah said, 'Fancy.'

Once he had gone she phoned Laura and told her nothing except to get over there as soon as she could. Laura was already dressed and arrived in ten minutes. From the shower Sarah called the bare details of what had happened, then made muesli and toast while they discussed what to do now.

Laura asked, 'Do you think this man Teal had you under surveillance all along?'

'No. I really don't think he realised Ray was in there.'

'Bloody hell.'

'Well, it's not totally a coincidence. He knows that if he follows me around he might find something interesting sometime.'

'Anyway –'

'Yes, anyway – what next? We may well have seen the last of our friend Ray.'

Laura frowned. 'You think so?'

'I think he'll try to make it on his own. Face it, what are we offering him? He doesn't trust me, he now knows I'm liable to bring the bloodhounds on my heels, and you – I just have the feeling that he's a street cat who in the end can look after himself far better than by depending on us. He's not interested in helping us uncover a scandal in the world of nuclear power politics. He doesn't give a shit.'

'I'm not convinced of that,' Laura said.

'Well, I can hang around a couple of days, then I have to go back to Faulston and start writing copy. What about you?'

'I've just been handed my flat back. On a plate.'

'No.'

'Kate either wants to buy it or move and buy somewhere else. That was the deal we had. So I've done it.'

'Done what?'

'Told her I'm moving back. As soon as she raised the question, I didn't even have to think. I'd already made the decision. I just hadn't been forced to voice it.'

Sarah asked, 'Are you sure it's the right thing?' Glad herself, she wanted to appear cautious.

'No. But the only way I can go on seeing Martin is to stop living with him. Actually sharing a house got screwed up with too many other things. I'd always sworn to myself that I'd never again get into one of those situations with another person where we'd end up yelling at each other because we felt trapped. I guess I'm just not that afraid of being on my own.'

'It'd be nice to see you around dear old Clapham,' Sarah said. She hoped that one element in Laura's decision was herself. But it didn't show, and she knew better than to angle for an answer.

Laura laughed. 'I occasionally meet people I used to know. I tell them I've just been to the country for a bit. They assume I've had an abortion or a nervous breakdown.' She paused. 'There's one thing about falling in love at the age of forty – you tend not to let people know. It makes things a hell of a lot easier when you change your mind.'

Darling Martin,

It's not usually our style to write like that (the 'darling', that is), but I wanted to start this letter by saying right out what a lovely man you are. Before I get on to the heavy bits. Anyway, you are a very sweet man, always surprising in your range of feeling, and serious in the good way that makes me feel that my life is anchored in something worthwhile and not just a lot of froth.

When I came to live at the cottage I felt a strange certainty, a feeling that this was it for life, and I was happy with that. Now I'm not so sure. I don't ever want to say goodbye to you, and I think that in a peculiar way, living apart we'll be more together than ever. I don't want any aspect of our relationship to end, including the physical.

I don't know what changed things. I remember some of those early visits, the peace I found there, the visual excitement, the great satisfaction of your company. None of that has gone, and yet – it was like a long, gorgeous sunset, which I thought would be the background to the rest of my life. But night followed, and the dawn that followed the night was cold and sobering. It made me realise that nothing ever comes to an end, however much one wants to step back at a lovely moment and tell life – stop, that's it, I'm happy with that, let's leave it like that. It doesn't work. Life isn't a picture after all.

Ray wasn't the problem, he just focused things. The things that have happened since we met him have made me feel that the one time in my life when I'm faced with a matter of public concern, outrage, whatever, I don't want to just stand aside and pretend that I have more important things to do. Because what is happening around us is going to make all those important things look extremely trivial. Also, although I have been very scared at times, I don't want to give up because I'm scared. I want to see this through in whatever way I can.

I love you. However grim the face of things becomes, beneath all that I'll always love you. I'll be back at the cottage on Thursday, assuming you get this the day before, and we can talk then.

love, Laura

Dear Laura,

It seems cowardly to write this while you're away, but it's only since you've gone that I've understood clearly what I have to say. I still haven't worked out how to say it, of course. But I'll try.

I realise that things are never going to be the same between us, and when I ask, the same as what, I see how ridiculous the idea of things staying the same is. I used to think that life was a line, a series of blocks through which one passed in linear progression. Now I believe that life is a spiral, an infinity of intersecting spirals, and nothing is ever over.

I realise that I had much of my old age when I was a child, and this year, for instance, I have lived out part of my youth. I understand now the importance of the night when I dreamed about you and woke believing it real. It has been a difficult and turbulent year for me, and I suppose youth is like that whether one experiences it at sixteen or fifty-six or whenever.

Sorry to ramble. I accept that we may not live together all the time from now on. I don't know how we'll work it out in a practical sense, but I wanted to say that I don't regard this as negative. I feel about you as I always did, even in the many years when we had lost track of each other's existence, as someone who I would never not care about and, sooner or later, would need to be with again.

And one day again, will be.

love, Martin

Kate, the woman who was renting Laura's flat, had just left the scribbled note by the phone. It said, Ray, 23 Lansbury Buildings, Marigold Street, SE5, 4 p.m. today.

Laura checked the map book. There were hours yet. After thinking things out for a while, she phoned Scardale. Harold, doleful, effeminate, precise, informed her that Mr Knapp was staying at his London apartment for the moment. Laura rang the Brompton number several times but got no answer. Then she drove from Clapham through Stockwell, the map book open on the passenger seat.

A grey, drab day, pre-menstrual and downcast after her latest talk with Sarah. The story won't sell, Sarah said, but she was cagey about what she had told potential buyers. Laura had no choice but show tactful respect for whatever Sarah said, but Sarah was a careerist, and in the end career would win through. Maybe Ray wasn't worth the risk. All Sarah could offer was to make more tapes, any other testimony he could give, with no promise when or how it might be used. And, neither of them added, if.

This uninspiring proposal was all Laura took with her to the address. Marigold Street was not clearly signposted, and part of it had been demolished, leaving bits of waste areas fenced off by steel netting with guard-dog signs. Lansbury Buildings made no particular impression on the street until she came alongside it, when it could be nothing else.

She drove in through a crumbling brick gateway. The courtyard of barely grassed mud and fractured concrete was littered with urban scrap, a burnt-out car stripped of its wheels, a smashed-up pram, two supermarket trolleys, a lot of broken glass and domestic rubbish. Lansbury Buildings itself was a curved three-storey block like a giant brick sofa. Deck-access balconies ran along its front, its iron-framed windows were mean and dark, sightless under the awnings of the gaunt walkways.

Laura swung the Dyane round and drove away. It was 3.50. She parked in a quiet residential street where the other cars looked like reasonable company, and walked the few hundred yards back to the address Ray had left.

She entered the courtyard again. Two black teenagers and one white were kicking something around the rubbish-littered concrete. It was a chicken, white and flabby in its plastic shroud. They halted for a moment and looked at her, and one made a just inaudible remark at which all three laughed. Then they started booting the chicken again. Laura's skin prickled, and she concentrated on the numbers of the flats. Many of them were boarded up, and the whole hulk of Lansbury Buildings gave off the degraded look and rotting smell of deferred demolition.

As she looked at ground-floor numbers to get a bearing, movement to one side made her turn. Laura saw Ray in the shadowed entry of a flat whose window was shuttered with corrugated iron. He beckoned her. Laura went across, looking round instinctively as the furtive atmosphere got to her.

Ray had no access to the flat, he was just waiting in the shelter, stinking of decayed masonry and human waste, of an abandoned entry.

Laura said, 'This isn't 23.'

Ray shook his head briefly, and she realised, no, of course, the 23 was just to get her there, he would never be exactly where he said. She ought to know the pattern by now.

'What happened?'

His forehead was badly bruised, above and below the scalp line, and the dried blood had not been completely washed off.

Ray shrugged. 'Somebody got silly. Thought I had something worth stealing.' While he talked to Laura his eyes constantly roved the wasteland behind her.

Laura said, 'I heard what happened at Sarah's.'

'Did you know they were tagging her place?'

His voice was gentle but bleak, and his eyes said he owed nobody anything.

'Well –' Laura said, and the moment's opportunity to lie escaped her. 'We didn't realise it was still –'

Ray dismissed her confusion. 'It's OK.'

He looked at this slim, blonde woman, her neat straight hair, her handsome bone structure and nice skin, beginning to show fine lines around the eyes and mouth. She was not his type, and from one point of view she was an idiot. Still, he had to remind himself that it was dangerous to like her. Even if she was all he had.

The gritty wind pinched their faces, Laura's pale and patient, Ray's unshaven and damaged, sharp with a street hostility she had not seen in it before.

'Forget this Keeling woman,' he said, compressing the words into a single bullet of sound.

'Her name's Sarah.'

'OK. Forget Sarah.'

'Why?'

'She's bad news. She'll use me. She might even shop me.'

Laura was shaking her head urgently.

'She's the only hope we've got. If we want to get your story out.'

Ray's eyes said, come on, let's stop joking.

'You don't want to?' she asked.

Gently, reasonably, Ray said, 'Somebody's going to kill me first. I don't want to die for somebody's good cause.'

Laura was irritated, and vaguely hurt. 'Why did you bring me out here? To tell me that?'

'You're the only person that can help me.'

'Why should I?'

'Because if you keep me alive there's always the chance the story might come out. But if I stay in this country I'm dead. You see what those kids are kicking around over there? That's me.'

After a long moment Laura said, 'All right.'

Chapter Nineteen

Godfrey Knapp returned on foot to The Boltons from his solicitor's office off Cadogan Square. The trees were shrugging off the last of their wizened leaves, and a glossy film of damp emphasised the dirt of the pavements. Knapp chose to walk because for the moment the prospect of human company, even that of a taxi driver, nauseated him. Over his chalk-stripe suit he wore a camel-hair coat, and on his head a suede hat with astrakhan trim. The usual cigar jutted from his full, angry mouth. People automatically stepped aside for him on the pavement. Knapp had never seriously contemplated the alternative, and maybe they realised.

The solicitors had only confirmed what he knew. The divorce case was watertight, airtight, tight as a gnat's anus. With a contemptuous stare Knapp had refused any suggestion of trying to discredit the adultery evidence. He did not even wish to know which of the many women he had laid over the years had been cited, or how much they had been paid for the work. Or, indeed, how long Dorothy had been hoarding that evidence against the day when it would suit her to use it. He shat on all that, it was beneath him. The one thing that could never wound Godfrey Knapp was human action, because he had long since learnt there was no bottom to its squalor.

But unless he could raise the money, in effect buy Dorothy out, Scardale would have to go. And he could not raise hundreds of thousands of pounds. Scardale would pass from his family, pass from his life. His world would shrink to the Brompton apartment and winters on the Riviera, the empty padded idleness of so many of the scrofulous old bastards he himself had always derided. He would never be able to go within a hundred miles of Scardale again, and everybody would know.

The irony was that with the disposal of Scardale he would become a very rich man. The expenses of the estate would cease to drain his funds, and with the right buyers – Arabs, or an entrepreneur who would timeshare the place (although this thought made him heave) or milk its hunting, fishing and leisure potential – Knapp would acquire a great deal of liquid wealth to play with, even after Dorothy was settled. He had good tax lawyers, and financially the future did not disturb him. But the soul was about to go out of his life.

The session with Laura rankled, eating away at his self-image. He had fallen in love, and in consequence the grisly milestone of sixty seemed a piddling zero. But he had achieved the freedom of her naked body only to find himself unable to rise to it. As soon as he arrived in London he called a Knightsbridge service he sometimes used, and in a brutal half hour for which he paid generously he restored his confidence in his own carnal powers.

But it was Laura that he had failed with, and still Laura that he wanted. A morose fearfulness was overtaking him. He wondered, on another level, once it became common knowledge that Dorothy was twisting the knife in him, how many more enemies would creep out of the woodwork.

As if to confirm the accuracy of his presentiments, ten minutes after Knapp got back to his flat the phone rang, and a quiet well-bred voice asked if he was free to talk.

Knapp frowned, trying to identify the voice. He gruffly demanded, 'Talk about what?'

'It's Charles Hayes-Langham, Godfrey.'

'Charles! My dear chap, I didn't spot you. Are you in town?'

Hayes-Langham was a business colleague, a man Knapp

shared a couple of boards with. Outside boardrooms they rarely met. Silently Knapp wondered what the old pimp wanted. Money? Lunch? He'd already heard about Dorothy and wanted to sound him out about Scardale . . .

'I just wanted a private word, Godfrey. A tip-off, you might say. Ah –'

Knapp rattled his index finger on the ear-piece of the receiver. He was not in the mood for insider dealing, if that was what it was.

'Someone's been asking questions.'

Knapp growled, 'Questions?'

'Yes. Asking me questions. About you. And not only me. A mutual friend of ours has also been visited.'

'Concerning what?'

'Various activities of yours. Over quite a long period. I told them nothing, of course, I know nothing –'

'Who were these people?'

'Let's just say they didn't identify themselves.'

'You mean I'm being investigated.'

First the investigation, then the smear. Nothing you could put your finger on or refute. Then just let the dry rot spread, and another life putrefies out of the public view.

'I thought you ought to be forewarned, old boy.'

'Charles, many thanks. I owe you.'

'Not at all, old boy. Do the same for me when my turn comes.'

Knapp hung up. An intense loneliness enveloped him. So this was how they would come at him. Later, he questioned the incentive behind the call. Not friendship, that was for sure.

A few weeks earlier Knapp had run into an old friend in St James's Square, and maybe it had been an omen or, as it now seemed, a stroke of luck. His name was Rex Appleton, and although he never disclosed what he did, Knapp knew perfectly well. His external resemblance to a downtrodden city gent – the masochistic humour, the crumpled suit and cropped unassertive moustache – was so pronounced as to conceal totally the fact that the parallel ended there. They had been at school together, where Appleton's nickname had been Steamer, referring to his ability to fart silently and at will during lessons. Their acquaintance had been renewed during Knapp's intelligence-farming days in the Middle East, and at the end of this brief meeting in St James's Appleton had told him the wine bar where he could always be contacted.

Knapp checked the address and number, called and without giving his name said he would meet Appleton there at six that evening. The discreet voice at the other end said that seven was more usual. Seven then, Knapp answered, that was fine. The place was called Grappa, all chianti bottles in baskets and a modest frontage that made it look as if a party of four would crowd it out. Just off Curzon Street, Knapp recognised it as the kind of middle-bracket place where operatives of different branches of Five would assemble. Even the ones whose headquarters were south of the river would come back here for the class, the aura, the connections.

Appleton was already there, a rodent-like figure in a well-worn striped suit, with thinning grey hair, pop-eyes in a chubby pink face, and a ginger moustache trimmed till it was no more than stubble. As Knapp entered the bar heads turned at his large, baroque presence, and Appleton leapt up with boyish eagerness in an act of surprise mirrored by Knapp's own startled greeting.

'Godfrey, old man – a drink, a drink. This is tremendous. What'll you have?'

Godfrey had a dry martini, and Appleton, as if to say why didn't I think of that, also had a dry martini. They chatted for a few minutes so that Appleton could positively link Knapp to the anonymous phone message. The one convention they had to observe was to betray no knowledge of who Appleton actually was. In fact Knapp did not know who he was, not any more. But he was in the organisation somewhere, and useful? Knapp would soon find out.

241

'Remember Beirut, eh? That nightclub, what was it called? Where that woman went round picking up coins with her quim. And old Eggy French heated up a dollar with his fag lighter under the table, and put it down for her to spread herself over. Boy oh boy, what a scream!' Appleton laughed himself an unhealthy mauve and wiped the threads of perspiration from his gleaming cheeks, gasped and laughed some more, then grew reflective and said, 'Dear old England – what's happened to her?'

Knapp's polite chuckle also terminated efficiently, and he remarked the speed at which Appleton was putting away his martini, a sign that they would not be staying. Minutes later Appleton collected his coat and bowler hat, and they stepped out into the cold evening. Keeping to neutral ground, with mutual assurances that neither of them had pocket recorders running, they headed at Appleton's suggestion for the park. Knapp proffered his crocodile cigar case, and they both puffed at the fine Jamaica tobacco as they walked along.

'It's simple enough,' Knapp said. 'Somebody's up my arsehole, and I don't like it. You know a character called Harry Teal?'

'Vaguely familiar, old son. The odd meeting in the line of work. Why?'

'I have an idea he's something to do with it. What I need to know is, why am I under investigation, and what do I have to do to kill it? Because my affairs in the near future are going to be complex, and I don't want some bright bleeder using my bones as his career ladder.'

Walking faster to keep up with Knapp's long strides, Appleton said, 'You don't have any idea what it's about, old boy?'

'I have a suspicion. But I don't want to prejudice things. I also know how to clear myself, and I have a very attractive bit of trade to offer. With one stipulation. The aforesaid Mr Teal gets nothing out of all this, except maybe a kick in the nuts.'

Appleton was bright-eyed and eager. 'Can you leave it with me, old boy?'

'Only for twenty-four hours. Otherwise the trade I'm able to make may slip out of my grasp.'

'Willco, old son, if at all possible.'

They arranged their next contact, then went their separate ways through the twinkling Mayfair night, Knapp to an informal dinner engagement, Appleton back to the office.

The room in which Appleton switched on an adjustable desk lamp, blinking thoughtfully at the pool of light which appeared on the veneered surface in front of him, reflected impeccably that peculiar British mix of humanity and sadism which says that power, at least in public, should adopt a dowdy, even mediocre, front. It could have been the room of a local government clerk or a junior tax inspector. It needed redecorating, it always had, it always would. It was a room unburdened with any style. Power had no need of fashion.

Appleton dialled a number and after the bleep spoke into the recording machine at the other end. His fussy voice articulated the words precisely.

'Reference Dark Lady. Am in possession of data of great import. Require approval to act. Must expedite for quick kill. Will wait on this extension. 531. Appleton.'

He leaned back in the not very comfortable swivel chair and relit the cigar Knapp had given him. The duty officer would patch through the message to whoever needed to hear it most. And Appleton would be ordered halfway across London for a powwow, in a chauffeured car more than likely, with a big cheese in a penguin suit. But by midnight he would have what he wanted.

It was the ultimate ploy, to go to a man and set things up in such a way that he thought he had come to you. Beautiful, in a modest sort of way. Fishy sort of character, Knapp, but a chap who would never give you a bad cigar. That was one thing about people like old Godfrey – not over-endowed with life's more foxlike qualities, but decent to the core.

Knapp was gambling, and he knew it. Beneath his dinner-party geniality a dark current ran through his mind the whole evening. His back was to the wall, and in that position the only ethic was his own survival.

In the world he moved in he could not afford to be a laughing-stock, or – even by the flimsiest of associations – a traitor, not even suspected of being a dishonourable man. Once you were tainted like that, people began to drop you, doors closed, your name vanished from conversation. He had seen it happen to others. Shit, he had done it himself. It was the law. And if he had to taste blood in order to survive, well, one man's blood was much like another's. He had no debts, and a man without debts could choose his own loyalties.

When he arrived back at The Boltons around midnight, Knapp flicked his answering machine and found a message from Laura. She had to see him, it was urgent, she would come however late or early, could he ring her? It was a London number. Just to hear her voice again he reran the tape several times, then went to the phone, settled in the adjacent armchair, and tapped in the code.

Laura crossed the river by Battersea Bridge. She parked in the courtyard of Knapp's building, announced herself and waited for him to release the house door.

A few uneasy minutes passed while Knapp served some mulled wine and they discussed his recipe for the mull with a pretence of interest. It was nearly one in the morning, but they were both stone-cold awake in a way the wine would never touch.

Finally Knapp asked, 'How do I pay my debt?'

'Don't put it like that, Godfrey,' Laura said. 'You must be following the news. You know what's going to happen to this country.'

Knapp said, 'Apart from Scardale, I have never felt particularly English. As for British' – he gave a deep cynical laugh – 'a word employed by the English to insult the conquered Gaelic peoples. *Sind Sie ein guter Deutscher?* And Scardale, as a matter of fact, was always to me an enclosed terrain, not a part of some other land mass, but a country in itself.'

Laura said, 'At least you're not one of those people that use patriotism as an excuse for power and greed.'

They were both, at that moment, thinking of Harry Teal. Neither had any idea what was in the other's mind.

'That,' Knapp answered, 'I think you can safely say.' He inhaled the spiced breath of his wine. 'And now, the details of our business.'

It turned on a boat, and Knapp had a boat, a 25-foot speed launch which he kept moored in a marina beyond Saltmayne. It turned also on a landfall on the Spanish coast, and Knapp had himself taken the boat along the Mediterranean twice.

'It seems simple,' Laura said.

'Things always do in the end. Does he have papers?'

'He has contacts in – He can get false papers.'

'But that's not our concern.'

'No.'

'The schedule?'

'Nothing specific. Just soon.'

'I'll have to work on it.'

'He needs to get out of London.'

'I can hide him at Scardale.'

'So it's possible.'

'Oh yes,' Knapp said. 'It can be done.'

'This story has to come out in the open some time,' Laura said. 'And he's the key.' She was earnest, over-defensive, but she had to make this point constantly.

'I shall need three days,' Knapp said. 'You can bring him to Scardale then. Until that time – well, I suggest that whatever hiding-place he has now he continues to use.'

'I'll be in touch,' Laura said.

'Yes.'

Knapp had gone blank, tiredness or drink seeming to catch up with him. But in reality, now the business part of their meeting was over, his mind had reverted to their last encounter and the remorseless goad of its memory.

His lasting emotion, and he was damned if he was going to gloss it over, was rubbished pride, the galling memory of two bodies unable to satisfy each other. *'Comme au long d'un cadavre un cadavre étendu.'* Christ, how it galled.

Laura stood up. Knapp, gentleman and ladykiller, rose with her. She made a move, he moved. Towards the door. Yes, he thought, but I can't let it go like this, there are things people sometimes don't understand.

'The last time we met –' The voice downbeat, ponderous.

Laura smiled slightly, but it was hardly a smile. 'No, don't let's say anything about it.'

Knapp watched her, his eyes beady in their search for rejection or disgust, almost hoping to find it. Or even worse, a shrugging indifference, unforgivable.

'I can't leave it like that.'

'Godfrey –'

Laura's mind raced through the choices ahead of her. She had already paid her dues, he had no right to demand more. No good, appeals to integrity were never any use. She could treat him with revulsion – if that's your idea of a deal, forget it – and walk out. But she would never get past him, the choices weren't real.

Knapp already had the stertorous breathing of a strong man going out of control. His hands gripped her shoulders, wanting, maybe even needing, a struggle. His body pressed down on her while he mauled her like a blow-up dummy. He wanted her to be impressed. That was the trouble. For the first time Laura disliked him. He had no interest in the person inside her body, as long as she was impressed. But the dislike cleared her mind, made it easier to use him. As his hand grabbed one breast and his face came down towards her neck, Laura had an idea.

'Only if you wear a condom.'

She whispered it. Her voice was controlled and indicated an indifferent willingness. Knapp was staggered and tried to brutalise his way out.

'I don't use those bloody things.'

'Well I do.'

Knapp looked robbed. She had snatched the initiative away from him.

'You never insisted on it before.'

'I'd hate to get AIDS from you, Godfrey.'

It was a light, stinging remark. Knapp knew better than to show that he felt it. He said nothing, his hands slowly easing their grip on her shoulders. There was something Laura had not seen in him before, an unstable shadow somewhere within his eyes, and she suddenly feared that the evening might not even end with rape. But for the moment she had got him reacting to her, and she wanted to keep it that way.

She asked, 'Don't I have any rights with you any more?'

Knapp scowled. Laura had found that thin vein of sensitivity and honour inside his grossness. His deep voice was pompous but compliant. 'Of course.'

He released her and went to the bathroom. He had lied about the condoms. When you screwed the range of women he had over the last twenty years, condoms were the better part of valour.

The apartment was very warm, and the carpets and furniture had a clean, soft comfort in which nudity would not seem ridiculous, so while he was gone Laura stripped, folding her clothes carefully on an armchair.

Knapp wanted a bed beneath them. When they finally lay together Laura handled him like a doctor a patient. She needed to do very little to stimulate him. The main impulse was the desperate sexuality that made his breath rapid and short and his chest pound ominously. Knapp was so determined not to lose his erection this time that he wanted no delay. Laura rolled the condom on for him, manoeuvred herself on to it, sank her nails in his buttocks, and it was all over. Even the groan of his orgasm was brief, and as Knapp attempted to prolong it the sound resembled a cry of anguish, loaded with dissatisfaction.

With the same poise Laura slid herself off, and left Knapp to dispose of the limp rubber with its bulb of yellow ooze. She cleaned herself with a tissue, which she left on the Italian-tile coffee table, and got dressed.

As she was leaving, she said to Knapp, who had put on his gown and was already sinking into a pit of terrible loneliness, 'You will keep our bargain now, won't you, Godfrey?'

Knapp, grim, said, 'Naturally.'

'Because if you don't, somebody will come and kill you.'

They parted without a goodbye. Afterwards Laura thought what a stupid thing to say, silly and melodramatic. But it might have to come true.

Scraps of late autumn mist still drifted like dry ice in the hollows of Streatham Common. Godfrey Knapp paced an area in front of the big house where Appleton had indicated they meet. Imposing, blowing cigar smoke on the air, Knapp admitted to himself how little talent he had for the secret life, the finicky deviousness you had to use, the cultivation of paranoia as a trick of the trade.

But making a deal to save his arse, that was something else. Come on, you creepy little bugger – ah, there he was now, a small, round, beetling figure, Appleton, crawling across the common like a bug on a sheep turd. What a twisted little wreck he must be inside, Knapp thought, under the boyish humour. All these Intelligence people, the school sneaks, peaching on the dormitory wankers, peering under the bog doors . . .

'Morning, Rex, so glad you got back to me so quickly.'

Appleton's mobile face twitched amiably.

'Sorry to drag you out here, old boy. Safe places and all that. Taking a stroll, bumped into an old chum – In case anybody wants to know.'

They walked, Knapp diplomatically clipping his stride to match Appleton's short pigeon-toed steps.

'What's the form, then, Rex?'

The nervous eyes and the snout nose wrinkled up at Knapp.

'Bit dicey, old son. Somebody's opened a file on you. Do you really have no idea why?'

He was full of an anxious concern that was not worth its weight in toilet paper, as Knapp knew well, and was intended to know.

'Of course I bloody do, Rex. Let's stop pissing about. We go back too far for that. What was this fuck-up in Faulston all about? Some little escapade of C Branch, a trial run that went wrong and was intended to go wrong? Eh?'

Appleton looked round apprehensively and steered Knapp along a path which lay open to the acres of wet grass and the traffic noise from the main road.

'Better hush a bit, old son. You know how it is. 'Fraid I can't comment on organisational matters. You know the form. Always moving the furniture around. Don't know where half the stuff is myself now. Strictly *stumm*, all that.'

Knapp sniffed loudly. 'On my bloody doorstep too. So I get tarred with that brush, and now some cock-happy bastard from – what? – F3, something like that – is telling people not to know me any more.'

Appleton's eyebrows and forehead fought each other for wrinkles. He looked as pained and shifty as if Knapp had just flashed at him. Later Knapp would realise that trying to impress Appleton with his knowledge of departmental names – probably out of date now anyway – was a sign of insecurity. But by then it would be too late.

'Strictly *stumm*, old lad,' Appleton repeated.

'There's somebody they want, Rex. We've seen his face on the television screen.' Knapp wagged a finger at Appleton's chest. 'And I know why they want him.'

Appleton murmured, 'All very interesting.'

'Can you call the dogs off me?'

Appleton's gloved hands fidgeted with his hat and scarf.

'Tricky, old son.'

'You realise what I'm offering?'

'Question of evidence, Godfrey old boy. People upstairs don't like being made fools of.'

'Are you suggesting I'm inventing this?'

'Course not, old chap. Know you better than that.'

249

'He's all yours, Rex. Do your career no end of good.'

'Oh, never mind me, old boy. Just waiting for the pension. Growing roses in Surbiton, that'll do me.'

'I'd only want to make one condition.'

'Give it a shot, old chap.'

'This man Teal. I want it kept away from him. And I want a document from you detailing the service I'm performing. Something I can use.'

'Asking the earth, old lad. Putting things on paper. Tut tut.'

'I'm not working for promises.'

Silence, but they continued their circuit of the damp leaf-strewn paths for some time. Suddenly Appleton dropped his fussy old-maidish pose, clapped his suede-gloved hands together, and said, 'All right, Godfrey old boy. You've got your deal. This is what you do.'

Chapter Twenty

From the lake – '*lac de sang, hanté de mauvais anges*' – with its fringe of pine wood, Knapp stared at Scardale, and reflected that once this other business was over he would find a way of avenging himself on Dorothy for forcing him to sell the place. His eyes, still clear for long distances, spotted two vehicles moving across the winding estate road, the Land-Rover – Ritchie's jeep – and the blue Dyane. Some sheep trotted away from him as he crossed the pasture towards the house.

They were waiting for him on the gravelled drive, Ritchie, Laura – pretty and businesslike as she greeted him, as if they were just friendly acquaintances, and how he hated her for the way she could switch him off like that – the Keeling woman, and a stranger. Keeling he'd been right about all along, she was up to no good, but he thought he'd torpedoed her. Maybe Mr Teal really was as dumb as he looked. And the stranger, called Peter English on the telly, nasty eyes and a plausible face, obviously taking this bunch for all they had.

'Well, we are all met,' he boomed on approach. His eyes moved quickly from one to the other. 'We'd better not make this a social event.'

'Just take us there, Godfrey,' Laura said.

Knapp bridled. Her coolness, her tone of voice – he could tell from Ritchie's relaxed bearing that the poor sucker didn't suspect a thing. 'I didn't anticipate a party.'

Laura said, 'We'd all like to see the place.'

Knapp looked at Sarah Keeling. Pride demanded that he make one condition. 'Not her.'

'Godfrey,' Laura said, 'we'll play this our way.'

While she spoke, Ray went over to Knapp and fixed him with eyes that said, *If you fuck me up, I'll kill you.* Then he pointed. 'You ride in the jeep.'

Knapp shrugged. They all got in the two vehicles.

A couple of minutes from the house Knapp told Martin to stop. At first sight there was nothing. But anyone knowing what to look for would have picked out a mound which was not part of the natural undulation of the pasture. Knapp led them round one side of this.

A cut in the ground appeared, a few concrete steps leading down to a metal door. He undid two locks and pulled the handle, which also served as a lever operating a heavy bolt into the steel frame. He switched on the light and descended several more steps into the shelter. The others followed. Sarah gave Laura a sideways glance and grinned. 'The real thing.' She opened a leather case, which hanging beside her shoulder bag nobody had noticed, and aimed a compact Japanese camera. Knapp wheeled and barked, 'No photographs. I must insist, I absolutely insist –' Ray, at the same moment, raised his index finger and shook his head. Sarah paused, then coolly put the camera away again. OK, her job was words. By the time she left here she would have plenty of them.

The shelter smelt of cold, damp, incipient mildew, beneath the odour of polished linoleum and imperfectly dried-out mortar. Immediately inside the door one room, its breeze-block walls postered with plastic-sheeted maps of the region, gave into what appeared to be two others. The barely adequate fluorescent strip in the low ceiling made a puddle of yellow light amid the thin dusting of footprints on the shiny floor.

'A small thing but my own,' Knapp said.

His voice rebounded, verging on the comical, off the bleak walls. The others came in, their steps loud in the underground

252

stillness. Knapp levered the door shut behind them. To Ray he said, 'Nobody will find you here.' His words were offhand and conveyed scant esteem.

They spread out and looked around, for something to do. Knapp ignored them. He had been here earlier in the day to install a camp bed and chairs, a small store of food and bottled water, a hot-air blower, a portable toilet, and to check the power supply.

It was some time since his last visit. The shelter had been installed only partly at his own expense, through an excellent deal he had put together by offering the facility as a civil defence sub-regional headquarters. The Ministry of Defence had provided half the cost, and Knapp had netted himself the rank of senior co-ordinator (personnel) in the post-holocaust hierarchy. In the panicky days of the early eighties he had greatly enjoyed the regular practice weekends out here. Ordaining the lives and deaths of half a million fellow-humans was much too important to be left to civil servants whose biggest problem was controlling their greenfly. That Thatcher woman was said to love her simulations down in the bunker, and Knapp could understand it.

But somehow the impetus had gone, and it became a bureaucratic routine like anything else. The focus of Knapp's personal survival came nearer. Bugger World War Three, his problem was his sixtieth birthday. And although with the Caunder reactor and the Polaris base along the coast this whole area was a prime target, the underground sessions had become repetitive, palled into a clockwork perfection increasingly cut off from reality. The shelter had virtually become a discarded toy.

And now, impatient with his estate agent's role, he said to the others, 'When you're ready.'

Laura turned to him. 'I'm the only one leaving.'

Knapp's objections died unborn. 'Very well.'

'The keys,' Laura said.

Indifferent, Knapp handed them over. Laura gave them to Martin.

'If this is all some safety measure,' Knapp said, 'you may rest easy. No one will come here. The helicopter will touch down at 0600 hours tomorrow. You know the rest.' To Laura he said, 'Could you give me a lift back to the house?'

'Sure.' With a brief, confident 'See you' to the others, Laura accompanied Knapp outside, to the grass bent by the wind and the far-off grey fulness of the lake under the louring sky.

'I'm not happy about that Keeling woman,' Knapp said. 'I think she'll balls it for you.'

Laura asked why. There was always that grain of doubt about Sarah, and he had stabbed his finger right on it. As they got in the car Knapp elaborated. 'For the sake of a story she'll sell you and your principles. She's the only one who's going to make anything out of this business.'

'You're a dreary man, Godfrey,' Laura said as they drove back to Scardale. She realised that once this was all over she would never meet Knapp again, or have anything to say to him. She suspected, without surprise, that he felt the same towards her.

Knapp disregarded her uncomplimentary words and asked, 'How do you feel about this place?'

Sensing that he was about to ask her in, Laura said cautiously, 'Very nice.'

'I know you won't tell anyone else if I ask you not to, so I do ask you – I have to sell Scardale.' He hoped that she would be shaken by the news. But Laura had gone off Scardale. It was a mausoleum, the temple, although pretty enough, of an insatiable ego.

'Why?'

'It's held together by my wife's money. She's divorcing me. I can't maintain things here, so . . . It's already on the market, in a discreet sort of way.'

'Where will you go then?'

'I have my place in town. I may go to the sun, somewhere. This country's about to be deluged by an almighty turd called – I suppose – stable government. There's no style, no taste any more. There are many things I am not, but one thing I am is a man of taste. In important matters.'

He struggled with the door. Laura leaned across and pulled the correct catch. As he got out she said gently, sadly, but killing, 'You're just a rich man, Godfrey. That's all. Just a rich man.'

'A very complex human being.'

Sarah Keeling said, 'Oh sure.'

'I mean it,' Martin answered. 'I've known Godfrey Knapp over ten years. He's one of those people with a deep vein of idealism which they'll only exercise if everyone else pretends not to notice.'

'So why is he getting involved in this?'

'Well, he has power, and he likes to let people see that. He loves this country, and he doesn't like what's happening to it. That's why he's helping us.'

'And you believe him?'

'Yes, I do.'

Sarah dropped the subject. She had never understood Martin. Beneath his direct, amicable surface there was something inviolable. And you only got news by violating people. Like it or not. Either he was hopelessly naïve, or he was kidding her. Behind the round lenses of her glasses her eyes gave off a momentary cynical sparkle.

A short time later Martin left the shelter. Sarah levered the door tight. Now it was only her and Ray. Self-contained and silent, he lay on the camp bed. Knapp had only been told to provide one bed. They had wanted him to assume that Ray would spend the night there alone.

'Whenever you're ready,' she said.

Ray said nothing. Sarah snapped open a bottle of mineral water and found a plastic cup. The hot blower had desiccated the air, and she drank till she felt her body tissues moisten again. She put the cup at one end of the shelf, marking it down as hers. You could soon stop being a person in these places.

Ray said, 'I'm going out.'

'Why?'

His eyes were all boredom and threat. 'Because I want to piss, lady, and I'd sooner do it on the grass than in the toy-town shithouse they've got down here.'

No doubt he also wanted to look around. Sarah waited by the door, irrationally afraid although she had the keys and she knew that if he ran, he now had nowhere to run to. But it broke a taboo, and when he returned she went outside herself, taking some Kleenex, and squatted in the spiky grass some distance from the shelter. The prospect of using the portable toilet with Ray only a few feet away had been worrying her too.

She seized another opportunity. The next time he went outside, she took some hurried pictures of the shelter interior. After his initial prohibition, Knapp had neglected to confiscate her film.

She asked Ray again if he wanted to start. She had enough tapes for ten hours, and she had no intention of wasting any of them. Ray, looking thin and sly, did nothing to hide his reluctance. But this was part of the deal, Laura's deal. No tapes, no boat, no escape to Spain. He had no way out, and he knew it.

Day and night lost all meaning, except as marks on their digital watches. Long before what was technically evening, after long spells of question and answer into the recorder, they were both exhausted. Ray insisted they sleep in shifts. He would take the bed for two hours, then let Sarah have it for four, and the same again. There was no dimmer switch, so the strip lights all had to go off. The two chairs were canvas on tubular aluminium frames. Sarah stretched herself between them, hugging herself into as much comfort as she could, and contemplating with satisfaction the material she had taped. When it was her turn on the camp bed she curled up with the hardware in her leather bag, as snug in her arms as a favourite soft animal.

When the project first took shape, Sarah had feared this long subterranean night, the prospect not only of rape, but a

256

more general aggression, psychological rather than bodily. She had overcome it by counting on her ability to make mental contact with Ray, and it had worked.

By leading him through careful and subtle questions she had built up a profile deep enough for a book, and she had treated him with such respect that in the end he was the intimidated one, he was the one who didn't want the talking to stop. And once he was in Spain she would be able to take things further. If they could expose the Faulston incident it would be the story of the decade. Sarah expected this high to keep her awake, but she passed out immediately. When Ray woke her and she pressed the light button on her watch, it was already five in the morning. He had let her sleep through.

The chill white sky was blotched with ragged purple cloud, and some time before six Ray had the shelter door open so he could scan for the arrival of the helicopter. Ten minutes before the hour the distant buzz of a lightweight two-rotor machine homed in on Scardale, circled and came slowly and elegantly down on a patch of flat lawn fifty yards from the house.

'OK, this is it.'

Ray admitted no ceremony, zipping his jacket as he strode away into the cutting early morning wind. From the pocket he took a black SAS-type hood and pulled it over his head. They were taking no chances with the helicopter pilot.

Sarah ran after him, her various bags flapping from her shoulders. She saw Godfrey Knapp emerging on to the wide steps of Scardale's frontage, hands jammed in pockets, customary cigar fuming. She also saw, further down the road, Laura's Dyane, stationary. She tried to catch Ray.

'Listen, I just wanted to say –'

He looked sideways. His narrow eyes said he had no use for her now.

'Thanks,' she said. But he didn't want to know about her thanks. She went on, breathless, 'In Spain I'll put something together. You're the key to something really important –'

Even through the hood, she could read the wolflike leer of his face. He said, 'When you come near me again, don't be empty-handed.'

Sarah wanted to lift the moment, to share her excitement with him. She wanted a bond between them. But Ray didn't give a fuck, he wouldn't take it, and there was no time now.

The group assembled, Knapp, Ray, Laura walking up from her car, and the helicopter pilot shuffling his feet by the surprisingly small, frail-looking Robinson machine. The foreshortening made the cabin look no higher than his head, and the tilted two-blade rotor seemed to add only another four feet to the helicopter's height.

Knapp, taking pleasure in his ability to fix these things, had obtained a few hours' use of the lightweight chopper from a television executive friend who had a decent country place not many miles away. His credit was still good in that quarter, at least. He went over to have a chat with the pilot, put him at his ease and explain the route, referring to a map which he spread out on the downcurved screen of the Robinson's cabin. He also handed him a plain envelope containing a large sum of money to compensate him for the early hour. Knapp then called, 'Everything's ready to go.'

His statuesque bearded face was an impenetrable mask of arrogant boredom as he watched them approach the helicopter, Sarah, Ray, Laura, three out-of-place windswept figures, washed-out from lack of sleep and outwardly uncertain of what they were doing there.

'She goes too.' Ray spoke direct to the pilot, ignoring Knapp. He indicated Laura. The compact Robinson was only a two-seater. The pilot shook his head. Knapp intervened with a surly shout: 'This wasn't discussed.'

Laura said, 'We weigh about eighteen stone between us. That's not much more than you, Godfrey. We can squeeze in.' She looked closely at him. 'Is there any reason why I shouldn't go?'

'Absolutely not. If that's what you want.'

The pilot objected. 'I could lose my licence for this.'

'I'll see you're all right,' Knapp said, and gave a magisterial but unconvincing wink as the pilot opened the passenger door.

Laura got in first, then Ray. They had to disregard the seatbelts, but Ray immediately reached for the headset and handed it to Laura, not even waiting for the pilot. As the slender blades began to whirr Laura looked out. Knapp was already halfway back to the house. She gave Sarah a brief wave as the grass flattened around them and the chopper rose on a cone of air.

From the steps of Scardale Godfrey Knapp watched the light copter bank and glide out, the wind already bearing away its noise, until it was like a large seed-head drifting away across the sky. He wondered if he would ever see Laura again. Something resentful and vindictive inside him said no. No, he would leave her behind with Scardale; no, he had taken everything he wanted from her. Yet already he was looking forward to a renewed pursuit of her once this business was over. Being in love suited a man like Knapp. Acknowledging the power of this strange force, he could justify anything he did.

> She turned away, but with the autumn weather
> Compelled my imagination many days . . .

That was it. So what the hell. The Robinson was a pinprick on the vast nothingness of sky. He spat on the gravel and went in.

Over the headset Laura asked nervously, 'Are you sure about the route?'

'I was told Oxhead,' the pilot said curtly. 'That's easy enough.'

Oxhead was an island, a mile long by half a mile wide, off the coast a few miles past the Saltmayne promontory, shielded by it from the worst of the sea's anger. From the plexiglass bubble of the Robinson the coastline soon swept towards them. Laura had no idea how far up they were, maybe three thousand feet, but the land was flat and dull

259

below them, the fields a continuum of greyish-green. They soon followed the land's edge beyond Saltmayne to where the humped shingle of Helbeach reached out along the curve of Limport Bay like a long brown arm ridged with muscle, separated from the mainland, except at its wrist and shoulder, by a thin saltwater lake.

She was suddenly anxious, afraid that when they were over Oxhead the visibility would be too poor. She steeled herself against panic. Pressed against Ray she could feel the wiry indifference of his body, and something hard at chest level inside his jacket. Oxhead lay a mile out from one end of Helbeach, and the pilot veered into the offshore wind as it came into view.

He took the Robinson down a gentle diagonal as they passed over the choppy grey water, and the oak and pine woods of Oxhead assumed distinct forms ahead of them. Laura concentrated hard on her recall of the map of the island. In case the pilot had his own ideas, she told him, 'Don't land till we say.'

The pilot gave a sideways look of snotty authority past the silent hooded figure. 'I'll carry out my instructions, if you don't mind.'

Before Laura could argue they were swinging over the open area in the centre of the island, where the trees gave way to a few acres of grass and the pilot looked for somewhere to touch down. Laura gripped Ray's arm. Without a headset he would never hear her. His narrow eyes stared through the slits in the hood as she shook her head and called to the pilot, 'Don't land.'

The pilot yelled back, 'I'm taking her down.'

He gritted his teeth and began to circle. The sooner he was shot of these two weird bastards the better. A job was one thing, but this was getting ridiculous.

The next thing he knew was an automatic pistol jabbed against his temple by the man in the hood. And the woman's voice, steely but gentle, over the headset.

'Fly back to the mainland. You know Lendra, the hill-fort? Put down on there.'

260

Chapter Twenty-one

At the small, self-consciously pretty town of Limport, rising steeply from its sheltered cove, Martin Ritchie took the second of the twice-daily boats over to Oxhead. He re-experienced the good feeling of leaning back on the slatted wooden seat as the asthmatic motor launch ploughed through the restless water. Zipped up against the wind, he watched the small lights of Limport quay glimmer through the thickening darkness that rolled in from the sea. Pellets of spray stung his face, and he revelled in it as at a salutation from an old enemy.

Once he had known very well the dashing waters of this strait, although the days when as warden of Oxhead he had crossed here by rowing boat were now many years gone. Yet this trip seemed to return that part of his life to him in a sort of living photograph. He knew the present wildlife warden on the island, and had phoned asking if he could go over for a night. They kept up a regular contact, and there was always a meal and a bunk in the modest warden's quarters which had once been his own home.

Oxhead was owned by the National Trust, with the exception of an inlet at the tapering end of the island which was a no-go area used only by the marines from the base over on the mainland. Much of the rest of the island was fenced off into reserves where the progressive extinction of many rare species was being resisted. The public sections were park-like, practically suburban, with evergreen-bordered walks and the occasional Gothic folly, all remains of the ambitions of a one-time owner to tame and adorn the wilderness. But beyond these decaying formal gardens the ragged trees of the island raved in the undying sea wind, the mists blocked it off from the outside world, and Oxhead hunched back into its primeval solitude.

Beyond Limport was a large onshore oil-field, extending by the year, and on clear days people could now see rigs tapping the same belt of oil several miles out to sea. It was only a matter of time before the rigs came to Oxhead, and if the Limport Yacht Club had its way the new loading terminal would also be on Oxhead rather than the mainland. The oil companies admittedly made a lot of public obeisance to 'the ecology', and naturalists were employed to advise them and lend credibility to their concern. Martin had never been easy about his involvement in all this. But as always, you had the choice between doing a thing and not doing it. For the moment he spared himself a final judgment.

Oil preoccupied the early conversation he had with the warden, an emotional ginger-bearded man who, with his invalid wife, had become almost a recluse out there. From Oxhead even the events at Faulston seemed remote. Apart from the trippers who came over in the more frequently run summer boats, paid their landing toll, walked the ruined gardens for an hour and then left again, only the very determined came here – the hardcore nature observers who had access to the reserves, and people seeking a landscape which could still convey a primordial aloneness. Both the latter were agreeable to the warden. They talked on, and he then in passing mentioned some other activity in the last twenty-four hours.

'A lot of coming and going. A helicopter set down in the military bit, and I never heard it take off again. Then a boat came over, it looked like one of the marine boats, but it put in at the wharf, and I got a phone call from the regional HQ saying some special guests would be staying at the lodge tonight, but not to worry, they'd take care of themselves and preferred not to be disturbed.'

'Oil people, you think?' Martin asked.

'Shouldn't wonder.'

'I'd like to do a night patrol. Is there anything I need to know about?'

'I don't think so. Hasn't changed since you were last here.'

'You'll join me?'

'I won't, if you don't mind. Annie sometimes wants things during the night, and it's not fair . . . You're sure you can find your way about?'

Martin smiled. 'Fairly sure.'

Later Martin left the warden's house. Even in the dark he made a friendly note of bushes he had planted in his time there, well grown now, and how they had a vegetable plot where he had once cleared a large patch of builder's debris, thistle, and scraggy hawthorn. Places lived.

He headed out into the island. Although around the moon there was an aureola of filmy lemon light, the sky was clear and the cold air had a crisp stillness which sharpened his senses. The familiar smell of Oxhead – the mulch of vegetation and mud, the pines, the odour of sea-wrack – flooded back and gave him the sensation of a distant place that was still home. But after some minutes the task he had come there for had pushed all these old associations aside.

The lodge was a rebuilt wing of the great house which had once stood on Oxhead in its days as a private estate. Fire had destroyed all but a fragment, which had been restored, modernised and walled off from the rest of the island. It was occupied permanently by a couple of grace and favour residents, elderly genteel people who loved nature and solitude. A caretaker ran the place, guests came and went, mainly in summer, and as a matter of efficiency as well as courtesy they contacted the Oxhead warden on arrival. You met all sorts, Martin remembered, some of the nicer members of the eccentric wing of the upper class. But visitors who came at this time of year, who were to stay incognito, to the extent that the warden had been warned off any approach, had to be worth a look. They were no more oil people than he was.

It was much more than ten years, and every step Martin took reminded him of how much older you were near fifty than below forty. But he could still scale a six-foot wall. He even remembered, from his last trip, a section where the stone was crumbling, and the moonlight made it easy to get up and hoist himself over.

He had to be careful now. There was plenty of shrubbery here, but neatly tended by the caretaker, not made for hiding. But the moon cast long shadows, and further on there was a patch of wooded ground, away from the lodge, and Martin knew all these places as if he had grown up there. He chose the route his action would have to take, then scooped up a handful of gravel from the path and moved into position.

The lodge had three storeys, and the lighted window was on in the middle of the three. Martin whirled the gravel through the air. There would be no second chance. As the small chips of stone pinged against the glass he withdrew into some laurels from which he could see the window.

The curtains were not drawn, and two faces immediately appeared in the square of yellow light framed by dark creeper-covered wall. Maybe a bird or a bat had crashed against the window. These were eerie places at night. Or maybe something else.

The two men rapidly disappeared again. Before they could get down to the lodge door Martin ducked through the shadows and made for the deeper cover. The moment had been long enough. Next to the round startled face of someone Martin had never seen before he had clearly identified the heavy menacing face of Harry Teal.

He picked his way back along the boundary of a swampy reserve to the end of the island closed off by the military. At one point broken ground and cliffline erosion made the wire fencing unworkable, and it was easy enough to find a way into the restricted area. There was a small installation here, a couple of Portakabins, and a light on in one of them, no doubt because they were mounting an overnight guard for what Martin made out in open terrain some fifty yards away – the humped black shape of a helicopter.

Back at the warden's house Martin had an hour's chat about the island's wildlife. The warden was a photographer, and they looked over his latest work. After planning some activity for later the next day, and Martin cueing the fact that he might go out for a dawn watch, they turned in. Martin set the alarm on his watch at 4.30.

He settled down in the spare room. For a moment, in the darkness, his body seized up as the presence of this house, and the silence outside, enveloped him. It was not the dry, placid quiet of Macemoor, but a silence embracing great forces, underlaid by the deep breath of the sea. He knew it all so well. He had lived here with Eleanor, and they had been happy in that easygoing kind of happiness where ultimate knowledge is avoided, the last veil not torn aside. He had often wished he had never left the island, but now after a year of Laura he knew he was no longer the contented man who had once lived here. There was no regret in the knowledge.

When he went out into the still dark early morning, a grey light was breaking over the sea, and the dry tassels of dead sedge rattled in the wind along the watery inlets. A flock of Brent geese put up at his approach, and he trained his glasses on the plump dark fowl, a hundred brace of wings clapping the cold air as they fanned out into wedge-formation and disappeared over the island.

The eerie silhouettes of peacocks, a hangover of the island's more stately phase, strutted about, their cries raucous and accusing, as he made for the unwooded high ground, the tonsure of Oxhead, where the helicopter was scheduled to land, and from where he could also watch the strait across which Godfrey Knapp's boat would travel. They had estimated that twenty-five minutes after the helicopter left Scardale, Knapp would take his boat out of the Limport marina. Within fifteen minutes of being on the island, Ray should be leaving again.

Except that now it all had to change. Although it was technically safer than the mainland, they had prepared for Oxhead to be a problem. The Limport police or the coast-guard were sometimes about, or there were landing assault exercises often staged at odd hours by the marines. There was no shortage of reasons for alternative plans.

Martin heard the gentle whirring of the light helicopter long before he saw it. He sighted it, then tracked it in with his field glasses. Regretting what he was about to do, he unzipped his parka and pulled out a red and white checked scarf. As the helicopter dropped in on its landing path, he waved. They were not low enough for him to see anybody in the cabin, but he knew they saw him from the way the chopper levelled out and circled round. He only stopped waving when it banked away and whirled back out over the sea again.

Lendra. The pilot asked 'What now?' as he huddled behind the Robinson for shelter from the wind.

At least the automatic pistol had been put away, and the hard case in the black hood was already scouring the view from the hill-fort for his next move. The pilot had two concerns, getting the Robinson, and himself, back in one piece. Not in that order. Then the hooded man turned abruptly and barked out, 'Strip!'

The pilot froze, wondering why, picturing the conse-quences, shouting in his mind that if they wanted him to strip, they surely weren't going to kill him. Were they?

He watched as the woman laid a hand on the hooded man's arm and shook her head. The expression on her face said, not necessary.

'Shoes.'

While the pilot removed these, the hooded man gathered some large stones from the flinty ground. He forced several rocks into each shoe, then went to the edge of the crown of the hill-fort, and flung one shoe out into space so that it bounced over an outer rampart and vanished in the bushes on the lower escarpment. Further along he threw the other shoe in another direction. Then he came back to the pilot, whose feet were already soaking and painfully cold, and said, 'You better go and look for them. And don't try to fly this again. I'm going to disable it, not badly, so you won't need to make an insurance claim and tell anybody about this. Just enough to make it unsafe to fly. Understand?'

'Yes, yes, thanks.' The pilot nodded gratefully.

'You'll be able to fix it yourself. Just a matter of time.'

'Right, right.'

The pilot nodded eagerly and was already scrambling down the coarse white grass of the slope. Ray got into the cabin of the Robinson, thinking to disconnect a few wires. But in the end he did nothing. By the time the pilot checked everything and got off the ground, this would all be over.

'OK, let's go.'

They had followed it all through on the map, the footpath down from the corrugated slopes of Lendra, across a brief buckled patchwork of fields to where the brown ridge of Helbeach curved in to join the mainland again, a wall of cobbled stones topped by the grey slate roof of the sea and its promise of freedom.

Soon after the helicopter, the boat. Much of Oxhead was fringed with gravel beaches, and for some way out mudbanks underlay the tide. But Martin knew the spots where the landshelf dropped away to give adequate draft to a boat, and Knapp had been given precise directions where to bring it in, at a point where Martin would be waiting to give him a line to sail on.

The power-boat – the *Fanny* – nosed forward through the idly breaking water. The day was overcast but settled. Knapp killed the engine and drifted the boat in through the deep water, squinting as he swept the overgrown edge of the island. Something was wrong.

He had seen the helicopter fly over, and through rubber-armoured binoculars he had watched as it quite clearly did not put down, but heeled round and hightailed back to the mainland. By radio telephone he had called in Appleton at his operation centre on Oxhead. Appleton was confident of the plan's security, and guessed they were playing silly buggers to test Knapp out. He instructed Knapp to stay with it, play a straight bat and keep in touch.

So when Martin Ritchie appeared at the water's edge, Knapp already knew that Ray was not waiting there. Whenever he thought of this cold-blooded, pasty-faced killer, the word 'Ray' conjured up in Knapp's mind the manta, the sea vampire, shadows of underwater death. Feeling comfortable in his designer boatwear and corduroy cap, and enjoying the game-playing aspect of all this, he lifted his head from the cockpit as the *Fanny*'s buffer tyres jarred against the stone bank.

'Where are they? What's up?'

'Change of plan.'

Knapp thickened his mouth in scornful intolerance. Something about Ritchie had always irritated him. Maybe it was the fact that he had never been able to feel superior to him, never been able to discount him as a nonentity. Even after he had screwed his bloody woman he still could not shrug him aside, and it rankled.

'What sodding change?'

'I'm coming aboard.'

Judging the moment when the tide would lift the boat against the rock, Martin got in.

'OK, skipper,' Knapp said. 'Which way?'

Martin pulled out a map and indicated the stretch of Helbeach they were to sail for. Knapp shrugged and woke the Volvo inboard engine to life. The power-boat kicked effortlessly away and glided back out to open water.

Martin sat on a bench behind the open-backed cockpit while Knapp stood, below deck level, at the chromed wheel. All the controls were electronic, state-of-the-art material, but

268

for this stage Knapp only needed hand and eye.

As they breasted the more generously heaving waves out from Oxhead, he called above the engine noise, 'Why this pissing about? Who had a problem?'

'That was the way they wanted to do it.'

Knapp half-turned his head again.

'I could have handed the boat over at the island. What was wrong with that?'

'Precautions,' Martin said.

Knapp's eye rested on the radiophone. Had they assumed treachery, out-thought him, and by chance hit on an evasion that might work?

He ground his teeth. If Ray got away, Appleton and his friends would form the inevitable conclusion, that he, Knapp, had conned them. But that made no sense. Why should he have gone to them in the first place, only to betray them now? No, Rex Appleton understood everything. He was there himself, on Oxhead, on top of the whole shooting-match. Knapp shook off his moment of fear. It was going to be all right.

Chapter Twenty-two

On Helbeach the pill-boxes were a relic of the World War Two years when this entire range of coast had been fortified against invasion and later used for simulated beachheads in preparation for D-Day. Years after the barbed-wire entanglements and weapon fragments had been cleared up the concrete pill-boxes remained, gradually pitching over into the shingle, their gun slits like the blank eyes of monstrous heads, helplessly sinking.

Helbeach itself was a dense ridge of brown pebbles, all of uniform size in any one place, but graduating from the dimensions of large potatoes at one end to small polished beads at the other. Extending out under the sea, the bank had always been a nightmare to shipping, an anvil of small stones on which storms pounded stranded boats to matchwood. But approached from landward the sea disappeared from view as Helbeach's brown hump became a desert horizon, with the one strange detail that from its further side came the drawn-out echoing groan of millions of pebbles being dredged back by the tide and hurled forward into the shingle mass again.

Reaching the bank, Laura and Ray, his hood now discarded, crunched their way up the long mound of pebbles. It was more of a hill than it seemed, constantly slipping under their feet as they mounted to the crest of the ridge and the slope down to the moaning grey water. Since leaving the helicopter they had not spoken, not even to question why

Martin had warned them off landing on Oxhead. The plan was clear, and they set their faces towards the next stage.

Laura spotted the boat, and turned to direct Ray's attention. But he had already seen it. Martin, with his exhaustive knowledge of Helbeach, had no trouble coming in at the correct pill-box. Laura remembered the spring day when they had trudged the length of the bank, searching out the life that clung on in the stony waste – ringed plovers breeding there, tough succulent plants, scores of small bizarrely-shaped life-forms that flew and crawled and survived on the gigantic shingle dune. Aiming straight for a particular pill-box would give him no trouble.

Laura removed her hat and shook her straight blonde hair into the wind, to cool her head for a minute, then pulled the woollen cap on again. For this moment she closely watched Ray. She had never known anyone with less of a need to communicate. 'It's going to be fine,' she said.

His narrow eyes, still hard in spite of the sea-wind's moistening, rested on her. All he said was, 'Yeah.'

She wanted to match his terseness, his Zen-like indifference. Words were lies, who needed words? But she could not do it.

She said, 'I suppose this is goodbye.'

He stared at her as if unbelieving that she expected him to answer.

'Right. Goodbye.'

The power-boat's engine was close now.

'You're not the world's most charming man,' Laura said. 'But I hope you make it.'

Suddenly and fleetingly, the lines of his thin unshaven face deepened as his eyes and mouth smiled at her, wryly and secretively, the first smile he had ever shown her. It said, this is all I'll ever give you, but take it. Laura could not help smiling back.

The *Fanny* was drifting in now, its shapely bow, royal blue below and white above, slicing the troubled water. Even in the dull morning light the craft's wooden trim, stained to a golden colour and well varnished, looked neat and jaunty. The two men in the boat were shadowy, Knapp in his sailor's hat, Martin waving.

Ray shot Laura a last glance, then hit the water. The boat was on low revs, as near in as the shelf of the bank allowed. Martin was waving, and Laura waved back as Ray half-ran through the violent green water. She only saw in Martin's wave what was expressed in her own. Only later she realised that she was wrong, the one thing it said, above all else, was goodbye.

Sarah Keeling had taken the Dyane from Scardale and driven to a hill called Telegraph Mount which was in fact the other end of the long range whose more noted extremity was the earthwork of Lendra. From a lay-by off the little-used road Sarah studied the bay beyond Helbeach with the binoculars Laura had left in the car. She watched, because she knew what to look for, everything as it happened – the return of the helicopter, the boat arriving at the pebble bank, Ray's departure. She saw, small even in the ×8 magnification glasses, Laura alone on Helbeach after the boat had put out again.

Their plan dictated that now Knapp would touch back in at Oxhead, where he and Martin would jump the boat. After that Ray was on his own. Martin would reappear at the warden's house, and Knapp would return to the mainland by the morning service boat.

Telegraph Mount gave a wide view of the Oxhead strait and the sea beyond. A heavy tide seemed to be running, and even as Sarah watched she sensed the sea changing – the whitecaps more frequent, the waves gnashing, the roar of the Helbeach pebbles deeper and more anguished as the sea chewed and spat them out again. Knapp's boat carved its way through the tidal race, bobbing on the water towards Oxhead. It seemed to curve away from the island, Sarah assumed for a straight run-in to the landing-point.

Then she stopped breathing and fought to keep her eyes

from blinking, from a moment's interruption of her sight of the boat. There was no return curve, no run-in to the island. They were making for the open sea.

'Head away from the island.'

They were half a mile out now, breasting the waves at fifteen knots. When Knapp's hostile face turned from the red digital flicker of the instrument panel Ray added curtly, 'That way.'

He pointed towards a grey nowhere in which the horizon was all but lost. Knapp demanded, 'What do you mean?'

To Martin Ray shouted, 'Why didn't you let us land on the island?'

Gripping the boat with one hand, Martin raised the other in a reassuring gesture. 'It was just a feeling. Playing safe.' His lips were numb and his face peppered by spray, easy conditions in which to lie. 'Only suspicion. It seemed best –'

He knew that Ray still regarded him as incompetent, and he played up to that now. Above all he did not want to let Knapp know anything.

The indented coastline of Oxhead was unfolding to their left as the boat ploughed on. They were already past the drop point. Having received no answer to his question, Knapp yelled, 'You're not giving me any bloody orders!' and lunged the wheel. Simultaneously Ray's hand slipped inside his pocket and out again, and the Browning automatic was a few feet from Knapp's head. His lips hardly seemed to move, but his voice bit through the crashing of the sea.

'You're going all the way. And if there's any shit I'll spread your brains all over that fucking deck.'

It might have been the rougher weather now they were out in open water, but Knapp's skin was waxen and his eyes glassy. He offered Ray no confrontation. His shoulders seemed to contract, his whole body was smaller, as he turned back to the wheel.

The wind had risen to force 5, and the sea was patched with long shadowy waves and everywhere flecked with whitecaps.

Ray turned to Martin. His distrust, his determination to make it, now overrode everything.

'Right, you. Get that dinghy, get it pumped up.'

There had to be a dinghy on board, that had been one of Ray's requirements for the boat. It lay, part-inflated, under the slatted wooden seat in the stern. Martin looked round for a pump.

Knapp called, 'It's here,' indicating the inside of the cabin. He glanced round. Ray held the Browning, still flush with a dozen 9mm rounds, casual but ready to strike. Knapp kept one hand on the wheel and reached for the pump. He sensed Ray about to come forward and get it himself. The boat heaved. His left hand almost slipped from the wheel as he leaned forward for the pump.

Earlier, it seemed half a lifetime earlier, Knapp had asked into the radiophone, 'Why not pick him up as soon as he leaves the helicopter?'

'You mean an ambush? Strictly taboo, old son. Look at it like this. They do a swift shufti of the island, spot a man with a gun hiding behind a tree, and we're all in the shit. Then of course there's the chance he might take the pilot hostage, at least as far as the boat. We don't want a body on our hands. Especially the wrong body.'

Appleton paused, and across the phone line Knapp could picture his rabbit-like face twitching.

'So what, then?' Knapp said. 'I let him take the boat?'

'Let him take the boat, old son. You get off at the island. We want him out there on his own. Then we'll intercept.'

The *Fanny* was rolling away from the sea as it came at her starboard bow. Ahead lay the waters of the eastern Atlantic. The forecast for Biscay was fair, but Knapp had never bargained on having to test it out. He cut into the wave flow to avoid too great a periodic roll, and wondered where that bloody police boat was, and what good it would do him now.

The lurch of the *Fanny* had thrown Martin on to the deck as he struggled to get the dinghy out. It jammed under the seat because it was already part-inflated, its orange Hypalon tubing saggy but not flat. On his knees Martin pulled it into the open deck area and looked up as Knapp reached the pump from a shelf inside the cabin. It was a foot-pump, with a metal cylinder and heel-rest, and two feet of tough rubber air-pipe. As Knapp gripped it he swung the wheel with his left hand so that the boat slewed round and bounced on a breaking wave, pushing its whole level into a crazy tilt.

Then Knapp let go of the wheel altogether and spun round, flailing the pump at Ray's head. He swung it by its pipe, and the cylinder caught Ray already off balance, smashing against his wind-stiff hand. The Browning flew sideways, seemed to hover in the air for a moment, then was gulped down by a rearing green wave. Ray staggered, and Knapp whirled the pump by its tube again, round his head, towering over Ray, this time aiming to cave his face in.

The wheel jerked clockwise, anticlockwise and back again as the *Fanny* was taken by the sea and tossed by every thrust of the waves. Knapp's arm, raised to bring the pump down on Ray's head, suddenly overbalanced him into a stumbling collision with the cabin wall. Ray measured his own steps and went after Knapp.

Once his hands were on him the sickening pitch of the boat made no difference. His fists worked brutally on the older man's body. The boat had heeled round into the path of the running sea and was being thrown along like driftwood.

'You'll kill him, you stupid bastard!'

Martin had his arms round Ray's shoulders, trying to fight him off. Their bodies rocked ludicrously as they shouted and gestured and struggled for balance. Knapp was a half-collapsed figure clutching the side-rail for support, his face bloody and sick as each roll of the boat hurled him within inches of the waves. Ray turned on Martin and lashed a blow at his cheek from which he tottered back the length of the open deck. Only the rail kept him from going over.

Then the dinghy went. First it stirred on the deck, then the wind plucked it from the boat and tossed it on to the water twenty yards away. Only half-inflated, it bobbed on the swirling water, a big orange scrap of ocean garbage.

Ray's head went up. The wind had deadened his ears, and for a moment he was unsure of the direction, but then he saw it. A helicopter, the rotor noise increasing all the time.

He was blown. He had known all along that it would be down to a race. Fuck it, then. His face sharpened, the vicious mask of the trapped wolf, the cornered rat, his teeth bared and his skin flecked with the spittle of the murderous sea. Let them come for him now. He was ready.

Martin was looking round, checking, assessing. Ray looked at Martin now and saw betrayal. As he advanced unsteadily towards him, Martin reached down and forced his boots off. He could see the dinghy. The same sea that washed it along would carry him after it. There was a dip in the stern rail. He made his own decision, chose his moment as if Ray was not there, stepped into the gap, and dived.

While he was still in the water, the salt burning his nostrils and the current tugging his clothes and heaving him about like flotsam, he heard the boat's engine whine up into a purposeful roar. Floundering to stay afloat, he saw its tail spin round as Godfrey Knapp took control again. For a moment Martin thought they were going to bear down on him. But the *Fanny* swung to one side and shot away through the water.

Martin swam to his limit and finally caught hold of the slippery orange skin of the dinghy. Just as he dragged himself into it the power boat's backwash hit him. Frozen and retching, he lay there like a child in a cot, rocked by the scissoring water. At that moment the helicopter passed overhead.

Then they would meet up on the pebbled ridge of Helbeach, when it was all over. And what? Go home? But where was home now, for any of them?

Her chest so tight she could hardly breathe, Sarah Keeling's hands shook with cold, with an excitement that she was scared to come down from. She was troubled also because the boat had not put in at Oxhead. So she stayed on and watched.

The sea, so far off, appeared flat, except that the orange dinghy lifted into view then dropped from sight again, drifting diagonally to the coastline with the huge tide now running on to Helbeach. Knapp's boat had vanished into the watery horizon, and Ray had thrown Martin and Knapp out in the dinghy. That had to be the explanation.

She watched for a long time, until she could make a clear sighting of the dinghy. She watched in disbelief as it bucked along on the current, buoyant but flimsy, with the ghostly sadness common to all abandoned seacraft, drifting, empty.

Harry Teal was worried. Not personally, *professionally*. That was the only way he ever worried. He called to the pilot of the Wasp, 'How far will this thing go?'

'About 150, there and back.'

'Miles or k?'

The pilot wasn't quite sure who this character was, but he knew nothing about choppers. Holding the sarcasm, he said, 'Miles.'

'Never fear, old son,' Appleton said, patting Teal's knee. 'He can't go as far as he thinks.'

To underline the *he*, Appleton pointed down at the *Fanny*, now with only two men aboard. Teal asked, 'How's that?'

Appleton cupped his hand round the mouthpiece on his personal intercom, as if this would aid audibility.

'Simplicity itself. Our pal Knapp said he would doctor the fuel gauge. A few more miles and they run out of juice. Our gendarme colleagues will then come floating along and apprehend this villain. And then you're away, my young friend, you're a made man.'

Teal chewed his fleshy lower lip.

'Why didn't Knapp come back to the island? What's his game?'

'You don't think he's gone native, old chap?'

'I never trusted him. I still think he was using you, Rex.'

277

'You may be right, old son. But for what?'

'Perhaps we're about to find out.'

Teal gnawed his lip and his eyes bulged with intensity as he watched the unfriendly waters several hundred feet below. The Wasp could make 100 m.p.h. with no trouble, and it pleased him to think of the effect the chopper's presence must be having on the nerves of the two men in the power boat below.

He would have the bastards. Teal had still not worked out what Rex Appleton's motives were, but it didn't matter now. Appleton had come to him because of something departmental, a favour done is a favour owed, this is bigger than both of us, protocol of that kind. But the pay-off would come when he, Harry Teal, finally nailed the arse of this man who had dominated his life since God knew when. He would squeeze every last drop of moisture out of that son of a bitch.

Appleton glanced at his watch. He had been visibly more time-conscious than usual this morning. Behind the city gent façade which kept the world on such agreeable terms, the mind of Rex Appleton was calculating to the second the precise countdown pulsing through the circuits of a timed detonator bonded to several ounces of C4 plastic explosive which during the night had been tamped into the engine housing of the *Fanny*. Unknown to Knapp, unknown to Teal, known only to himself and the SBS people who had done the job. My God, Appleton thought, I hope they got the right boat.

Maybe it was nerves, or a total absence of nerves, that prompted him to open a conversation when he judged that the remaining seconds were well into two digits.

'Choppy old sea, Harry. You ever do any sailing?'

'Sailing? No.'

'A dry-land man, like me. I tell you, even being up in one of these things nearly gives me the runs. It's before your time, but there used to be a chap called Pinky Fairweather, out East in the old days –'

A sudden orange glare below. The pilot's reaction was

278

impeccable, faster than conscious thought. His hands and feet, almost as if in a defensive flinch, pressed the controls and banked the Wasp away from the flash of danger below. It looked like a fire, but only for the briefest of milliseconds. After that a raging vermilion flare filled the space where the *Fanny* had been.

From its increased height the Wasp circled straight back. By a strange accident its return curve coincided with the post-explosion scatter of debris, and something soft and mushy slapped on to the helicopter's front screen. It was human flesh, and it stuck on the plexiglass at the end of a bloody smear. The pilot felt his stomach start to rise, and quickly activated the wipers.

He took the speed right down, and they circled the pillar of dirty smoke which the sea wind was already strewing across the air. Just another raft of maritime waste, the remains of the *Fanny* and her occupants now rose and fell with the play of the waves before disappearing for ever.

Harry Teal, white-faced and sick, looked helplessly at Appleton, needing a lead to be given or at least words to be spoken. But Appleton had his freckled hands over his face, and seemed to be shaking, but was giving nothing away. The pilot of the Wasp, without referring to either of them, veered away from the dispersing wreckage and pointed the chopper landwards.

A fine sharp rain beat down now, and both extremes of Helbeach, ten miles apart, faded into the clouded drizzle. Not far ahead the pebbled spine, brown and glistening, resembled smooth sand, but for the two women tramping its length the shingle jarred the ankles and dragged down the spirit.

Sarah had reported everything she saw. They had been through all the speculations till there was no more to say. The dinghy could be a freak, nothing to do with Knapp's boat. But there had been an inflatable on board, they knew that. As for the colour, these things were nearly always orange. To make them easy to spot, right? And it worked. But if it was from the

279

Fanny it might have gone overboard by accident. Or evidence of a capsize. Or Knapp and Martin had left the boat and . . . But Sarah repeated, 'I looked and looked, and couldn't see anybody. It doesn't mean –' But they didn't argue about what it didn't mean.

Wet and bedraggled, they were unable to quit the strange no man's land of the shingle ridge. It was the only place which offered insulation from, on the one hand, the complexities that awaited them on the mainland, and on the other the harsh simplicity of the sea.

They had not discussed it, but Laura knew she would not leave here till dark. As the pebbles crunched and rolled beneath her feet, she felt a growing desire to stay here for ever, to lie down here and die now. There were times when it was not right to die, but others when death was fitting, and she did not feel her life pulling her any further than this rainswept wilderness.

They decided to split up, to try and cover the whole length of Helbeach and meet up again hours later. Pinched by the wind and streaked with rain, they hugged, numbed by layers of clothing but passing a flame of sustenance between them.

'One day,' Sarah said, 'we'll finish writing this story.'

Laura answered, 'Yes, one day.'

They turned away from each other. As they walked away both women were crying, their tears streaming with the rain, and as Laura went further she began to sob loudly, to howl against the shriek of the wind and the insensate moan of the high tide as it clawed the shingle. She cried aloud till she had no energy left, and the sorrow and fear were wrung out of her.

Then she saw the dinghy. Running was impossible, but she forced her pace towards it. A flaccid bag of orange plastic, it washed limply back and forth at the crest of the tide, almost up to the summit of the bank. The rowlocks were empty. That was the first detail she noticed. The paddles were gone from the clamps. So somebody had tried to manoeuvre the dinghy on the open sea. She wondered if somehow Martin could have made it back to Oxhead. But the tidal drift was away from there, and nobody could have got through the freezing water across the current.

She dragged the inflatable beyond the reach of the tide, then walked on. She was scoured of all emotion now, in a bleak calm induced by the sight of the dinghy.

A quarter of a mile ahead another concrete pill-box jutted out of the pebbles. Only slowly revealed, as a hollow in the bank straightened itself out to her eye, a body lay on the slope in front of the pill-box, a sudden weird tableau of a soldier killed attacking a machine-gun post. Although the body was only a black shape huddled above the tide line in a dip in the shingle, she knew instantly that it was Martin. An electric force went through her. This time she found that she could run.

As soon as she reached him she pulled the collapsed body over. His face was livid, plastered with wet hair, eyes closed, bloodless lips slightly apart. She felt for his breath and pressed his wrist and neck for a pulse, but the skin was chilled, her hands too numb to feel anything.

She slapped his face and shook him, shouting words of anger and love and pleading into his ear. For a moment she accepted that he was gone, this was his dead body she was fighting, and despair, the onset of madness, reared over her. In a final gesture of refusal she plunged her mouth down on his, forcing stiffened lips together and gasping breath into him.

Somewhere in the cavity of his body Laura felt a response, a kick, a heave of life, and she roared air into him and pummelled him, hammering back the sleep of death into which she felt his body sinking.

Suddenly Martin writhed, and she briefly tasted bile and pulled away just in time to avoid the mix of salt water and vomit that jetted from his mouth. The power of the spasm racked his body over, and crouching with his face against the water-glossed pebbles Martin spewed his stomach empty.

His reactions were slow, and he was starting to shiver, but after what seemed minutes he focused on Laura and said in a

281

faint wind-chapped monotone, 'I was waiting for you.'

She helped him to his feet. The car was a mile away, and in the car there were dry clothes and hot drink. Suddenly the mile seemed nothing. The wind was behind them now, and even the awkward trundle of the pebbles underfoot seemed to ease their steps.

They passed the dinghy. Martin told Laura how the breakers moving in on Helbeach had finally thrown him into the water, and his only chance had been to strike into the current and swim for it. In the last stages of exhaustion he had dragged himself through the freezing surf and passed out on the shingle. He knew, he said, that he must not die until he had seen her one more time.

Later they would piece together the rest.